Katie's Choice

CASSIE DONN

Best wishes

Cassie
x

Copyright © 2024

All rights reserved.

Edited by Mary-Anne McNulty
Cover Design by Martina Doherty
Layout and format by Paddy Leonard

No part of this book can be reproduced in any form or by written, electronic or mechanical, including photocopying, recording, or by any information retrieval system without written permission in writing by the author.

*Dedicated to my late friend, Janet.
Thank you for the precious memories;
you were the best x*

Prologue

Katie repeatedly smoothed and pleated the corner of the crisp white cotton sheet as she lay in her private room at the North West Independent Hospital, on the outskirts of Derry City.

As desperate as she was to seem calm in front of her husband, Matt, he would know this action was a sure sign of her anxiousness. He put his hand on top of hers in an attempt to stop the cycle, and then, quietly taking hold of her hand, he softly brushed his thumb back and forth across the top of it. She finally lifted her eyes to him.

'I'm fine, love,' she assured him. 'It's only routine surgery. Straightforward, quick recovery. No problem.'

A hysterectomy. To Katie, it felt anything but routine.

She turned her attention to their son, Connor, as he paced the floor while trying to make idle conversation with his parents. But he wasn't fooling his mother. Katie watched him closely, noticing how preoccupied he was. If only she knew what was going on in that young head of his. Something was troubling him, but, whatever it was, he was keeping a tight lid on it. She knew better than to ask.

Suddenly, the room fell quiet as each retreated to his or her own thoughts.

Katie felt so responsible for these two people in front of her. They needed her. What if something went wrong during surgery and she was taken from their lives forever?

She could see the worry etched on her husband's face and felt sorry for him as he sat there. All their married life, Matt was there for her; her protector. She could pour her troubles onto him - no matter how big or small - and be comforted by his words of wisdom, his strong physique as he wrapped his arms around her, and his unconditional love. He adored her.

Katie wasn't aware she'd let a tear escape until Matt's finger gently stopped it as it rolled past her cheekbone. He'd think it was nerves about the surgery, not suspecting for a second that it was her guilt and shame that caused that tear to fall. How could she hurt this wonderful man? She closed her eyes and made a promise to herself: as soon as she got out of here, she was going to put her life back together again. She didn't quite know how it had all got so out of control in the first place.

She loved Matt. Always did and always would.

Her thoughts were interrupted by the staff nurse walking breezily into the room. Nodding at Matt and Connor, she said, 'You gentlemen mind leaving us for a few minutes?'

Once they'd gone, she handed Katie a urine sample bottle.

'Just one last thing, Mrs Cully,' she smiled. 'We know it's highly unlikely, but just for the record.'

'No problem,' Katie said, walking to the bathroom. 'After a number of miscarriages years ago, I haven't been able to conceive since... so I'd doubt very much if I were pregnant.' As she heard herself say the words, she suddenly had a wild and terrifying thought: *but what if I am?*

1

(Six weeks earlier)

With one hand holding her scarf tight against her neck, Katie opened her car door and threw her handbag onto the passenger seat. She started up the car and immediately switched on the heated seat; it was a cool day for the first week in October and the news from her consultant had added to the chill. She waited for her iPhone to connect, then called Carol.

'Looks like I'm for the high jump in a few weeks,' she told her best friend. 'Doctor said a hysterectomy's the only way to deal with these bloody fibroids - at least that'll be the end of the monthly nightmares.'

'Well, sure, there's no surprises there,' Carol replied. 'You won't know yourself. You OK about it?'

'Yeah, it's no big deal nowadays. A few weeks and I'll be back to my old self.'

'So have we time to get away for that holiday?' Carol asked, half holding her breath in anticipation.

'Can't see why not, but we'll need to make it sooner rather than later.'

'Great, I'll check it out tomorrow. Somewhere nice and hot; I can't wait!'

Katie stopped off to get a bottle of wine (Châteauneuf-du-Pape; a bit fancier than usual, but she felt the situation called for it). She wasn't going to let this worry her; Matt would do enough of that for both of them. She decided she would phone Connor later when she got her hospital date; no need to make a fuss.

Connor lived in Glasgow. He'd found a job there, in IT, after graduating from Queen's University in Belfast. Katie had always dreaded him leaving home; her one and only, her pride and joy. When the inevitable happened, Katie bravely hugged and kissed him goodbye, then burst into tears as she closed the front door and Connor and his girlfriend, Amy, headed off to the airport. She consoled herself with the fact that Glasgow was only a hop, skip and jump away. Flights were frequent and cheap; it could've been a lot worse.

Amy Kelly was a pretty blonde with large brown eyes. She was from an area known locally as the Waterside, which lay on the east bank of the Foyle - the river that ran through the heart of Derry. Despite growing up in the same city, Connor and Amy met for the first time at the bar in the students' union at Queen's.

She was petite compared to Connor's six feet stature, but what she lacked in height and breadth she made up for in cheek and cockiness; traits that Katie, in all honesty, found off-putting. If Amy had something to say, she came right out and said it - often quite bluntly.

Katie found this rudeness very disrespectful, but Connor pleaded with his mother to 'just let it go'. It took her all her strength to keep her mouth shut when Amy snapped at Connor in her presence. She was always complaining about her to Carol, swearing that one day she was going to let her have it.

'My Connor is far too good for that one, Carol,' she'd say to her friend. 'He has the patience of a saint. I honestly don't know why he sits and takes it; she is so bossy and spoiled.'

'Sure, don't they say opposites attract, Katie,' Carol would say in an attempt to soothe her friend. In reality, Carol didn't like this side of Amy, either. It annoyed her, the way she barked at Connor, but she knew it would do Katie no good to interfere in her son's relationship, so she would say: 'Your Connor just lets it go over his head, so there's no point in worrying about it.'

With Connor headed for Glasgow, Katie had secretly hoped things would eventually fizzle out between them, but, two weeks before he left, he announced Amy was moving there too; they would share an apartment to keep their costs low. That was over a year ago and Amy still had Connor where she wanted him: in Glasgow and under her thumb.

Katie was lifted out of her reverie by the sight of Matt as she pulled into the drive. He'd wanted to go with her to see the consultant but she'd insisted on going alone. She'd called him on the way home to give him the news, and, as she emerged from the car, he came and wrapped his big arms around her and kissed the top of her head.

'My poor love,' he whispered.

She felt a slight sting in her eyes; sometimes his big bear hugs had that effect on her. He was just a gentle giant - *her* gentle giant - and the kindest soul she had ever met.

She gathered herself and handed him the wine. 'Here, open this and bring out two nice glasses.'

Katie walked into her bedroom, kicked off her four-inch wedges and slipped out of her knee-length skirt and fitted top. She stood there looking at her reflection in the mirror. She was proud of her curvy body; at 43, she was still in good shape.

As she pressed both hands on her flat tummy, she thought of the pregnancies she'd had in the early years after Connor; the pain and loss she suffered when all of them ended in miscarriage. Fibroids, the doctors said. Katie had longed for another child and was willing to risk further disappointment, but she never got pregnant again. She and Matt had more or less accepted it wasn't meant to be - but this hysterectomy would make sure of it.

'Well, there's definitely no chance now, kiddo,' she said to the mirror. 'Not a hope in hell.'

She slipped into a pair of black leggings and a cream off-the-shoulder T-shirt, tied her long, honey blonde hair into a loose ponytail and made her way downstairs and into the kitchen.

Matt placed a large glass of Châteauneuf-du-Pape into Katie's hand and raised his glass to hers. 'Here's to my brave baby.'

'Did you really have to say "baby"?' Katie chided, taking the glass without meeting his eyes.

Matt stared at her, realising the impact of his words.

'Not another word, Matt. I'm fine really. You'd think I would know by now that my childbearing days are over. It's just the finality of it all, I guess.'

'Sorry, love, for being so insensitive. I'll call you "honey" from now on, shall I?'

At that, they both smiled. 'Yeah, that'll do,' said Katie. 'Let's order a Chinese; I'm starving.'

After they'd eaten, Matt, still sipping his wine, went into his small office at the rear of the kitchen to finish off some sketches for an office block he was working on. He'd promised his client the drawings in two days and he always worked better under pressure; a glass or two always helped, too.

Mathew Cully was a well-known and sought-after architect; widely liked and respected. He was meticulous - always dotting the 'i's and stroking the 't's - and had earned a reputation as a reliable, decent businessman. 'Old school', Katie described him. When he walked into a room, his presence was obvious; not just by his large frame but by the air of assuredness that surrounded him.

As Matt sat at his computer, he had a brain wave. After 15 minutes surfing the net, he came out from his office and back into the living room, beaming.

Katie looked up from the TV. 'What's up with you?'

'I've just had a great idea. Why don't we take a nice holiday before your op?' He went on, excitably, 'I know you always wanted to go on a cruise and there are great deals at the moment - I'll take time off; God knows I could be doing with it - and maybe Connor can get away from his work and we could all go in two weeks' time.'

'Hold on, big man,' Katie laughed. 'Has that wine gone to your head? If I thought it would only take a few glasses of Châteauneuf -de-Pape to actually get you to go on a sun holiday I'd have bought you a crate of the stuff years ago!'

The last few times they'd been away together they'd not gone far; Dublin for a long weekend at Easter and Matt's sister's summer house in Donegal for a weekend in August. The last time they'd sat together on a plane was when they'd visited Connor in Glasgow last year.

Matt wasn't keen on sunny destinations like the Med or Canary Islands, and, in recent years, it was virtually unheard of for him to take a full week off work.

Suddenly, Katie remembered her earlier conversation with Carol about them going on holiday together; this was going to throw a spanner in the works. She looked up at Matt, not wanting to burst his bubble; she couldn't possibly say she was planning on taking a trip with Carol now.

'What makes you think Connor will want to go on a cruise - or any holiday - with us? And he'll not leave his precious Amy,' she added sarcastically.

'Well,' said Matt, 'I meant for them both to come with us; my treat.'

'Are you serious, Matt? You think I'm going away to look at her for a full week, bullying our Connor? Absolutely no way!'

'Katie,' he sighed, 'you have to give the girl a chance. Connor obviously loves her. He's not that much of a pushover. She's not that bad. Sure, it'll be an opportunity for you to get to know her better. I'm sure she has a lovely side to her.'

He added: 'Connor couldn't love someone who's all bad, now, could he?'

For Matt's sake, Katie held her tongue and nodded. 'Hmm… I suppose we could ask them.'

Silently, she hoped they wouldn't go.

2

Connor hung up from speaking to his dad. He couldn't believe he was getting a chance to get away for a week in the sun. The rain and cooler temperatures were getting to him, but... he knew there'd be a high price to pay for a week of Amy and his mum together. Suddenly, the lousy weather seemed more appealing.

When Connor moved to Glasgow, part of him felt he needed space; not only from his parents but from Amy. When she'd insisted on moving with him, he'd tried as diplomatically as possible to convince her to stay at home - at least until he'd sussed things out.

'I don't understand why you'd rather go alone,' Amy had complained. 'Won't you miss me?' Then, after a beat: 'Don't you love me?'

'It's not that, babe. Of course, I'll miss you - and you know I love you - it's just… I mean, you'll be giving up a good job at the hospital and you have nothing lined up in Glasgow. It just seems silly when there's no rush. I don't want to be dragging you over there on a whim.'

As he'd hugged her to him, the panic rose in his chest.

'Well, I'm going with you,' she'd said firmly. 'You give your mum and dad the good news and I'll tell mine.'

Amy had just started a job in Altnagelvin Hospital. She'd done her placement there as part of her nursing degree and loved it. But, determined to follow Connor, she'd applied for a few posts in Glasgow. She had an excellent CV and references and was confident she'd secure a post - which she did, only two weeks after they'd arrived.

Despite his reservations, Connor had found it exciting, at first, moving in together; not having to go their separate ways after kissing goodnight.

They were in a new city; meeting new colleagues and new friends. They'd been here over a year now and life was going well… at least, that's what he told himself.

He heard the key turn as Amy bounced in, full of energy after her gym class.

'Have you not started dinner?' she snapped, looking pointedly towards the kitchen, which had neither smell nor sign of any cooking in progress. 'I told you I'd be back at half seven.'

'No,' Connor said apologetically, 'Dad's just off the phone. Guess what? He and mum are going on a cruise and they've offered to take us too; all expenses paid.'

'Well, that's obviously your dad's idea,' Amy said bitterly. 'Your mum hates me.'

'No, she doesn't,' Connor lied.

'Well, I don't care because I hate her, too,' she huffed.

'Look, Amy, she just doesn't get you. She thinks you're too outspoken.'

Her eyes widened. 'Oh, really? Well, do you know something? I don't think *you* get me either. What's up with you anyway? You always seem so distracted. I don't know where that head of yours is, half the time.'

She stormed off into the kitchen and started preparing food.

Connor called after her from the living room. 'Is that a yes or a no? I have to let them know as soon as.'

He sighed inwardly. Right now, he didn't care either way. A holiday? Yes. On his own with his parents? Maybe. Alone with Amy? No way. With Amy and his mum? A complete disaster.

When he looked back towards the kitchen, Amy was standing at the door, staring at him.

'There's that look again,' she said. 'You're not even in the room.'

'Aw, stop, Amy, I've things on my mind. So; what do you want to do?'

But she turned on her heel and the only answer he got was the banging of saucepans and dishes.

Connor pretended to watch the TV but he was totally oblivious to what was on the screen.

How much longer can I stand this? he thought.

His fingers tapped nervously on the armrest of the chair as he threw his head back and stared up at the ceiling. He wanted to get up and run out of the flat. He wanted to tell Amy to go back home again and leave him in peace. But he knew he would do neither.

Instead, he got up and made a fuss of her, told her how much he needed her; how much he loved her. Told her his life would fall apart if she wasn't in it. His pretence worked (as it always did) and, after a few tears and 'poor me's' from Amy, she was back on top of her game.

'Well, we can't look a gift horse in the mouth, can we?' she smirked.

'That's better, babe,' Connor soothed. 'We'll have a great time.'

'Ring them back and tell them we will go,' she demanded. 'With a bit of luck, your mum will get seasick on the first day and she'll have to stay in her cabin the entire week.'

'Now that's not nice, Amy. Mum's heart is in the right place. Just cut her a bit of slack. I swear you both could be friends if you worked at it,' he enticed.

She glared at him. 'So, I'm on a well-deserved holiday and I have to keep your mum sweet? I don't think so!'

Connor rolled his eyes, which earned him a thump on the arm.

'You know, it's all *her* fault.' Amy's look dared him to disagree.

'Yeah, of course it is, babe,' he sighed. *What's the point?* he thought.

Connor picked up the phone. 'Hi, Dad. Count us in!'

3

Katie rang Carol on her way to work the next morning, hoping her friend hadn't checked out their girly holiday yet.

'Carol, I'm in a bit of a dilemma,' she said. 'Matt, believe it or not, wants to take me on a cruise in two weeks' time; I know it's because I'm going for the op. I know me and you had plans, but the words wouldn't come out of my mouth. I'm so sorry.'

'Not a bother, Katie,' Carol reassured her. 'There'll be other times. When you recover, we'll get away; don't worry.'

'Thanks, but it gets worse: Matt has invited Connor and Amy, too. I can't bear the thought of it, but I'm going to have to keep my mouth shut.'

'Oh shit,' said Carol. 'A week on a ship… there'll be no avoiding them.'

'Yeah, tell me about it! Though Matt keeps telling me there'll be almost 3,000 people on board, so it's not like it's just us and them.'

'You'll be grand. Just go for it; it'll be great.'

Katie was always first to arrive in the office at the City West bank, where she held a senior post. She'd usually bring a bag of buns from the local bakery and have the kettle boiled, ready for her colleagues. She liked getting in first; liked starting off her day organised and prepared.

She was sharp-witted (sharper still when it came to the job) and had an air of authority about her that was reinforced by the way she dressed; smart and chic. Her staff liked and respected her. Any time Sam Taggart, their boss from head office in London, came over to have a meeting with them, the others felt intimated, but Katie rose to the challenge every time. She was never afraid to speak her mind, but always with poise and sensitivity towards her colleagues. Sam liked this assertive quality about her. He liked a lot of things about her.

As Katie waited on the kettle to boil, she thought about the cruise conversation she'd had with Matt and Connor the previous night. Then she remembered Sam telling her he and his wife had cruised a few times and loved it. She sat there, contemplating whether to ring him and ask him had he ever sailed with 'Golden Lands'.

They spoke from time to time on the phone. His voice had a very distinctive tone; deep, clear and very posh. She could tell from his picture - which she'd seen in one of their corporate booklets - that he was handsome, but when they'd finally met in person, her first thought was that the photos didn't do him justice. He looked about 45 - though Katie guessed he may be older. He was almost as tall as Matt but much leaner; definitely a gym-goer.

His thick, dark hair was turning grey at the temples and he kept it a bit longer than most men his age. It was heavy on top; a bit unruly. She liked the way he ran his fingers through it, brushing it off his face when he was thinking.

And he had the most amazing brown eyes she had ever seen. She couldn't remember him ever wearing a tie; just an open neck shirt - and always a nice suit. And his shoes. Italian leather. She liked his style.

Sam had been visiting the Derry branch for the past two years, and over that time they had become very friendly… maybe overly friendly. There was a slight tension between them that was unmistakeably flirty. It made Katie feel alive to think that Sam liked her; fancied her, even.

They'd last met two months ago; Sam had insisted on walking her to her taxi after their business dinner that evening. But, instead of the gentlemanly kiss on the cheek that she'd been expecting, he kissed her full on the mouth. It only lasted a split second before Katie nervously pulled away, said goodnight and got into the taxi. She'd texted Carol as soon as the taxi took off. *Holy shit… SS (Sexy Sam) just kissed me!*

She hadn't seen him since that night but they spoke frequently on the phone; mostly about business and ending up with a few pleasantries. The kiss was never mentioned. It was put away in a box; probably the best place for it.

She was brought back to reality with the phone ringing. 'Hi Katie, Sam here,' he said in his posh London drawl.

'Oh, hi, Sam,' she said, smiling. 'I was just thinking about you.'

'Something nice, I hope,' Sam said jokingly; Katie could sense him grinning into the phone.

'Well… you go first. It was you who rang me, remember,' Katie said, her tone flirty.

Finally, after talking purely business, Sam asked, 'So what's on your mind, Katie?'

'Well, Matt and I are thinking about going on a cruise; actually, Connor and his girlfriend are coming too. Just wanted to run it by you, the expert,' she laughed.

'Yeah, good choice. You know what I think of cruising; it's a great holiday.'

'Have you ever sailed with Golden Lands? Matt got a really good deal - it's five stars - and I have to say it does sound lovely. We plan to go in two weeks' time; October 23rd, I think.'

As Katie rambled on, a broad smile crept across Sam's handsome face.

'So, what do you think? I suppose it will be too late if you say it's not so good, because Matt is booking it as we speak,' she added.

Finally, he spoke. 'I think it's a great idea, because one: it's a great cruise line, two: it's a great price, and three: Jill and I are going with Golden Lands as well... on October 23rd.'

Katie felt her heart pounding in her chest. 'What? You're not serious; the same date. Oh my God, I'm going to have to ring Matt right away. With any luck he's been delayed in confirming it. I'll have to make up some excuse for why I can't go.' Katie couldn't hide the total panic in her voice. 'How am I going to get out of this? I can't believe it. Oh my God.'

'What's the problem?' he said, amused. 'The ship is big enough for all of us, Katie. I promise I'll pretend I don't even know you. But I can't promise I won't be excited seeing you every day in a lovely bikini.'

'Stop it, Sam. I'm being serious. I don't know how I'm going to get out of this. I'm going to ring Matt straight away.'

'Up to you. We're all booked... and I certainly have no objections,' said Sam, cool as a breeze.

After saying their goodbyes, Katie put her hands over her face. She didn't want Sam and Matt in such close proximity. It wasn't that she didn't trust herself - she would never do that to Matt - it would just be too weird. Matt had never met Sam and Katie had never met Jill and that's the way she wanted it to stay.

Think hard, Katie told herself, pressing the heel of her hands into her forehead. No; she needed to talk to Carol first.

'You are joking me!' squealed Carol down the phone.

'What am I going to do?' said Katie. 'Carol, there's no way I'm going on that ship. Could you just imagine running into Jill every day? She's probably so drop-dead gorgeous I'd feel like a plain Jane beside her. And then seeing him all 'lovey-dovey' with her...' Katie suddenly heard herself ranting and stopped. 'Aw, don't listen to me; you'd think I really fancied him.'

'Well... do you?' her friend enquired.

'No. But, you know I like him. He's so easy on the eye; actually, he's bloody gorgeous. And he has a great sense of humour. It's just everything about him; I shift a gear when I see him - or even hear him on the phone, for that matter.'

'Well, first of all, you need to ring Matt and see if he's booked yet. With a bit of luck, he's had a busy morning.'

'Right. And then what? Jesus, I can't even think straight, Carol.'

'Um, tell him there's a seminar in work you need to go to and that you'll have to put the holiday off for a week. Or say you heard bad reports about that ship, so maybe try another company.'

'Yeah, I'll say someone in work went on a Golden Lands cruise and the food and entertainment were very poor; you know how he likes his food, so that might work. Thanks. Right, I need to go and see if I get him before it's too late; I'll get back to you.' Katie hung up and phoned Matt straight away.

'Hi, darling,' said Matt. 'It's all booked. I even managed to get us an upgrade to 'aqua class', which gives us a few privileges.'

Katie's heart was racing and her stomach felt sick. She couldn't start backtracking now. He was so excited, so she had better sound excited too.

'Great stuff!' Katie answered, trying hard to muster up some enthusiasm while the words *fuck, fuck* went through her head.

'Aye, we're all set,' said Matt, hardly able to contain himself.

Katie met Carol after work; she needed a glass of wine before she went home. Seeing the look on her friend's face as she walked into the bar, Carol stood up and gave her a big hug.

'Jeez, Katie, you'd think you were about to go to prison rather than a luxury cruise,' Carol observed.

'It *is* going to be like a prison, Carol. I'll be afraid to go out in case I run into Sam. And then there's Amy; I can't bear that one!'

'You need to stop this now, Katie,' Carol scowled. 'Get a bit of perspective. Have you told Sam you're booked?'

'Yeah, I phoned him. He thinks it's hilarious. Keeps on talking about seeing me in a bikini and watching me from afar. I told him I'm going to pretend I don't even know him.'

'Why? What's the problem, Katie? He's only a work colleague you have a bit of harmless flirting with. You'd think you were having an affair with him, the way you're going on. Is there something you haven't told me?'

'Don't be ridiculous; it's nothing like that. I just want to relax and not have to look over my shoulder all the time.'

'Well, I think you should introduce Matt to Sam and his wife,' Carol suggested. 'At least that way, you'll not spend the entire time worrying about bumping into him. He will have to behave then… if that's what you want him to do. I've a funny feeling you might just enjoy being eyed up by Sexy Sam.'

When Katie arrived home, Matt opened the door, a big smile on his face.

'I'm really looking forward to the cruise,' he said, pecking Katie on the cheek.

'Aw, me too, love,' she replied. 'It'll be great.' *Not*, she thought.

4

With one week to go before the cruise, Matt got an urgent phone call from a client he'd been working with for some time.

'Look, Matt,' Jim Bates said, 'there's no way round it. I can't wait 'til after your holiday; this is life or death to me. I need this brought forward. It has to be before the board by next week.'

Matt felt sick inside. How was he going to tell Katie he couldn't go away? She was so excited; buying bits and pieces for the trip and looking happier than he'd seen her in a long while. He knew he was about to disappoint her; something he always tried to avoid. Maybe Carol would take his place? Katie loved going away with her friend. And it wouldn't cost Carol anything. It would be his loss… in more ways than one. But he really didn't have a choice.

'Oh no, Matt, that is so unfair,' Katie wailed when he broke the news to her.

'There's no way out of it, love. This is a really big client and it's a really big contract involving a lot of money. I'm gutted too, honey, but I've seriously no choice. Would Carol take my place? I'll change the name on the ticket so it won't cost her anything. Sure, you two will have a ball.'

Suddenly, Katie pictured herself and Carol on the sun-loungers, champagne in hand and Sam close by (with Jill, of course). She could feel her heart starting to flutter. *What is wrong with you?* she asked herself. Snapping out of her daydream, she looked up at Matt. He was studying her face, puzzled.

'Well, I'd better ring Carol, then, if that's how it's going to be. See what she thinks.'

'Are you sitting down, Carol?' Katie asked, lying on top of her bed. She didn't want Matt around when she asked her, as she was unsure how her friend would react, knowing Sam was going to be there. Maybe she would refuse to go, not wanting to be part of anything that might 'happen'.

'What's up now?' Carol asked.

'You doing anything in the last week of October?'

'Why, you need me to do something? Please don't ask me to keep the dog,' she groaned.

'No, I was wondering if you'd like to come on the cruise with me? Oh, Carol, I *need* you to come on the cruise with me!' Katie said, her voice shaking with panic and excitement.

'Huh? What are you on about?'

'Matt can't go. He's been given a work deadline. He's offering you his holiday - free of charge.'

Katie ranted on. 'I don't know whether to laugh or cry. I *so* did not plan this to happen.

'But if you were with me, things could run more smoothly. We could have good fun and I won't have to worry about Matt noticing Sam's lusty glances.'

'Hold on, Katie,' Carol said firmly. 'Do I have a choice here? I mean, it's a lovely gesture and everything, but I'm not going away to be a cover for you as you walk yourself into a holiday romance - and a bonkers one at that, given your potential lover has his wife with him, you have your son and future daughter-in-law with you and - above all else - you have a husband at home. It's crazy!'

'It's not going to be like that, Carol,' Katie stressed. 'I'd never be that stupid. I know I'm just getting a bit carried away. Look, it's been sprung on me, so now I'm springing it on you.

'Just think about it and you can call me back in a wee while.'

5

Carol Devlin added milk and instant coffee to her favourite mug and filled it up with boiling water. As she sat on the high stool at the island in the centre of her kitchen, she slowly sipped and thought about Katie and Matt.

She'd met Katie over 30 years ago, when they both ended up sitting nervously together on their first day at secondary school. It was the beginning of a great friendship and they'd been inseparable ever since.

After school, university beckoned for both. Carol went to Queen's in Belfast to study art and design and Katie stayed in Derry to do business and economics at Magee. But their friendship never suffered; they'd spoken on the phone practically every day and had met up during semester breaks.

When their studies finished, Carol, who loved bringing a room to life with colour and textiles, moved back to Derry to work in interior design, while Katie was offered a job working for Ulster Bank.

When the two friends met their respective husbands, they made up a foursome from time to time. Matt and Ciaran were happy to please their wives by socialising together now and again, but it was more than obvious they would never be bosom buddies.

Carol had a few skeletons in her cupboard that only Katie knew about. She loved the fun and the flirting, which had led to a few flings over the years - though she never gave her heart away.

Her friend never judged Carol when she strayed (in fact, she'd dug her out of a few holes). Ciaran was a bit of a cold fish. He wasn't a great one for showing warmth and affection and Carol knew Katie could see it; it was the reason she never scolded her for seeking it elsewhere.

Carol didn't have kids. It wasn't for want of trying, but it had just never happened for her and Ciaran. She adored Connor (her godson) and would often laugh and tell him how lucky he was having 'two mammies'.

She brought herself back to the question at hand. *Should I go on this cruise or not?*

She weighed up the pros and cons: five star was not to be sniffed at. Heat on the bones in October and food and drink on tap! So, why not? Well... it was OK for her to fall by the wayside now and again; she could handle it. But *Katie?* The guilt would kill her, and if Matt found out, it would destroy him.

Despite Katie's insistence she would never cheat on Matt, Carol's gut told her otherwise. Something was different about Katie when she spoke of Sam, and Carol had never seen her like this before. It was an accident waiting to happen and Carol wasn't going to be the one to push Katie onto the road.

Her logical self was saying *don't go*, but her carefree self was fighting for a say: *Katie is entitled to a little bit of excitement, as long as no one gets hurt. We won't always turn heads! And maybe it's better I'm along with her to keep an eye...*

Katie sat, anxiously picking at her gel nails in anticipation of Carol ringing back with her answer. Unable to wait any longer, she rang her.

Carol took a deep breath as she saw Katie's number flash up on the screen; she didn't want to disappoint her beautiful friend, who'd do anything for her and who Carol had needed more times than she cared to remember.

She put the phone to her head and, without even saying 'hello', blurted out: 'Right, Katie, I'll go. I'd rather it was just me and you, but it's not. I can't say I'm over the moon about it, but maybe you need a bit of flirtation with this fella Sam. I just pray you get it out of your system and it stops at that.'

Katie couldn't believe it; she'd resigned herself to the fact that Carol wouldn't want to be part of her possible infidelity (however slim the chances) and had been wondering who else she could ask rather than forego the holiday. She dreaded the thought of going alone with Connor and Amy.

'Really, Carol? I thought you were dead against it. Oh, thank you, thank you! I swear I'm not going to step out of line.'

'Liar,' Carol laughed. 'Well, you're not always going to be young and irresistible; every dog has its day.'

'Oh God, I've nothing to wear!' yelled Katie, full of excitement.

'Don't you start,' said Carol, before signing off with a breezy, 'catch you later, hon'.

Katie jumped off her bed and walked over to her mirrored wardrobes that ran the entire length of the room. She pushed the hangers back and forth, squashing all the clothes to within an inch of their lives; not one thing appealed to her. She stared at them, wishing they could reinvent themselves.

The look she wanted was 'hot, cool, rock chick', but everything in there said 'elegant, classy businesswoman'. No; Sam was used to her dressing that way. She wanted a 'sexy, no effort' look. She needed to be stunning.

She imagined herself walking around the ship wearing gorgeous outfits and Sam watching her. Sam longing for her… Sam wishing he was with her rather than his wife.

Katie sat back on the bed, still looking at the bulging

wardrobes. *What the fuck is wrong with me?* she thought. *Am I going through a mid-life crisis?*

It was 'Sam, Sam, Sam', morning noon and night.

She had to keep a lid on things with Carol. Her friend wasn't stupid and Katie feared if she knew what was really going on in her head she would bail out of the trip.

How did a little bit of fun and flirting become so all-consuming? Katie wondered.

Not for the first time, she found herself wondering what Jill looked like. Was she skinny? Was she fat? What was her dress style? Was she outgoing and bubbly? Was she much younger than her? She knew no one could catch a man like Sam without being a jaw-dropper.

She needed to get a grip. Get out of this silly mood. Look forward to the holiday for what it was and ignore this teenage excitement running through her veins.

Katie got off the bed and picked up her phone, forcing herself to sound more upbeat and positive.

'Carol, fancy a bit of shopping to get us in the holiday mood? I seriously need some new clothes. Town opens late tomorrow night; what you think?'

'Yeah, sounds like a plan,' said Carol. 'And would you get the details of where we're actually going on this cruise? I want to make sure everyone is green with envy when I tell them where I'm off to.'

The next evening, after their successful shopping trip, the girls stopped off for a nightcap and a quick bite in Badger's, the popular bar across from Foyleside shopping centre. Katie was like a six-year-old examining her purchases and didn't care who was watching as she pulled bikinis, sarongs, flip-flops and lacy knickers out of her bags and sprawled them all over the table. Then, getting more excited, she lifted a pale lemon silk halter top from a Coast shopping bag.

'I have to look at this again,' she said. The edges were piped with soft black leather and the neckline scooped into a V shape that would show just a little cleavage; it would also show off her toned shoulders and arms. She was secretly thinking, *yes; Sam would like this.*

'That will be stunning with your black leather leggings,' said Carol. 'An outfit like that would take you anywhere.'

A knowing smile spread across Katie's face. 'Yeah, I love it; just what I was looking for.'

'So, what did Sam say when you told him that Matt wasn't going on the cruise?' Carol asked, picking a large prawn from the skewer and popping it into her mouth.

'I didn't get around to telling him.'

'So, he still thinks Matt is going?'

'Yes, well, to be honest, I've been up to my eyes. I haven't even spoken to him since this all changed. I was going to email him, but I'd be afraid someone else might read it and add two and two together and come up with ten. I don't have his personal account.'

'Good,' Carol said firmly. 'And I hope you never get it… his email address, I mean,' she smiled impishly as she licked the sauce off her fingers. 'So, poor ol' Sam is in for a right ol' shock.'

'Ah, same boy won't let it fizzle him,' Katie assured her.

'What's he like, anyway? Apart from being tall, dark and handsome.'

Katie's face lit up with a wide smile and she became animated as she told Carol that everyone in her office fancied him.

'Sounds like a real charmer,' Carol smiled. 'I'm looking forward to meeting him.'

'Hey, hands off, you! Join the queue. Jill is first… I'm second.'

'You just said it, Katie, and don't ever forget it: the wife will always be number one.'

'I've my own number one at home, Carol. Matt is the love of my life. I'm just being a bit silly.'

'For all you know, that boy could have a bird in every branch,' Carol warned. 'You just need to be careful. There's nothing wrong with a bit of excitement, but there's a price to pay for everything.'

Katie didn't like the way the conversation was turning; her bubble was starting to burst.

Wanting to change the subject, she fumbled through her handbag and produced a blue cellophane folder. 'By the way; here's the itinerary. Venice to Rome, here we come.'

'I'll drink to that,' said Carol, raising her glass and clinking it against Katie's.

6

'Final check,' Matt shouted as Katie rushed downstairs, grabbing dirty laundry with one hand and her earrings with the other.

'Passports, euros, cruise documents, insurance; all here,' he said, filing through the blue leather travel folder provided by Golden Lands.

Connor and Amy had arrived home two days previously and Matt was driving them all to Dublin airport. Connor arranged the suitcases in the boot of the car, leaving the roof rack empty for Carol and Amy's luggage. He'd enjoyed staying at home the last two nights, with his mum busy spoiling him. He felt relaxed; felt he could breathe more easily.

Katie got into the back seat, letting Connor sit up front with his dad.

'All aboard,' Matt said as his four passengers settled back on their three-hour journey.

Amy did her best to be civil, knowing a week would be challenging enough with her future mother-in-law without getting off on the wrong foot. Connor smiled to himself as he listened to Amy talking to his mum and Carol, all sweetness and light, when, in truth, Katie always got the worst word in Amy's mouth.

Carol and Katie chatted easily, with Carol trying not to leave Amy out of the conversation. Katie, on the other hand, didn't seem to be making the same effort. During a 'pee stop', Carol pulled her friend to one side and whispered, 'Come on, Katie, I think you're being a bit stiff. Amy is really trying to be friendly towards us; you in particular. We've a week together, so for fuck's sake be nice. Offer it up!'

'Alright,' said Katie.

'Good. We're almost at the airport now, so that's the worst part over. Just grin and bear it.' Carol showed off her own perfect teeth in a wide, false smile.

Matt pulled in at the drop-off bay. Katie insisted there was no need for him to come inside; he had a long journey home and best to be on his way.

After wishing them all *bon voyage*, Matt turned lastly to Katie, his two arms smothering her body. She snuggled into his chest.

'You're going to start me off if you don't let me go,' she sniffed, lifting her head and looking into Matt's kind, handsome face.

'You have a great time, honey, and don't be worrying about me. I've so much work on; you'll be back before I get a chance to lift my head.'

'Come on, Mum,' Connor called over to her. 'The gates are closing. Dad, release her now!'

'On my way,' shouted Katie.

'Love you, big man.'

'Love you too, princess.'

With five sets of hands waving and blowing kisses, four went one way and one went the other.

7

Day One

The ship sat proudly on the dull brown waters of Venice.
'Oh my God; how does that thing even stay up on the water?' Amy asked, looking at the older women for some reassurance.

'Yeah, you would wonder how it does,' said Connor. Apparently, this vessel is 1,047 foot long and weighs 122,400 tonnes.' Amy's face turned the colour of death as she gasped at the ship in horror.

Katie actually felt sorry for her. For the first time ever, she saw Amy's vulnerability.

'Well, someone's certainly done their homework,' said Katie, nudging Connor to play it down. She almost felt like consoling Amy with a hug, but feared she might be pushed away. As usual, Carol came to the rescue.

'These ships are as safe as houses. Sure, how does an aeroplane stay up in the sky? Same thing. Anyway, let's leave all that to the professionals; I can hear champagne popping.' She slipped an arm through Katie's and Amy's and, with the porter carrying their luggage, they all headed towards the floating village for a week of who knew what!

It was organised chaos as they went through embarkation. The queues moved quickly as everyone signed up, smiled at the camera for their ID cards and got their assigned 'state rooms'.

Before they knew it, they were being welcomed on board by what seemed like every nationality of smiling young men and women, holding silver trays with champagne or soft drinks, eager to please their new travellers.

They looked around in awe at the crystal chandeliers, sweeping staircases, glass lifts and mahogany furnishings. Such luxury!

'Oh yeah, I could get used to this,' Carol smiled.

Katie was so carried away by the buzz of the ship (and the champagne) she even lifted her glass to Amy and wished her a great holiday. Suddenly, it dawned on her that Sam could be nearby. She knew his plane was due an hour or two after theirs, but she had lost track of time with all the excitement of their new surroundings.

'Shall we go to the rooms?' Carol asked. 'I'm dying to see our new abode above the waves.' She, too, could feel the champagne taking effect.

'Yeah, our luggage must be there by now and there's a mini bar to keep us topped up,' Katie smiled.

Carol winked. 'This place is getting better by the minute.'

The four of them took the glass lift to the tenth floor, the people milling beneath them becoming smaller and smaller.

Carol opened the door to her and Katie's state room with a wide smile. It was finished to the highest standard and decorated with soft, neutral colours. A large flat-screen TV was built into an oak unit facing their perfectly dressed twin beds; a welcome greeting for 'Ms Cully and Ms Devlin' flashed on its screen.

While Carol went to check out the en suite, Katie opened the sliding doors to their balcony and leaned over the railings to the neighbouring state room occupied by Connor and Amy.

'Happy so far, you two?'

Connor appeared on the balcony. 'Wow, Mum, this is amazing. The room is great; very compact, but they've thought of everything. Amy's having a shower. She's in great form.'

Um, why shouldn't she be? Katie thought.

'Well, we're going to get organised, so I'll leave you two to do your own thing. No doubt we'll see you at the pool area,' Katie smiled at her son. The happiness of knowing she would be seeing him every day for the next week made her heart float like a feather. She'd missed him so much since he'd left home.

Katie went back inside and opened up the mini bar, which was stacked with beverages and mixers. She lifted out a couple of gins and tonics and reached for two cut glass tumblers that sat on the shelf of a wall unit.

Carol stepped out of the bathroom, drying her hands on a white fluffy towel.

'Good minds think alike,' she smiled at Katie as she took the drink from her.

'So, what's the game plan? Do you want to unpack or shall we drink this on the balcony and then head out for a nose around?'

Reality was starting to kick in and Katie wasn't sure if the flutters in her tummy were nerves, excitement or both.

'What if we run into him?' she said, as Carol opened up her suitcase to look for a bikini.

'You're a bit late wondering about that. He is on the ship, isn't he?'

'I assume so. I didn't spot him - remember, I've never seen him in anything other than a suit.'

'Well, he'll be wearing a lot less this week,' smiled Carol. 'Right, drink up, Katie; let's get changed and get out of here.'

Katie rose with a sigh. 'My nerves are shot to shit; I need to get this over and done with.'

After choosing colourful bikinis and matching sarongs, the girls checked their looks in the long length mirror. Happy with what they saw, they headed off to the pool bar on deck 12.

Loads of people had the same idea; some were already laid out on sun loungers, cocktails in hand. They made their way to the bar and got two seats partly in the shade; the searing afternoon sun shone brightly in the clear blue Venice sky.

There was a medium-size pool in front of them, with two Jacuzzis at each side of the top end. Beyond that was a stage where a four-piece band, decked out in bright floral shirts and beige slacks, was setting up for the 'Majestic Sail Away' set for five o'clock.

Katie scanned the deck for Sam, but couldn't see him.

It's a wonder he's not at the bar, she thought. *Then again, maybe he's one of those men who behaves totally different with the wife at his side.*

Each attractive woman who walked by, Katie took her from the feet up, wondering if it was Jill, but each time, she settled down with someone other than Sam.

Carol knew Katie was pretending to be cool but she could see a mile away that her friend was on tenterhooks.

'No sign of 'Sexy Sam' yet?'

'Not yet. I think I might throw up at any minute.'

She had no sooner spoken when a beautiful, blonde, tall, slim woman walked through the automatic door leading from the lift area to the pool deck. Katie's gut feeling told her it was Jill.

'I bet that's her,' she said to Carol under her breath, lifting her gin and tonic to her mouth and taking a large gulp.

She watched as the other woman glided elegantly into a shaded area and sat down at an empty table. The woman wore a bright pink and silver maxi dress that was slit high on both sides. One shoulder was exposed and showed off the silver strap of a bikini top. She wore long, silver earrings and carried a large, soft, silver leather bag that had a bunch of diamanté keyrings jangling from one side. She looked about 35. Katie suddenly felt very plain by comparison.

'I thought you didn't know what she looks like,' said Carol, hardly able, either, to take her eyes off the blonde lady.

'I don't! I heard she was tall, blonde and good-looking, so I just feel it in my water. Time will tell; I'm quite sure Sam will be here soon, too.'

'I don't know about you, Katie, but I need another drink.'

8

Carol waved to the smiling bartender and ordered two more G&Ts as Katie took a lipstick from her makeup bag and applied it without the use of a mirror.

Carol smiled. 'It never ceases to amaze me how perfectly you can do that; I'd have it plastered all over the place.'

She took the lipstick from Katie and was mockingly drawing on larger lips around her mouth when a male voice sounded from behind.

'Hello, Katie.' It was him.

Katie tried hard to keep her composure; not easy due to the combined effect of nerves and daytime drinking.

'Hi, Sam. So... you made it.'

There he was in all his glory. Katie didn't know where to look first; at his handsome face or his long, muscular legs. He wore a pair of stonewash blue denim shorts and a pure white, lightly creased linen shirt, its last few buttons undone and hanging out over his shorts. He oozed sex appeal.

'I sure did,' he said. 'So, what do you think so far?'

'Very impressed. I think we'll manage a week of this for sure.

'Oh, sorry,' Katie quickly added as she realised Carol was staring at her. 'This is my best friend, Carol.'

'Pleased to meet you, Carol.' Sam took her hand and kissed it.

'So, where are the hubbies, then?' he asked, looking around.

'At home where all good husbands should be,' Katie smirked, gathering some Dutch courage.

Sam looked confused. 'Oh. Why's that?'

'Matt had to work, so Carol took his place.'

'Right. Very good!'

'Where's Jill?' Katie asked.

'She's in the room, unpacking. She likes to be organised.'

'She'll be here shortly'.

The two friends looked at one another and the relief on Katie's face was clear; even Carol felt herself breathe a bit easier too.

'Are you having a drink with us?' Katie offered.

'Yeah, go on, then. I'll hang out here until Jill comes down.'

As Sam called the bartender over and ordered his drink, Carol spoke quietly into Katie's ear. 'Thank God you were wrong about yer women over there. Even I was a bit worried; she's way too much competition.'

'Here's to the two virgin cruisers,' smiled Sam, clinking his glass to theirs.

'I've been called a lot worse,' Carol laughed.

The mood soon livened as Katie, emboldened by the alcohol, held court with funny stories, switching her attention with ease between Carol and Sam as all three of them laughed. Her boss seemed mesmerised by her frivolousness, vibrancy and confidence.

In mid conversation, Katie turned her head as something caught her eye; the beautiful blonde lady was waving in their direction. Quickly, Katie looked behind her to see who she could be waving at; to her total devastation, Sam waved back. A guilty smile spread across his handsome face.

The blonde got up and made her way towards them, her maxi dress parting to reveal long, toned, tan legs. As she moved closer, Sam muttered, 'Oh, I didn't realise Jill was already at the pool deck.'

When she reached them, Sam reached out and kissed her full

on the mouth before introducing her to Katie and Carol.

What he didn't mention, however, was that he and Katie were work colleagues. Instead, he made out they had just met five minutes ago - he even pretended to get their names mixed up: 'Let me see, ah, Carol, right?' he said, pointing to Katie.

Jill smiled as Katie introduced herself. She was even prettier up close. Her blue eyes sparkled under her long black eyelashes, and, as she smiled, her full pink lips gave way to perfect white teeth.

Katie could have stared at her for much longer, but Sam hastily made their excuses.

'No doubt we'll see you girls around.'

Sam and Jill walked off hand in hand, making such a striking couple that other people sitting about turned their heads to gaze after them.

As Carol's eyes followed them, she noticed that Jill's smiling expression had turned into a frown.

9

The two girls sat there in total silence. As Katie nervously chewed the end of her straw, Carol pulled hers out of the glass and took a large swig of the gin.

'Holy fuck, this is going to be good. I'd say there might be a murder in paradise.'

'Why?' asked Katie, hope rising in her voice.

'That Jill one had a face on her like a busted bagpipe. There's more going on there; I'm telling you that for nothing.'

Just as Katie leaned in to gossip some more, Connor and Amy emerged from the automatic glass door and made their way over.

'Thought we'd find you here,' Connor smiled.

Katie's face lit up as she greeted her one and only. He had Matt's dark brown eyes and broad smile. Connor had a happy-go-lucky air about him that Katie was delighted to see; she'd thought him a bit distracted -stressed, almost- when he'd come over from Glasgow.

He was losing his boyish looks and becoming a man; and getting more handsome with it. It did her heart good just looking at him and she couldn't help but throw her arms around him and squeeze him to her. Connor was well used to this. He hugged his mum back with the same ferocity and kissed the top of her head, which was second nature to him after years of watching his dad do exactly that. *God, life is strange*, thought Katie, as she released him and offered Amy a seat beside them.

'You have to get your own drinks, darling. Just order and give them your ID card. With the drinks package, you can't buy anyone a drink, but the good thing is it's already paid for.'

'We're like the Royals,' laughed Carol. 'Not a pound between us.'

Katie had to act normal, but she was dying to hear Carol's take on Sam and Jill. She scanned around occasionally, half wanting to see them walk back to the pool area.

The conversation flowed easily as they all sat at the bar, more happy cruisers coming into the bar area and settling down nicely. Then a voice on the tannoy instructed them all to get ready for the emergency lifeboat drill.

They each had to go to their state room, pick up their lifejacket and go to the assigned muster station for the mandatory safety drill.

Back in their room, Katie and Carol, both giddy with alcohol, fought with their lifejackets and helped each other belt up. They then went outside to the corridor to wait for Connor and Amy. When her son and his girlfriend appeared, Katie had to stifle a laugh; the sight of Amy's petite frame housed in a large orange lifejacket looked faintly ridiculous, and was made even funnier by the ghostly pallor of her terrified face.

'Whose fucking idea was this anyway?' Amy said through gritted teeth, as if she could read Katie's mind.

'If this thing sinks, you won't need to bother getting me into a lifeboat; I'll have a heart attack on the spot.' Her voice was shaking, and she was almost in tears, so much so that Katie had to gather herself and offer some reassurance. Connor already had his arms around her.

'It's OK, babe, everyone has to do this. Sure, these big ships never sink. It's just safety regulations.'

'Oh, really? What about the Costa Concordia, like that didn't sink? All I can see are the photos and TV footage. Oh my God, I'm going to be sick!'

Katie and Carol rushed Amy into the toilet in their room,

where the poor girl was so violently ill that Katie had to sponge her face with a wet flannel.

'Come on, now, Amy pet,' Carol soothed. 'Everything's fine; you just have yourself all wound up. This will be over in ten minutes and we can all relax and get back to partying.' Her sympathetic words and soft expression had the desired effect; Amy took a sip of water and a deep breath and they made their way out of the room and towards their designated area.

Half an hour later, they were back on the deck enjoying the music of the band and the breathtaking experience of waving *arriverderci* to beautiful Venice as the ship took sail towards its first destination 200 nautical miles away: Split, Croatia.

After the drill, Sam and Jill headed to deck 15, which was more suitable for those who wanted a quiet sailaway, without music and with fewer people.

Jill was still in bad form and Sam was still trying to lift her spirits, but she was having none of it.

'I knew if I came down early, you'd be up to no good,' she moaned, as they headed to the far side of the ship.

'Honestly, Jill, this has to stop,' he said, exasperated. 'I told you; I went down to deck five to reserve a table for speciality dining and I was speaking to them for no more than two minutes before you came over.' He gave a deep sigh.

'I simply stopped for a beer and was only being friendly… in fact, they spoke to me first. I couldn't be rude, now, could I? Don't forget, we'll be spending a week with these people.'

'Indeed, we shall not,' she snapped. 'Them nor anyone else. You are away with me; this is our time together.'

Sam knew better than to tell Jill that Katie was a work

colleague and that she was here with a friend and not her husband; her jealousy and paranoia were getting out of control and no matter what Sam did to try to reassure her, it never worked.

His first marriage had broken down -mostly due to work pressures on both parties - but their divorce was amicable.

At the beginning of their relationship, Sam idolised Jill, never got distracted in her company and simply couldn't take his eyes off her.

Although she knew Sam loved her, Jill couldn't control the jealousy that clawed up her beautiful back and into her busy head. 'Mr Jealousy' reminded her time and time again that Sam was a married man when he'd first come on to her; if he'd done it then, he could do it again.

Although he'd explained repeatedly that his marriage was over when he'd met her, Jill knew any woman would fall at his feet - just like she had.

Sam had it all. Then again, everyone thought Jill had it all, too. *But did she have Sam?*

The deeply satisfying state of being in love with him had turned into an obsession.

That wonderful feeling of happiness and contentment had somehow mutated to insecurity and jealousy; a fear and a neediness that caused many a fight. That urge to argue, attack and blame led to them not speaking for days on end and to so many tears on her pillow. His claims of innocence never fully reassured her.

Deep down, she hated herself for putting a damper on the first few hours of the holiday they'd eagerly planned and were looking forward to. She didn't know why she allowed herself to get so jealous. Sam was only making polite conversation to a few girls at the bar whose husbands were probably on their way to join them. And it wasn't to say that they were raven-haired beauties; Jill knew she stood out in a crowd.

As she sipped her champagne with the early evening sun on her back, she made a conscious decision to lighten up and be happy. They both needed this break. A beautiful week lay ahead if she didn't let her jealous heart spoil it.

'I might go for a nap. All today's activities are catching up on me... want to join me?' Sam asked with a 'little boy lost' look in his eyes; a look Jill could never resist. She smiled back at him and took a long sip from her champagne glass. Leaving the remains on a nearby wooden decking table, she took his outstretched hand and walked to their suite.

After their evening meal, Katie and Carol retired to the champagne ice bar and sipped their cosmopolitans, enjoying chatting to other guests while Connor and Amy checked out the casino.

The bar seemed to be the hub of the ship. The bartenders mesmerised everyone with their cocktail-mixing skills, pouring them from a height into several glasses simultaneously while appreciative guests whistled and flashed their camera phones at their juggling expertise.

An eight-piece band played on the grand foyer on the lower level, and loads of people filled the floor, strutting their stuff and dancing off the delicious food they'd savoured from the main dining room or one of the ship's five speciality restaurants.

'It's a bit "coupley",' Carol said, screwing up her nose as she looked around the bar. 'I wonder what the captain looks like?'

'If he's tall, dark and handsome,' Katie answered, 'he'll not be safe while you're around.'

'If I've to look much longer at happy couples staring into

each other's eyes, he'll not be safe if he has one foot in the grave and the other one shaking,' Carol laughed.

'Don't see the love birds about; I thought this area would be their scene.'

'Mmm,' Katie said. 'Sure, they could be anywhere; there's things going on all over this place. Maybe they went to the show that's on in the theatre.'

'Yeah, or maybe they're all curled up after a bit of make-up sex. Hmm… lucky Jill.'

'Yeah, maybe,' Katie sighed, suddenly wishing she was somewhere else.

Connor and Amy had spent a few hours at the casino, spending more chips than they were accumulating. When Amy's numbers came up on the roulette table, she squealed and slapped the counter like a cowboy.

'Yes! Yes! Yes!' she cried, pulling an invisible chain down from the ceiling above her seat. She threw her arms around Connor's neck, bursting with excitement. Casinos weren't really Connor's thing, but he was enjoying it all the same. The champagne was flowing but he took it easy, knowing Amy would need looking after. Sure enough, she soon began slurring her words and getting more and more rowdy.

'Think we should hit the sack, babe,' he said. 'We've been here long enough.'

'No,' Amy pleaded. 'Wait another wee while, babe; I'm feeling lucky.' As she spoke, she slid off her stool, and if it hadn't been for Connor's quick reflexes, she would've landed flat on her face. She was a bad loser, but, in her drunken state, insisted she would win next time.

'Right. Ten more minutes then we'll call it a night,' Connor said firmly.

He didn't actually mind hanging out for another while, because Amy was firing champagne into her like there was no tomorrow. That meant she'd be fast asleep as soon as she hit the pillow.

And that suited him just fine.

10

Day Two (Split)

The ship anchored in Split at 7am. Katie and Carol had never been. The daily news bulletin informed them that Split was the second largest city in Croatia, built inside a former Roman imperial complex called the Diocletian Palace.

They woke early and went for breakfast. They were looking forward to getting off and exploring one of the Adriatic's most amazing seaports and the medieval old town.

They decided to laze on the deck for an hour or two, then go ashore and check out the churches, palaces, cafes, shops and galleries.

Katie left Carol at the poolside to catch the mid-morning rays as she went to the shore excursion desk to buy their tickets for the tour.

As she leafed through one of the tour brochures, she felt a tap on her right shoulder and turned around to be met by Sam's devilish smile.

'Oh, hi, Sam; how's you?' Katie wished she'd redone her lipstick.

'You girls going ashore?'

'Yeah, we're stepping off around noon. We haven't been to Split before; it's supposed to be lovely.'

'Definitely a place to see. You'll enjoy it. So, what did you get up to last night?'

'We sat at the champagne bar for an hour or so after dinner.

We were tired, though; it was a long day and we'd too much drink; first day madness.'

'Oh, I know. We ended up having room service and an early night. Up bright and breezy this morning.'

'Lovely!' said Katie, feeling her heart sink a little. 'You going ashore?'

'We will in a while. We've been here a few times before, so we'll just have a walk about, you know, get off and stretch the old legs. I've just left Jill in the spa so she'll be busy for two hours,' he said, pointedly.

'That's nice. We're hanging about the pool for an hour or so if you fancy a bit of company.'

'Yeah, I'll walk back with you and have a coffee and a chat.'

Katie got her tour tickets and she and Sam headed for the lifts.

'What floor are you on?' she asked.

'Twelve... same floor as the pool deck.'

'Oh, lucky you. That's where all the suites are, isn't it? Butlers and everything! I hear they're very expensive; are they worth it? We're on the tenth floor. The room is great and we've a nice balcony, too.' Katie found herself rambling on a bit as they got into the lift and Sam pressed for floor 12.

'You're welcome to come see it if you'd like?'

Katie froze. 'What? Are you mad, Sam? All we'd need is Jill to walk in; how would you explain that one?'

'Jill's at the spa; she'll be a while.'

Then, looking very serious, he added: 'And, by the way, I want to apologise for yesterday. You probably wondered why I didn't mention we were work colleagues.'

Katie said nothing; just looked up at him, eyebrows raised.

'You see,' he went on, 'Jill can be a bit insecure and I don't want any extra hassle. I should've explained this to you before we came away, but I thought Matt would be here and maybe you would be a bit standoffish yourself. I was thrown by your friend being here and I had to think on my feet and my instinct told me to pretend we were strangers. Sorry.'

Katie didn't know what to say, but before she got a chance to speak, Sam continued.

'To be honest, I couldn't believe my luck when you said your husband couldn't make it. I mean…'

'Why?' Katie interrupted. 'What difference does it make? Sure, your wife is here, isn't she? You'll not get looking out of your eyes by the sounds of things.'

At that moment, the lift stopped and Sam walked through the parting door. Casually, he said: 'My room is to the left; come on and I'll show you.'

Katie swallowed hard. She wanted to say no, but instead she followed him, trying to appear as calm as he sounded. He chatted easily as he walked past the first two state rooms before stopping at room 1202. She was glad there were no butlers around, as they would know she wasn't his wife.

As if reading her thoughts, Sam continued to reassure her. 'Jill is laid out getting a facial or a massage; stop worrying. She left her key card in the room, so she can't unexpectedly land back here. I told her I'd see her at the pool bar at 11.30. She knows I plan to go to the gym for an hour.'

He opened the door. 'After you,' he said, stepping aside.

Katie's mouth fell open as she walked into a beautiful lounge. It was a sea of soft cream furnishings: sofa, coffee table and organza drapes. Three arched pillars separated the open-plan lounge from the spacious and luxurious bedroom. A balcony ran the length of the entire two rooms and was furnished with cream decking furniture and deeply padded cushions. It was all so relaxing and romantic.

A door to the left opened into a large bathroom with a Jacuzzi and a matching gold-plated double shower. Jill's cosmetics dominated the 'his and hers' sinks, and a black silk nightie hung on a gold ornate hook on the back of the bathroom door.

Katie felt like a traitor, standing there in another woman's space.

'It's absolutely gorgeous,' she said, turning to Sam, who was standing outside the bathroom door watching her, a soft smile on his face.

'Yeah, it is that for sure.'

'I need to get ba-back; Carol will think I got lost,' she stammered, completely overwhelmed by what she was feeling, thinking and sensing. As she moved to the door, Sam's eyes seemed to pierce right through her. He then moved his gaze slowly to her lips and back up to meet her eyes again.

As their eyes locked together, a feeling of pure desire surged through her, the intensity of which she'd never experienced before - not even with Matt. Sam walked towards her and she stood there; motionless.

Slowly putting his hands on each side of Katie's face, Sam's lips met hers. The kiss, soft and gentle at first, quickly became more passionate as his hands moved over her body; first to her neck and shoulders, then down to the curve of her hips before stopping at the small of her back, where he pulled her forcefully towards him. Breathlessly, he broke off the kiss and moved his mouth to Katie's ear. 'Oh God, Katie,' he growled. 'You have no idea how much I want you.'

Katie couldn't believe this was happening. Part of her wanted to run out of the room and never look back… but then there was the part of her that didn't want him to stop. Finally, she came to her senses.

'Jesus, Sam, what the fu- what are we doing?'

He stopped, looking earnestly into her flushed face.

'Should I apologise, Katie? Will we pretend this never happened? Just like we pretend there's nothing between us every time we meet?'

'I need to go, Sam,' she said. 'I shouldn't be here; I'm not thinking straight. This is mad; *we* are mad!' She wiped her mouth with the back of her hand and walked away from him, neither of them uttering another word as she opened the door and nervously checked right and left before darting off down the corridor.

Katie decided to go to the toilet and take a few minutes to gather herself. Luckily, they were empty; obviously a lot of people were away sight-seeing. She looked at herself in the mirror. Her face was flushed and her lips were pale; a look of panic and shame stared back at her.

She took her bronzer, lipstick and eyeliner out of her small handbag and quickly applied them, then crouched down and hung her head under the hand dryer, running her fingers roughly through her long, limp hair in the hope of restoring some volume. Then she stood up straight and checked her appearance, satisfied she looked a lot better than she had when she first walked in. She left the bathroom, picked up a bottle of water from a small fridge sitting at the end of the corridor and walked as steadily as possible over to Carol, who was lounging on the pool deck. She wondered if she should keep the last 15 minutes of madness to herself.

'Oh, you're back,' Carol said, lifting her eyes from her book. 'What time are we getting off?'

I was getting off 15 minutes ago, Katie thought, drily.

'We've to meet up at noon in the public lounge,' she said, with as breezy a tone as she could manage. 'I'm going to sit for a wee half hour and then we'll need to get organised.'

'Perfect,' said Carol, returning to her book.

Katie laid herself back on the sun lounger, relieved Carol was engrossed for now. Her brain was in turmoil, not able to take in what had just happened.

What if Jill had come back? What if someone had seen me leaving Sam's room? What if we'd gone further? What if he ignores me the rest of the week?

'Katie, are you going deaf?' She opened her eyes to see Carol's face in line with hers.

'Jesus, Carol, you scared me there; I must've nodded off,' she lied.

As they got ready to go, Katie was glad she'd said nothing to her friend about what had taken place in Sam's suite; she'd go mad.

Suddenly, she was struck with a pang of guilt; she hadn't given poor Matt a single thought.

As the girls made their way towards the stairs, Katie felt Carol nipping her upper arm. She followed her friend's gaze: Jill was walking towards them, obviously making her way to meet Sam.

Her blonde hair was scraped off her fresh, make-up-free face. She wore a pair of denim shorts that were frayed at the edges and a little white vest top; so simple, but still effortlessly glamorous. Gold flip-flops and a large gold leather bag completed the look.

Jill smiled as she approached them. Katie had no intention of staying for a whole chat, but Carol had other ideas.

'Oh, hi,' Carol said pleasantly, slowing her step. Katie knew she meant business.

'Hi, ladies,' Jill said, self-consciously running her fingers through her damp hair. 'I'm just out of the spa; I must look a sight.'

Katie felt a pang of jealousy; Jill looked years younger and even prettier than she had the day before, if that were possible. Totally blemish-free and not a wrinkle in sight.

'There's hardly anyone around, so you won't be scaring too many,' Katie said, smiling.

Jill looked slightly taken aback at the cattiness of the comment. Carol stepped in.

'You look fab! Au natural suits you. You have a lovely day; probably see you around later.'

'Yeah,' added Katie. 'See you later!'

'Enjoy your day, too,' Jill said quietly, walking off towards the pool area.

Katie knew she was in for a telling off.

'Jesus, you were a bit rude there!' Carol scolded.

'I know,' said Katie. 'Don't know where that came from; I think I'm becoming a total bitch.'

Annoyed with herself, she made a mental note to catch herself on and stop all this nonsense.

'She looks amazing; even with no make-up.'

'Yeah,' Carol agreed. 'I only stopped to get a closer look at her and see what kind of personality she had… but you put a quick end to that,' she tutted, rolling her eyes and shaking her head.

'I know; I feel bad now. I can't handle this; I hope they stay out of our way this week.'

'C'mon, let's get a coffee and get out of here,' Carol sighed, knowing there was nothing more to say about it. What was done was done.

Sam spent a half hour in the gym after Katie had left. He felt the adrenaline pumping through his veins long before he pumped iron.

Holding Katie, kissing her and getting the response he wanted was like a tonic to him. He knew there was a deep attraction between them but he wasn't quite sure he'd succeed in getting her to take the next step. She may have rushed out of his room in a frenzy but he couldn't believe he'd managed to get her there in the first place. He knew there was risk involved, but he wasn't particularly thinking with his head. Sam always seized the moment, be it in love or war.

He had a quick shower, threw on shorts and a T-shirt and headed to the pool bar. Jill was already there. He slowed his pace and took a long look at his beautiful wife, sitting tall and straight on the bar stool sipping a glass of ice water. Any other man would be praising the Lord every single day for a woman like this.

Recently, though, he found himself comparing her to Katie. Jill lacked spontaneity and Sam wondered where their spark had gone. Was it just that he was starting to get bored with her? In stark contrast, Katie's vivacity excited him no end and drew him to her like a magnet.

He approached his wife. She should be all relaxed now after her facial and massage, but as he drew nearer, he could tell by her expression that she was not in good humour.

'Hi, honey,' he said, panicking slightly that she'd somehow found out what he'd been up to.

Did someone see Katie coming out of their room?

'That Katie one…' Jill began.

Sam felt the blood rush to his head.

Holy fuck! Does she know something?

'I just bumped into her, there, and she was so rude; said I'd scare people because I've no make-up on.'

Phew.

'You don't need make-up, honey,' he soothed. 'I'm always telling you that. You know I prefer you like this; a natural beauty.' He kissed her perfect mouth.

'She probably didn't mean it like that. God only knows what's going on with her; you shouldn't let her bad mood influence your day.'

'No. She probably fancies you and that's why she said it,' Jill sulkily replied.

'Jill, seriously…she doesn't even know me.'

She looked at him and tried hard to let her feelings go. She was being unfair.

'Yeah, you're right, I know. It's *her* problem; not ours.'

'That's better,' he said, relieved. 'Why don't you get changed and we'll go off and try and find a nice restaurant, maybe try some of the local fish?'

'Sounds great,' she smiled. A large weight lifted off Sam's square shoulders.

11

Amy was sleeping soundly beside Connor. Though only 9am, he'd been lying fully awake for the past two hours; ever since the ship had anchored. In truth, he had barely closed his eyes all night. Deciding he couldn't lie there any longer, he snuck out of bed and got dressed without waking Amy, leaving a note explaining his absence so as not to provoke her rage.

Just off to get a coffee, babe. Back soon!

He got dressed and slipped nervously out of the room, afraid she would stir and insist he got back into bed.

He went down to the fifth-floor café and found a nice easy chair by the window where he could relax and gather his thoughts. All was quiet until two male officers walked in, busily chatting to each other as they took a table next to the glass counter.

Connor imagined what that life would be like; getting up every day, donning a pristine Navy uniform and smiling at a new bunch of passengers, week in, week out.

Right now, that lifestyle seemed ideal to him.

As he stirred from his daydream, the younger of the two officers - a handsome, fair-haired guy - got up to leave. As he walked past Connor, he said, smiling, 'have a nice day, sir', in what sounded like an American accent.

'Thanks,' Connor said, smiling back. His eyes followed the young man as he walked, tall and straight, towards the lifts. He reckoned he must be 6'2"; definitely an inch or two taller than him. Connor turned his head towards the window again, lost in thought. Then reality kicked in and he remembered Amy would probably be waiting impatiently on his return.

As Connor came back into the room, Amy stirred.

'Aw, I need a Panadol, babes,' she moaned, rubbing her temples with her fingertips. She studied him. 'Why are you dressed?'

'I just popped out for a coffee. You were sound; didn't want to waken you.'

'Did you see your mum? What are they up to today?'

'I'd say they'll be off sight-seeing. You getting up? Come on; we should get off, too.'

'In a bit… I've a better idea right now.' Smiling, she pulled back the duvet and patted Connor's side of the bed.

'Babe,' he said, 'let's just get organised and get off the ship. It's a beautiful day out there and Split looks lovely. I fancy a walk around.'

Her face clouded over. 'Here we go again. You'd fancy just about anything other than me.'

'Aw, stop, Amy. It's ten o'clock already. The morning's almost gone and we leave this port at six. We don't have much time here, babes.'

Amy threw the duvet off herself and almost took his shoulder with her as she pushed past him and stormed into the bathroom.

Connor drew back the curtains and opened the balcony door, then stood outside leaning over the railings. Despite all the people around him, and all the buzz, he had never felt so alone.

12

Katie and Carol had joined a group of passengers and spent a pleasant day being led around all the cultural hotspots of Split by a helpful tour guide. Before returning to the ship, they'd spent the last hour nipping in and out of shops, buying knick-knacks and souvenirs.

All the while, though, Katie had been constantly looking over her shoulder, or scanning the restaurants and coffee shops, bracing herself for the sight of Sam and Jill. She didn't want to see them.

'One of the best things about getting off the ship is getting back on it,' Carol said, stifling a yawn as she showed her pass to the crew member. Their next destination, lying 152 nautical miles away, was Dubrovnik.

'I don't know about you, Katie, but I'm shattered,' Carol sighed.

'Yeah, me too. Let's just go for a nap. I'm even too tired to drink - and that's saying something!'

Katie lay on her bed listening to Carol's deep breaths as she slumbered peacefully across from her, but she couldn't get her own eyes to close - nor her brain to stop chattering.

She'd put her phone on silent mode before lying down, but now she lifted it to text Matt. As the screen came to life, she was shocked to see two texts... from Sam.

The first, at 6pm: *Can't stop thinking about this morning...xxx*

Then, at 7pm: *U ok, gorgeous? Thinking of U and ur beautiful smile... xxx!*

Katie re-read the texts, then quickly deleted them. She lay

looking at the ceiling. What was she getting herself into?

After dinner, Katie, Carol, Connor and Amy took up a spot at the champagne bar. To anyone looking on, the foursome might seem relaxed and enjoying each other's company. But, in reality, each one of them was wrestling with inner thoughts they couldn't say out loud.

Katie: *I hope Sam and Jill don't show up here. This is all too close for comfort.*

Carol: *I'm going to have to confront Katie; there's something going on with her.*

Amy: *We're away two days and Connor has barely looked at me, never mind made love to me.*

Connor: *I'm on the right side of the water, so why do I feel like I'm drowning?*

'Now, that's easy on the eye,' Carol said, nudging Katie and nodding to the two officers who were walking down the curved staircase that led to the champagne bar.

Katie turned her head; the young, tall, blonde-haired one was especially striking.

'Oh, to be 20 years younger,' she laughed, turning back quickly so as not to be caught staring.

Amy, straightening her back and tilting her head as she sipped her champagne, stared provocatively in the officer's direction. It was way too flirty for Katie's liking.

How dare that one eye up that blonde officer in full view of my Connor, Katie thought, turning back to see if the officer was connecting with Amy's gaze.

He wasn't. Her relief quickly turned to shock, however, when she realised the handsome young sailor was, in fact, looking straight at Connor.

Katie's eyes shot quickly back to her son; he seemed to have caught the officer's eye but quickly avoided it by reaching for his drink and asking Amy to pass him some ice.

But with that split second of eye contact between the two men, something stirred inside Katie that left her feeling very unsettled.

She scanned the faces of the other two, but they seemed totally oblivious; Amy and Carol were happily watching the bartenders do their juggling act. She glanced at Connor, sipping his G&T and nervously dusting down the knee of his jeans.

Connor, she'd noticed, had not been himself over the past few months. Their chats on the phone had become shorter and shorter and she often wondered if all was okay between him and Amy since they'd moved in together. But if something was wrong, he'd never said.

She'd hoped the holiday would do him good -let him recharge his batteries- but she wondered now if this could be about something else; something she'd never imagined in her wildest dreams. A mother's gut is never wrong, she mused, but with every breath in her body she hoped she was.

'I feel a dance coming on,' Carol said, shimmying towards the bar counter.

'Yeah, it's 70s/80s music tonight; you old girls should enjoy that,' Amy teased, all chuffed with herself.

Connor felt his mother's eyes on him and could almost hear the cogs of her brain turning. He quickly got off his seat and, placing each hand on Amy's waist, lifted her off her stool.

'Good idea, babes,' Amy smiled. 'We can practise that new jive you've been trying to teach me.'

As they walked off hand in hand, Katie knew (for now, at least) she had to ignore the crazy, nagging thoughts that had invaded every corner of her brain, and so she tucked it away in that little secret filing cabinet in the back of her brain - alongside the file labelled *Secret Liaison*.

'C'mon, I'm up for a dance,' she said, and with that, she knocked back her Cosmopolitan, flicked her hair over her shoulder and stood up like she was about to take on the world.

As they walked through the doors leading to the disco, 'Greased Lightnin'' was blasting through the speakers. Katie and Carol were immediately on the floor, giving it their all, while Amy and Connor went to the bar and ordered from the menu of popular 80s cocktails.

'Mum, you have to try these; they're dynamite,' Connor shouted, holding up a tray laden with B-52s and beckoning Katie and Carol off the dancefloor.

'Oh, go on then,' Katie said, though she was already feeling the effects of the alcohol she'd drunk during the course of the evening.

'We're going to be soo dead in the morning,' Carol said. 'But, what the heck? They look great!'

Whitney Houston's 'I Wanna Dance with Somebody' came on, prompting Amy to pull Connor onto the floor. When the song finished, he went to get another round in and Katie left the table to use the bathroom; she was feeling happy inside after seeing the young couple smiling at each other as they danced.

On her way back, she looked over at the bar to see if Connor needed a hand and noticed two officers who stood out from the crowd, all decked out in white jackets and trousers. Connor was raising his glass and clinking with one of them. She smiled to herself. It was nice, seeing him so friendly and relaxed; he was usually quite shy. But her smile faded when she realised the officer who was raising his glass to Connor was... Blondie. And there was that look again; its meaning was unmistakeable.

She made her way back to the table, with Connor following behind her with a tray of drinks.

'Right,' he smiled, 'we have another 80s classic: the Snakebite.'

'Wow, never heard of it,' Amy laughed, smiling up at Connor and eagerly reaching out to take one.

Katie could see how much she loved him.

Poor Amy, she thought to herself. *Poor Connor.*

She pushed her thoughts as far down as she could and tried to focus on the fun they were all having.

But the knot in her stomach was tightening.

13

Day Three (Dubrovnik)

Connor's eyes opened. His head was pounding and he had no memory of going to bed.

He glanced at the digital clock on the bedside locker - 9am - and then at Amy, who lay unconscious beside him.

They'd arrived in Dubrovnik at 8am; he couldn't believe he'd slept through it. He wondered if he should sneak out, like he'd done the day before, and go for a coffee. Slowly sliding his long legs out from under the duvet, he almost crawled out from the top end of the bed. Amy didn't stir.

He went into the bathroom, noticing his shorts and T-shirt folded neatly on the shelf under the sink. Funny; he didn't remember leaving them there last night. He smiled; even in his drunken state he must have been anticipating this morning's getaway. He freshened up, got dressed, slipped into his Nike flip-flops and eased out the door, standing for a moment outside with his ear cocked to the door to ensure all was quiet within.

Connor ordered a latte in the café and sat down on a comfy chair that was by the window but which also had a clear view of the lifts. There were more people around this morning; some getting takeaway coffees while others sat with a newspaper or book.

As the ship was docked that day, the gangway was open and streams of people were heading off to wander around the beautiful walled city that lay before them. Connor was looking forward to doing likewise. He finished his drink, checked his watch and was about to get up to go back to his room when the lift door opened… and there he was. The handsome officer was walking towards him but seemed otherwise occupied, chatting away on his phone.

Connor felt shy all of a sudden. He thought about their eye contact at the champagne bar and their brief encounter at the disco… but he didn't know how to approach this situation.

He'd known for a while he was attracted to men - for more than a while, if he was being totally honest - but he'd never acted on it before. Homosexuality wasn't really talked about in the Catholic all-boys school he'd attended; Connor knew, in a way he couldn't really articulate, he was different, but school was a laddish environment and he'd wanted to fit in. Almost without knowing it, he suppressed that side of himself, putting the vague stirrings he felt when distractedly staring at a boy in class down to admiration of his good looks rather than lust.

In his last two years of school, he'd even gone out with a few different girls. Nothing too serious and he didn't have sex with them - a few fumbles, just - but it was enough to convince himself he was straight… probably.

Then, when he went to university in Belfast, he met Amy at a party. They clicked right away, and when the earth didn't exactly move the first time they slept together, Connor put it down to first-time nerves and lack of experience. But, as time went on, things didn't improve in the bedroom department; there was no spark for him, and he had to work really hard to convince Amy he was into it.

Then, one day, when he was working out in the university gym, he found himself checking out the toned guy doing crunches on the machine next to him… and he realised this was something he'd been doing - subconsciously - for years.

Straight men don't do that, Connor, he'd said to himself. *You're gay.*

It was a relief to finally admit it.

Even then, he kept up the pretence - partly because he was afraid of stepping into that world, but mostly because he didn't want to hurt Amy. He thought his move to Glasgow was the perfect way to end the relationship, not thinking for a minute she would uproot everything and go with him.

He'd gone along with it because he couldn't summon up the strength to tell her the truth, but this last year in Glasgow had been torture. He felt so trapped and he knew things had to come to a head sooner or later… he just wasn't prepared for it to happen while he was on a cruise with his girlfriend. But the minute he laid eyes on that handsome crewman, he knew he was ready to make that leap of faith.

How could he be sure this guy was on the same wavelength, though? Connor was new to all this. *When in doubt, do nought*, he decided.

He was brought out of his reverie by the sense that someone was standing beside him.

Turning his head and raising his eyes, he looked up to see Blondie, smiling as he put his phone into the pocket of his perfectly pressed white trousers.

'Good morning,' he beamed. 'Nice day out there.'

'Oh, h-hi,' Connor stammered, not knowing where to look or what to say.

'I'm Chris, by the way.' Blondie reached out his hand.

Nervously accepting it, Connor introduced himself.

'So, where's that accent from?' Chris asked him.

'Ireland.' Connor wanted to kick himself for his one-word response but the ability to form a full sentence had deserted him.

'Well, New York is home for me, but, believe it or not, I'm a quarter Irish,' Chris said, looking very relaxed as he perched himself on the arm of the opposite chair.

This comes so easily to him, Connor thought.

'My great-grandfather was from Cork. I visited the ancestral home with my dad ten years ago; O'Malley's my name.'

At this, he took a wallet from his hip pocket, pulled a business card from it and held it out. Connor took it from him and glanced at it, noticing the email address and phone number in italics at the bottom.

Am I being chatted up, here? Connor thought. *Like, give me a call some time?*

Or maybe this was all part of his job; chatting to passengers, being friendly and polite.

'I've never been to the Big Apple; definitely on my 'to do' list,' said Connor, starting to relax a bit as he slipped Chris' card into the breast pocket of his T-shirt.

Just then, the lift door opened with the automated announcement 'level five' sounding across the café; out stepped Amy.

Connor froze in his chair as she strode towards him. He knew by the look on her face that she had something to say.

'Oh, hi, Amy,' he said, trying his best not to sound panicky. 'I thought I'd let you lie on while I grabbed a quick coffee.'

'So, this is where you got to,' she spat. Chris, clearly sensing the mood, got up to leave, but Amy, nodding briefly at him as she kept Connor in her death stare, said, 'So, what's going on here? Maybe you'd like to introduce me.'

'Amy, ah, yeah… this is Chris,' Connor replied, wishing the ground would open up and swallow him.

'Nice to meet you, Chris,' Amy said, ignoring his outstretched hand, 'but I need to speak privately with my boyfriend; do you mind?'

'Sure thing,' Chris answered, delighted to be able to make his exit.

As he hurried away across the fifth floor, Connor sat in his chair, mortified.

'What are you playing at, Amy?'

'I don't know, Connor. Why don't you tell me?'

She was furious, but Connor wasn't exactly sure why. He wondered if they'd fought the night before; maybe he'd said something stupid? He had no idea if they'd even come back to their room together. *Maybe she suspects?* For a split second, he wondered if he should come clean; get it all over and done with. But he couldn't do it. He knew it would be a total nightmare, especially as he had nowhere to run: they were on a ship in the middle of the Adriatic.

He felt like a total shithead. This would kill Amy... it would kill everyone.

Her last sentence just floated in the air between them; he had to say something.

'Amy, look, why don't you just sit down, *please*.' He reached his hand up to take hers, but she fiercely slapped it away. Connor's chin disappeared into his neck as he stared at the ground. Amy shifted her weight from foot to foot, then she started to tap her right foot; he knew this was a bad sign.

'No. You listen to me, Connor. It was bad enough waking up and you not there. Again. Half the time, I don't even know what you're thinking or feeling. You keep avoiding me. You don't want to sit and talk to me anymore. I... I just don't know where I stand with you.'

She went quiet. Connor slowly looked up into her face; her eyes were filling up.

'That's not true, Amy.' He tried to reach for her hand again, but she raised her palm and closed her eyes.

Then, her voice quivering, she said: 'I know I've been very demanding lately, but I thought you were going off me and it's been making me very agitated and angry.

'Then, when I woke up to find that you and my mobile phone

were gone, the penny dropped.'

Mobile phone… what the fuck is she on about? Connor thought, totally stumped.

Amy knelt down and rested her elbows on Connor's knees. Her voice softened.

'Honey, you think I'm seeing someone, don't you? You took my phone hoping to find some answers. Well, babe, I can explain everything, and it's not what you think.

'One of the doctors at the hospital has a bit of a crush on me, but I swear to God, nothing has happened. Those are just drunken texts; they mean nothing. I'm sorry I was so mad just now, but you shouldn't have taken my phone. I realise now that I overreacted and I understand you're just feeling insecure and probably very jealous. But I love *you* and only you, babe. So, can we put this behind us? Please?

This was all news to Connor. But… he suddenly realised she'd just thrown him a lifeline.

He felt relief and shame in equal measure. Relieved she wasn't on to him, but ashamed he was prepared to let her take the rap for his behaviour. Right this minute, he couldn't care less if the whole hospital fancied her, but he'd have to play along as he couldn't think of any other way out of it; this wasn't the time or place for a confession.

'Yes, babe,' I thought you were seeing someone behind my back,' he lied.

'No, my love; you are the only one for me!' Amy whispered.

Crisis averted. But Connor knew he had to tell the truth about the phone.

'I didn't take your phone, Amy.'

But she held out her hand. 'It's okay, babe, I forgive you. Just give it back.'

'It must be in the room, babe,' he insisted. 'I would never, ever go through your phone.'

'But I've searched everywhere.'

'Maybe you lost it last night. Let's check at the purser's desk.'

Connor helped Amy to her feet, wondering how he was able to stand up straight himself; his insides were shaking. Hand in hand, they walked in silence to the desk, where, sure enough, her phone was produced; it had been found in the disco by one of the cleaning staff.

Amy was annoyed with herself for jumping to conclusions about her missing phone; and now Connor knew Dr Morrison had a crush on her. But at least she'd had the sense not to tell him she actually snogged the doc one night at a leaving party.

With things smoothed over, Connor and Amy spent a pleasant day together exploring Dubrovnik, enjoying a scenic boat ride before wandering around the beautiful old town and finishing up at the gorgeous Sveti Jakov beach where they drank cocktails and swam in the sea.

Back on the ship, Amy suggested they stay in their room that evening with a nice bottle of champagne and an in-house movie.

'Great idea, babes,' Connor agreed, distractedly patting his T-shirt pocket to make sure Chris' card was still safely tucked inside. Amy's wish was his command; nothing new there.

Katie and Carol had also been spending the day in Dubrovnik, where the steep climb up the ancient stone steps that carried them to the highest point of the beautiful walled city had taken its toll.

'We should have thought about this last night when we were downing those B-52s,' Carol puffed, using the breathtaking scenery as an excuse to stop and catch her breath. 'Talking of drink; we must suss out that wee bar we read about.'

They walked on a bit and, before long, they saw the sign for the *Bar with a View*. As they stepped through the entrance, they gasped in tandem at the sight that met them: the place was set among the rocks; parasol-topped tables scattered throughout that took in the amazing panoramic views overlooking over the Adriatic.

From one of the photo stops, teenagers were jumping off the rocks and diving 50 or 60 feet into the sea beneath. It was really scary to watch, but these young ones had absolutely no fear as they dived in and swam to the nearest rock below before making the climb back up to do it all again.

The girls sat there and had some lunch before making their way back down to the town, where they quietly joined a *Game of Thrones* walking tour and hoped no-one noticed they were freeloading.

They were so impressed by Dubrovnik's charm and beauty that they made a pact that they would return there for a week's holiday in the near future.

Back on the ship, Carol suggested they eat in the main dining room that evening for 'a 'wee bit of eye candy'. A very handsome Italian sommelier had been giving Carol a run for her money in the flirting department for the past two nights and when he saw the girls come into the restaurant, he made his way over.

'Buona sera, senoritas. Lovely to see you this evening.'

'Buona sera, Alfredo,' answered Carol, smiling as he lifted her hand to his and placed a gentle kiss on the back of it. So as to not leave Katie out, he reached for her hand and did likewise, but it was more than obvious he only had eyes for Carol, which Katie was delighted about.

She was glad her friend was getting a bit of attention, as it relieved her from some of her own guilt.

When they'd placed their food order, Alfredo came back with the bottle of wine he'd recommended. He stood there proudly, silver chain and tastevin around his neck, pouring a little wine into the tasting cup and swishing it, then breathing in its flavours before sipping it. Next came the explanations: the grape, the region, the year and the characteristics of the vino.

As the night went on and the other diners left the restaurant, Carol and Katie settled back and enjoyed the fun with Alfredo and a few other wine waiters who'd come to join in.

Carol, who considered herself a bit of a connoisseur, kept the banter going as more wines were brought to the table. Before long, she had Alfredo's chain around her neck and was tasting wine from the tastevin.

It was after midnight when they decided to call it a night, and as they got up to leave, Alfredo asked Carol if he could walk her to her room.

'Why don't you two sit here for a while,' Katie suggested. 'I'll go on up; take your time.'

Carol didn't need much persuasion. 'Right; I'll have one for the road, then.'

'At your service, senorita,' Alfredo smiled happily, lifting a fresh glass and filling it with velvet Burgundy.

Katie was happy to leave her to it because Sam had been sending her texts throughout the evening. Not wanting to draw attention, she hadn't had a chance to read them properly, but at a quick glance she could see they were not just flirty but actually pretty dirty.

Back in her room, she almost suffocated with excitement as she lay reading his texts. No answer was expected and she knew better than to respond; she was taking no chances with Jill. Just as she was happily nodding off to sleep, she heard whispering voices coming from outside the door; it was Carol and Alfredo saying goodnight.

Carol came through the door and closed it gently behind her. She looked at Katie with a 'cat who got the cream' face, then slid down the back of the door in a mock faint.

'Italia, 12 points!'

'Get into bed, you dirty stop-out,' Katie laughed, adding, 'I want a *blow-by-blow* account.'

They were still giggling like schoolgirls just before they drifted off to sleep.

14

Day Four (Montenegro)

Once again, Connor endured a fitful sleep and found himself lying awake as the ship anchored, at 8am, in Kotor, Montenegro. Just like the previous morning, Amy lay comatose beside him.

He tiptoed to the bathroom, unplugged his phone from its charge and lifted his T-shirt en route. Quietly locking the door, he took Chris' card from the pocket of his T-shirt and stared at it, heart pounding in his chest. *Will I? Won't I?*

Typing Chris' number into his phone, he composed a text.

Hi Chris, sorry about yesterday morning. My girlfriend can be a bit neurotic; I suppose I need to take some responsibility for her behaviour too… if you know what I mean?! Connor.

He read and re-read the message. *Nothing too incriminating there*, he thought, deliberating about whether or not to send it.

'Connor?' he heard a voice from the bedroom. Shit... Amy was awake. Panicking, he hit the send button and quickly unlocked the bathroom door.

'In the loo, babe,' he shouted back, splashing cold water over his face and flushing the toilet, then opening the door and making his way back to bed, where Amy lay, all smiles at his return and her impending love session.

After lunch, as they strolled around the pretty town of Kotor, Connor kept his phone in his shorts pocket, making sure it was on vibrate. From time to time, he imagined a buzzing sensation against his leg, but each time he checked his phone, there wasn't a peep from Chris.

As the hours went by and his phone remained silent, the disappointment became unbearable. Connor tried to console himself with the fact that Chris would be busy working; he probably didn't even have time to check his phone never mind answer a text.

It was different for him; he was on holiday and had too much time on his hands. Actually, he was probably getting carried away with something that was most likely nothing. *Get a grip*, he told himself, as he and Amy made their way back to the ship in good time for the 5pm departure.

He'd never expected to find himself in a situation where he was eyeing up a potential male lover while on holiday with his girlfriend. The plan had always been to 'out' himself to her long before now, but he'd never been able to pluck up the courage; he knew how angry and hurt she would be.

He was a total mess. He longed for peace of mind; to be free to be himself and to feel safe and accepted. God, how he would love to have someone to talk to. Someone who understood. Because, right now, fear, doubt and insecurity were his only friends.

Climbing the steps of the ship, he reached into his pocket to take out his ID card... and felt a vibration on his fingertips. Eagerly lifting out his phone (glad that Amy was a few steps in front of him), he looked down at the screen.

I understand... had one of those myself one time. Chris.

Connor's brow furrowed. What was that supposed to mean? Text messages could be so ambiguous.

He was no further forward, but at least they'd opened up the lines of communication; that had to be something.

As they walked back to their room, his pocket vibrated again. He increased his step, telling Amy he needed the bathroom. He couldn't wait to read his phone.

Playing volleyball tomorrow? I'm a bit of an expert... lol... maybe I could sort out that girlfriend of yours... accidentally on purpose... lol... Chris.

Connor felt his pulse quicken; Chris's meaning was becoming clearer.

15

When the ship had docked in Kotor that morning, Katie and Carol had been in no rush to get off, opting instead to spend the morning lounging by the pool.

'I swear, my belly is getting bigger by the minute', Carol said, disgusted.

'No carbs today, then?' joked Katie.

'Ah to hell with it, Katie. Sure, we're on our holidays.'

As she spoke, the pool waiter stopped at their loungers. 'Something from the bar, ladies?'

'Two pina coladas, please,' Carol promptly replied.

'It's only 11.30,' Katie laughed.

Then, in unison, 'but it's five o'clock somewhere!'

'Oh God, every day we're starting a bit earlier,' Carol groaned as the waiter returned with their cocktails.

There's not much to do in Montenegro,' said Katie. 'An hour or two walking around this afternoon will do us, so we'll just take it easy and enjoy these.'

Just as she put her head back and closed her eyes, her phone bleeped. A text from Sam.

Jill off kayaking...not back until 1.15. Fancy a coffee in 1202???

'Who's that? Matt?' Carol asked lazily.

'Yeah, he's just checking in,' Katie lied.

She looked at her watch, her mind working overtime.

I'll be there at 12, she texted back, not quite sure how she could pull it off.

'I'm having a ball, Katie. When you're next talking to Matt, let me know; I want to thank him personally.'

'Of course, Carol. He'll be delighted we're having such a great time.'

Katie sensed her friend's pensive mood and knew what was coming next.

'So, you seem to be handling the Sam and Jill situation quite well. At least we're not running into them too much.'

If only she knew!

'Yeah, well, it is what it is. I'm grand with it.'

Quickly changing the subject, Katie added, 'You know, I might go to the gym for a wee half hour before lunch.'

'You're mad!' said Carol. 'There's nothing would take me in there; but, then again, maybe I should,' she laughed, poking her belly with her fingers.

Katie knew there was no chance of that; she had her alibi.

Telling Carol she'd be back by 12.30, she left the pool, headed into the toilet at the end of Sam's corridor for a quick freshen-up and then knocked on his door.

Sam opened the door and Katie tentatively walked inside. Without saying a word, he lifted her onto the large bed and began kissing her with a vengeance.

Confused yet bewitched, Katie eventually looked up at him.

'You sure Jill has definitely gone on that trip?'

'Yeah. I put her on the bus myself and watched 'til it went out of sight. We have an hour or so.'

'No, I only have half an hour. I can't leave Carol too long - she thinks I'm at the gym.'

As Sam moved his kisses down Katie's body, she couldn't believe how comfortable she felt. *Why did being with him like this feel so natural?*

'We need more time, Katie. This is driving me crazy.'

'I don't want this to stop, either, Sam. But how? Without being caught out?'

She knew she should be lying back and enjoying their stolen

20 minutes of bliss, but the thought of having Sam to herself for a few hours suddenly took precedence. Her mind was buzzing with ideas and plans she knew would never work.

'What if I tell Carol about us? She won't be too pleased, but she'll cover for me.'

Sam, still savouring her shapely body, lifted his head and came up for air.

'Relax, sweetheart. Leave it to me; I'll think of something.'

Katie lay back and looked up at Sam, his upper body slightly raised over her, carrying his weight on his muscular arms and shoulders. As he moved slowly inside her, his stare never left her eyes. A burning passion rushed through them.

Afterwards, Katie reached for her bikini top, which in the heat of passion had managed to make its way up to her throat. *Strangled by a D-cup,* she smiled, pulling it down into place and shoving her boobs back inside. But what a way to go!

Straightening her bikini bottoms and pulling her sarong around her hips, she gave Sam a final kiss. Then she opened the door, checked right and left and almost ran down the corridor.

Sam tidied the bed and took a look around the suite to make sure there was nothing incriminating, then slipped his jocks back on and settled in front of the TV. He clicked into the interactive system and checked out the shore excursions for the next few days, searching for trips that would be around five or six hours in duration.

Jill was big into outdoor pursuits. She loved cycling, hill-walking and just about any kind of water sports. Sam took note of a few options she would enjoy… and which would give him and Katie an opportunity to be together for longer.

All he needed to do now was plant a few seeds tonight at dinner and convince Jill to sign up for a nice, long excursion.

16

Day Five (At sea)

There was plenty of entertainment happening all over the ship for the day at sea, but the girls opted to lounge by the pool to catch a few rays and get a ringside seat for the 'Officers v Guests' volleyball challenge at 12.30; maybe they'd even take part.

Connor and Amy arrived too late to the pool to nab a lounger, so took up two seats at the bar. Katie looked up from her book and spotted them. She made a pretence of going back to her reading, but every few moments she peered over the rims of her Christian Dior sunglasses, looking for signs to dispel the notions that were keeping her awake at night.

They're holding hands: good sign. They're chatting easily with one another: good sign. Now they're laughing: great sign!

Her head had been doing whirlybirds for the past few days. She found herself watching Connor - though she wasn't even sure what she was looking for. Maybe some effeminate trait. Or an unusual hand gesture or movement. But there were none.

She couldn't stop thinking about the glance that had passed between Connor and the young officer that night at the champagne bar. And then, later, at the disco, the way their eyes locked together... and that smile; its meaning was unmistakeable.

But why had she not noticed or sensed this about her son before? Are parents not supposed to know these things about their children? Had she been walking around wearing rose-tinted glasses?

For the hundredth time in the last 48 hours, she told herself she could be wrong. But what if she was right? She wouldn't love him any less; that wasn't possible. But, might it just be a phase he's going through? *Oh, God,* she thought, *I hope so!*

It wasn't shame that made Katie have this last thought; it was fear. Sure, attitudes towards gay people had definitely improved in the last ten years; things like the gay marriage act and the stamping out of workplace discrimination were proof of that.

But Katie knew that bigotry and prejudice still existed. She'd heard enough news reports about gay men being the victims of violent attacks to know that some elements in society still had a serious problem with homosexuality.

She remembered the debates that constantly raged on the radio a decade or so ago like it was yesterday. *Is it nature? Is it nurture? Is it a choice? Is it a sin?* Representatives from religious institutions - Catholic and Protestant - all had something to say on 'the gay issue', and the harder they thumped their bibles, the louder their voices carried.

Even now, the usual homophobic politicians and church leaders would occasionally pop up to spout their vile opinions, and Katie would shout at the radio: 'Give them peace, for God's sake. Live and let live.'

But now it hit her: this could be her Connor they were calling 'unnatural'; her Connor being beaten up by thugs on a night out in town for being gay. She looked over at him, unable to bear the thought of her lovely, gentle son being subjected to abuse, prejudice and ridicule.

She looked at Amy, and suddenly felt sorry for her, too.

She thought of the two gay guys who lived at the end of her cul-de-sac. They always seemed happy and content, but then again, what did she know? She wondered how society treated them. And how did their parents feel? Katie had always assumed having a gay family member was no big deal, these days, but now that it was knocking on her own door, it was a totally different matter.

She would sometimes see one of their mothers visit. Until this moment, she had never stopped to think how that woman coped with having a gay son. How did parents react? Was it hard for them seeing their son or daughter in a same-sex relationship?

Reality began to kick in. There would be no white wedding. No grandchildren. Katie's hopes of ever holding Connor's offspring suddenly came crashing down around her.

As if by fate, her phone rang and Matt's face showed up on the screen.

Oh, no... Matt. Oh, Matt! Katie was close to tears now. *How will he feel about this?*

Matt was a proud man. A man's man, working in a male-dominated environment. Would he be ashamed of Connor? Would he feel let down? Would he disown him? Would he blame himself for not encouraging him to play football? Blame himself for not insisting he followed in his footsteps? Was it her own fault? Did she mollycoddle Connor too much? *Oh, God, what will I do?*

Matt would know by her voice that something was wrong. No; she wasn't strong enough to take the call. Pressing decline, she sat back and closed her eyes, tears rushing down her cheeks like a burst dam.

Carol, who had automatically lifted her head towards Katie when she heard her phone ringing, watched her reject the call. Shocked by the state she was in, she immediately snapped her book shut and sat up straight to face her friend.

'Katie, what is it? Oh my God, are you alright?'

She reached out and gently removed Katie's hands away from her wet face.

'What is it, Katie? Tell me,' Carol pleaded.

Katie sat up, turned her back to Connor and Amy at the pool bar and faced Carol.

'It's Connor!' she cried, almost uncontrollably.

Totally confused, Carol looked up at the bar and saw Connor and Amy happily chatting away and then looked back at her distraught friend.

'But Connor is up there, Katie. He's fine. Look!'

Thankfully, Connor still had his back to them.

Katie took a deep breath and said, 'I think Connor is gay, Carol. No: I *know* he is.'

'What? Aw, for goodness' sake, Katie, that's ridiculous. He's a red-blooded man in love with, well, OK… a cheeky wee bitch.' Carol was trying to make Katie smile.

'No, Carol,' said Katie, sobbing and shaking her head. 'I don't have too much evidence - I don't have any, really - but I feel it right here.' She pushed her fist into an invisible hole in the centre of her rib cage.

Carol wished they were somewhere less public so she could hold her friend close to her, but with Connor nearby she just put her hand on Katie's knee.

'Katie, love, I really don't know where all this is coming from and now is not the time for me to ask; Connor will be over here any minute. So, let's just take a deep breath and smile because, apart from anything else, he hasn't murdered anyone… nobody's dead!'

Katie took a deep breath, let out a long sigh and wiped her eyes with the palm of her hands. Nodding at Carol, she gave her a sad, tight smile and said: 'I know. You're right; nobody's dead. I probably just need to wise up.'

A young cheerleader rounding up volunteers for the volleyball challenge approached them.

'You ladies interested in playing volleyball?' she chirped.

'No, I'm happy chilling here,' Katie said, with a fake smile.

'Come on, let's do it. It'll be a bit of fun,' Carol cajoled.

'No, you go ahead. I'll cheer you on from here.'

'Please, we just need three more to make up the numbers,' the cheerleader said.

Carol called over to Connor and Amy. 'Will you two sign up with me for the volleyball? Your mum's an old spoilsport.'

Connor checked with Amy and, surprisingly, she agreed.

The couple walked over to join Katie and Carol, and, as Connor sat at the bottom edge of his mum's lounger, he playfully pinched her big toe. 'OK, Mum?'

'Of course, darling.'

As Carol watching this touching scene between mother and son, she felt a lump gather in the back of her throat; secretly, she hoped Katie was wrong.

The passengers taking part in the game gathered at the right-hand side of the pool to await their opposition.

'Three cheers for our officers!' the entertainments officer bellowed through a bright yellow foghorn.

Ten young, lean crew members ran out from behind the bar area, punching the air with their fists.

Katie joined in with the onlookers cheering as they jumped into the pool one at a time. The last to hit the water, looking toned and tan in a pair of powder blue swimming trunks, was... Blondie.

Katie's heart almost stopped. She shot a quick glance over at Connor, who was clapping alongside Carol and Amy and not appearing remotely affected by the entrance of the handsome young man.

But Katie knew appearances could be deceptive. Like an eager schoolgirl focusing on a blackboard, she sat up straight and watched, determined to find the answer to her question.

17

Jill lay stretched out in a skimpy white bikini which showed off her perfectly tanned toned body. She held her sparkling ice water with one hand and held Sam's hand with the other.

They were not interested in the madness going on at the main pool area; being on the luxury suite floor, they had a more exclusive area for sunbathing and relaxing.

A generous-sized pool and hot tub sat on a spacious grassy area alongside a small cocktail bar. As it was a sea day, it was busier than usual, but its design of nooks and crannies gave adequate privacy to these more affluent cruisers.

Sam was lying back, casually reading the ship's daily newsletter. It set out hour-by-hour details of the day and night activities on board and also information on arrival and departure times, weather reports and recommended tours and attractions at the port in question.

They were due to arrive tomorrow in Taormina, Sicily, at 7am; Sam had already done his homework and was about to put his plan into action.

'There's a good tour for you tomorrow, darling,' he said, starting to read out the information about the tour taking in the Silvestri Spent Craters of Mount Etna.

'Oh great!' Jill exclaimed. 'You're coming too, right?'

'No, that's not for me, honey, but why don't you go ahead? I can entertain myself until you get back. You shouldn't miss it.'

'Yeah, I read about that tour,' she said, less convinced now. 'But it's over six hours. That's a bit long; even for me.'

'But you're here now. No time like the present.'

'Anyone would think you're trying to get rid of me,' Jill answered, suspicious. Sam was waiting for this. Jill wasn't one for doing things separately, especially day-long tours.

'Now, why would I want to get rid of you, darling? I just want you to do something I know you'll enjoy.'

'I'm not going without you, Sam. Just come with me; you'll enjoy it.'

'Really Jill, no. Look, just forget about it. We'll laze about on the ship instead.'

Jill was really keen to go and knew she was being silly, but this was hard for her.

'You don't mind being left alone all day?' she asked, knowing he wouldn't mind one bit.

'I'm a big boy now, Jill. Just go for it!' He tried to sound casual.

Sam held his breath, pretending to read through the newsletter as Jill gave it some thought.

'Ok, yeah; I'd like to go. I know it's not your thing, so, if you're sure?'

'Absolutely, darling. I'll go downstairs to the excursion desk and book it for you.'

Jill reached over and kissed him. 'You have me spoiled, honey.' But, deep down, she was already wondering if leaving him was the right thing to do.

Sam almost skipped down the corridor to the lift, his heart thumping with excitement. Once he got Jill's tour sorted, he just had to confirm his booking for the beautiful little boutique hotel he'd found on the internet the day before.

He'd already spoken to the receptionist and said he needed a room mid-morning and would be checking out later that day. He was confident and well-rehearsed as he explained he was travelling and just needed to rest up for a bit.

At the beginning of the conversation, the receptionist had

tried to explain the hotel's policy that guests could not check in to their rooms until 3pm, but Sam's charm and gentle persuasion had her eating out of his hand in no time; the room would be ready for him at 10.30am the next morning.

Katie was anxiously watching the game going on in the pool when her phone bleeped.

Probably Matt again, she thought. But it was Sam's name that lit up the screen.

To think I'm the only man on this ship who knows what lies beneath that beautiful black bikini.

Katie was afraid to look around; wherever he was, he obviously had a bird's eye view. She started typing.

So where are you spying from…lol?

His reply came straight away: *Upper deck - 9 o'clock.*

Katie turned her head a quarter to the left and looked up to see Sam raising his Ray-Bans from the bridge of his nose and back down again in a 'cloak and dagger' gesture.

She smiled to herself and looked ahead again towards the pool. Blondie was serving the ball to Amy; both enjoying every minute of it by the looks of things.

Maybe I got it wrong and it was Amy he had his eye on after all. Katie felt a relief wash over her; bad and all as this scenario would be, for some reason she could handle that better than Connor being gay. Her day was suddenly looking brighter.

Another bleep. *Jill away 2moro, I booked a hotel suite in Taormina, wanna share it with me?*

What?

Is that a yes?

Deffo!

Katie wanted to ask where Jill was going, but right now that didn't matter. She and Sam were going to have the time of their lives. There was a small problem, however: Carol.

When Katie looked back up, Sam was disappearing through a

small group of people who were watching the volleyball game.

The squeals and roars from the players and spectators were contagious and Katie joined in, her heart filled with lust and excitement.

18

Carol was delighted to see Katie in good form again. She'd noticed her texting quite a bit during the volleyball and guessed she was on to Matt; he must have helped lift her spirits. She hoped she'd not offloaded all that nonsense about Connor being gay, though.

She found herself paying extra attention to Connor and Amy and was pleased to find they seemed very content together. No; Katie had to be wrong. She was probably just feeling a bit homesick; or *Matt* sick. That would explain the faraway look she'd had periodically on her face over the last few days. Carol didn't want to bring the 'gay' word up again but she knew it couldn't just be ignored. But she decided, for now, to leave that ball in Katie's court.

On numerous occasions throughout the day, Katie began to tell Carol her plans for the next day, but she couldn't get the words out of her mouth. Maybe a few glasses of champagne later would help loosen her tongue - and prevent Carol from exploding when she found out what she'd been up to.

She'd noticed that Connor and Amy seemed all loved up earlier, which made her heart feel lighter. She wasn't quite sure if she was in denial or maybe just going a bit mad; she reckoned the latter was more likely the case.

The dress code for the evening was smart-casual, but as Alfredo had bagged the girls a special invite to the captain's pre-dinner cocktail party, they decided they would take the opportunity to wear the evening gowns they had packed for the trip.

VIPs, such as veteran cruisers and special guest artists, were among those invited, so they spent a little longer than usual doing their hair and make-up. Katie slipped into a tight-fitting long gold dress heavily beaded with tiny pearls and sequins. It had double spaghetti straps and fell to the floor with a high split on the right-hand side of the skirt. She finished it off with long, gold diamante earrings.

'Carol, I left three pairs of shoes at home so I could bring this with me; it weighs a tonne', said Katie. 'I'm glad I'm getting the chance to wear it now.' She admired herself in the mirror.

'Wow,' Carol gasped. 'That dress is one of my favourites on you; I forgot how gorgeous it is. It makes me sick you can still wear it so well after a week of eating and drinking.'

'Yeah, well, thank God for Spanx,' Katie replied. 'Half of my tummy is pushed up and giving me a grand cleavage.'

'Yeah, I can see that. You're going to have to pour me into mine.' Carol made a face as she lifted her black dress from the hanger.

'Breathe in,' Katie laughed as she tried to zip up the strapless boned bodice and Carol's breasts almost popped out.

'I can't breathe!'

'Take off your bra; you don't need it.'

'I can't go without a bra, Katie.'

'Yes, you can. There's plenty of support in this bodice.'

Katie pulled down the zip, unclipped Carol's bra and threw it on the bed. Her friend let out a deep sigh of relief. The zip went back up easier.

'There you go... perfect,' Katie said admiringly. 'Wait 'til

Alfredo sees you tonight. I can just hear him: "Bella, bella, bella",' she mimicked in her best Italian accent.

'Let's go, girl, and knock 'em dead!' Carol laughed.

They made their way to the sky lounge, where they were greeted by smiling, pristine staff offering appetisers, hors d'oeuvres and champagne. The room was buzzing with officers and guests alike, all dressed in their finery. A pianist played standards from the Great American Songbook on a baby grand piano while everyone mingled and the evening sun shone its last rays before slipping into the Mediterranean Sea.

'What the fuck are they doing here?' Carol sighed under her breath as she nodded towards the piano.

Katie looked over nervously, already knowing who she would see.

Jill stood there in all her beauty; the only thing missing was a halo above her head. She wore a stunning white silk Juicy Couture halterneck dress. Two front panels just about covered her small breasts and attached themselves to the waist of the full length finely-pleated skirt. The dress was completely backless, showing off the perfect shape of her tanned athletic back and shoulders. Her hair was in a loose fishtail plait hanging over one shoulder and her beautiful face was glowing and flawless.

Sam looked as gorgeous a man as Jill was a woman, standing out from the crowd with his white dinner jacket and black trousers. He had his arm around his wife's tiny waist and looked as proud as punch to be the other half of this picture-perfect couple.

Katie stared in awe, her mind working overtime. Is this the same guy who texted me a few hours ago wanting to spend tomorrow with me? Then it all made sense. Sam was using her, and she was totally falling for it.

But, then again, wasn't she just using him, too? A wee bit on the side, no strings attached, a bit of extramartial excitement...

'Holy shit,' said Carol, breaking Katie's spell. 'Don't tell me she can fucking sing as well?'

Jill had a cordless microphone in her hand and was whispering into the pianist's ear. His hands danced lightly over the ivory keys as he searched for a pitch that suited her; she finally smiled and nodded to him in agreement. Then, the intro to Nina Simone's 'My Baby Just Cares for Me' filled the room and everyone stopped talking, mesmerised by the elegant woman whose bluesy voice bounced off the microphone and almost lifted the ceiling.

For someone who appeared so shy and innocent, she held the room in the palm of her hand. She looked at Sam and moved a long, toned arm in his direction, sensuously swaying her beautiful body as she sang the last verse over again:

'I wonder what's wrong with baby,
My baby just cares for,
My baby just cares for,
My baby just cares for me.'

'Wonder has she done that before,' Carol muttered sarcastically, unable, like the rest of the room, to take her eyes off Jill.

Katie glanced at Sam, who was now standing at the side of the piano, his chest visibly expanding with pride. When Jill stopped singing, the room erupted and cried for more, but she returned to take her place beside her husband as he pecked her on both cheeks and slid his hand around her waist, giving her a little squeeze of approval.

Jill looked in their direction, the smile slipping off her face as she watched Katie watching Sam. Without taking her eyes off her adversary, she leaned her head on her husband's shoulder.

Katie thought she might throw up; she made her excuse to go to the loo.

'I'll go with you,' Carol said. 'I could be doing with some fresh air.'

When they reached the restrooms, Katie pushed open all the toilet doors to be sure they were alone before she spoke. Then she turned to Carol, who was watching her curiously.

Katie pointed to one of the cream wrought-iron chairs next to the glass sinks. 'Sit down, Carol. Just sit... and don't interrupt me.'

'Now you have me worried, Katie,' Carol said nervously, perching on the edge of the chair.

'Look, I'm going to come clean and you're not going to like it.'

'What, you're running off with Sexy Sam? Well, after that performance out there I'd say he's going nowhere.'

Carol didn't like the look that came across Katie's face.

'For Christ's sake, Katie. What's going on?'

'I've been with Sam twice in the last couple of days and I'm going to see him tomorrow off the ship,' Katie blurted, almost in one breath.

'What? You've been with him... and you want to see him tomorrow...' Carol looked at her in disbelief.

'I know, I know, it's mad, but I want to see him and Jill is away all day, touring... Sam has a hotel booked for us for the afternoon.'

Katie stood there trembling, chewing flesh from the inside of her cheek and wringing her hands together. Carol looked at her, then threw her head back and laughed out loud.

'Katie, you had better start at the beginning, because I'm totally lost, here. No, in fact, let's get out of here; I need a drink. And, by the way, I noticed the way she looked at you out there. Is she suspicious, by any chance?'

'No way,' Katie said insistently. 'I'd say that was her getting her own back on me for the other day when I wasn't too nice to her.

'She probably doesn't like me very much. OK, let's go to the cognac bar on level six; there's never a sinner in there any time we pass it. And not another word until we get there!' Katie marched out of the toilet, with a gobsmacked Carol in tow.

Once in the bar, they ordered two large brandies and sat at a small table at the side of the bar, where Katie spilled the beans about her encounters with Sam.

'So,' said Carol. 'You were off having afternoon delight while I sat reading my novel, oblivious?'

Katie wasn't sure if Carol was joking or annoyed, so she just went for the jugular.

'Do you think tomorrow will work out OK?'

Carol took a large sip of brandy, held it in her mouth for a few seconds, then let it slip down the back of her throat. She squinted over at Katie and shook her head, but she did it with half a smile on her face. It gave Katie the nerve to carry on.

'You could always meet Alfredo. I heard him say he's off work tomorrow. You could have a nice time with him.' Katie was hoping against hope that Carol would have someone to occupy her day.

'I would, but he's going home to see his *mama* tomorrow. He lives miles away, in the middle of nowhere.'

'Go with him, then,' Katie said encouragingly.

'Yeah, right, and what if *mama* is looking for a nice wife for her big son and she kidnaps me and makes me cook and wear black for the rest of my days? And, better still, what if *mama* is a young, leggy, dark-eyed beauty? I'm sure he has a girlfriend - or maybe even a wife.'

Katie was glad Carol was laughing about it all, but she still didn't have her answer. They sat in silence for another few moments before Carol spoke.

'You are something else, do you know that, Katie Cully?

Never thought I'd live to see the day. *Carry On Cruising* eat your fucking heart out!' she laughed, still unable to take it all in.

'So, should I do it? You think it'll be OK?' Doubt still niggled at Katie.

A broad smile came across Carol's face. 'Everything is possible! Where there's a will, blah blah blah. Right, drink up; I've a big date to arrange for myself for tomorrow.'

Katie jumped off her seat and threw her arms around her friend. 'Thank you, thank you. I know I'm mad, but I really want to do this.' She pulled Carol by the hand. 'Come on, I owe you a drink.'

'Aw, yeah, typical when there's a free bar.'

They made their way back to the sky lounge, where they each took a glass of champagne from a smiling young waitress. 'Follow me,' said Carol, making her way to the bar, where Alfredo was standing with a few passengers.

They passed the piano en route; Sam and Jill were still standing there, chatting to another happy couple. Katie pretended not to notice and continued smiling and talking to Carol in an effort to appear calm and collected, but, in reality, her heart was fluttering like the wings of a little sparrow in a birdbath.

Jill noticed them passing, and for the first time realised that the girls were on their own. No husbands or boyfriends. She felt sick to her stomach. She looked at Sam, her blood starting to boil. *Did he know they were here alone?*

As Carol approached Alfredo, he walked towards her with both arms outstretched. He took both her hands and greeted her with a peck on each cheek, then took a step back and, still holding her hands, studied her from head to toe. 'My beautiful Irish lady,' he enthused.

He was so besotted by Carol he didn't even notice Katie standing there. Feeling a bit awkward, she opened her gold clutch bag and lifted out her mobile phone. There were three messages from Sam. She slowly walked away to the far end of the bar, eager to read them.

The first, sent 20 minutes ago: *Hasn't she an amazing voice?*

Katie was incredulous. *If she's that fucking amazing,* she thought, *why don't you just stay with her?*

She read the second message, sent 10 minutes later: *Where are U?*

None of your bloody business.

And the final text, sent five minutes ago: *Can't wait to get my hands on U tomorrow honey... hmm xxx!*

Aye... just go and piss off.

Katie closed her phone without answering and made her way back to Carol and Alfredo, her lips tight with anger. She was completely confused; wanting to spend tomorrow with Sam but also wanting to tell him to take a long walk off a short pier.

What was the point of unsettling herself? How bad would she feel after spending a day in a love-nest with Sam? Then again, how good would she feel? Loads of women would give their right arm for an opportunity like this.

She couldn't help noticing Sam and Jill standing nearby, that arm of his still placed firmly around her slim waist.

He is one sneaky bastard, she thought, as she passed by them.

When Katie got back to Carol, Alfredo made a fuss of her, telling her how beautiful she looked. She thanked him and wondered if Carol had planned anything with him for tomorrow If Carol hadn't, she would text Sam and call the whole thing off.

'So, what's happening?' Katie asked as they walked to the dining room.

'He's all for it,' Carol smiled. 'We have to leave early - around 7.30am - so we'll get a taxi from the port, then his brother will pick us somewhere or other and drive us to his place.'

'That's a bit of a trek,' Katie said.

'Anything for you, my darling,' Carol joked, linking her arm through Katie's. 'So, when do you get your next set of instructions?'

'When he gets his hand surgically removed from his *amazing* wife's waistline.'

'What's up with you?' Carol said, shocked at Katie's bad humour.

'Ah, nothing. I'm just a bit pissed off.' She told Carol about the texts and how she was having a change of heart.

'Well, it's up to you, Katie. I'm sure Alfredo will get over it if I don't go with him.'

'I'll see.'

'So, when are you going to reply?'

'Don't know. I need to gather my thoughts; my head is all over the place. If he's that anxious, he'll text me again.'

As the hours passed, Katie felt like throwing her phone into the sea. It was 11pm now, and still nothing from Sam.

Carol looked at her impatiently. 'Will you for Christ's sake text him? Make up your mind; either you're up for it or not. You checking that bloody phone every two seconds is driving me crazy.'

'OK, OK,' said Katie. 'What will I say?'

'Just ask what the arrangements are for tomorrow. Simple!'

'So, you're assuming I'm going, then?'

'Of course you're going, Katie. You might be trying to fool yourself, but you can't fool me.'

Katie typed what Carol had suggested and hit send, then stood her phone up against a glass pillar on the bar counter, afraid she would miss his reply. Now she found herself in a state of panic at the thought of not seeing him tomorrow. *Maybe he's changed his mind.*

Against Sam's wishes, Jill had insisted on leaving the restaurant as soon as they finished their meal. Something was up with her but he had no idea what. All he knew was that he could cut the atmosphere with a knife.

He'd been on his best behaviour all evening; held her hand, praised her singing and showered her with attention. But the minute he closed their state room door, Jill started shouting at him, tears leaking from her eyes.

'You didn't tell me those girls are on their own,' she snarled.

'What girls?' Sam tried not to look like he knew full well who she was talking about.

'Those Irish girls. Oh, that Katie one is into you big time. She's probably your type, too... all tits and ass. I saw you looking over at her.'

'Jill, please, don't be ridiculous. *You* are my type, darling. Stop annoying yourself.'

'I don't want you talking to them again, Sam. Even if they stop to talk to you, you'd better get rid of them, do you hear me?'

Jill kept on shouting and ranting until she finally exhausted herself. She couldn't be reasoned with when she was in this kind of mood. Eventually, she got into bed and turned herself away from him, crying herself to sleep.

He stared at the ceiling. He knew he hadn't looked directly at Katie in the sky lounge, though he could see her in his periphery. *Was I that transparent?* he wondered.

It was midnight before he lifted his phone to text Katie.

Only getting a chance to text U honey. Jill's bus leaves at 9.30am. I can check into the hotel at 10.30am. I'll send U website and U can google the directions. It's easy to get to. I'll text in the morning. One more sleep! Ten more hours! Sweet dreams darling! Xxx.

As he switched off his phone, he said a silent prayer that Jill wouldn't call off her trip.

19

Day Six (Taormina)

When Katie and Carol woke up, the ship had already anchored in Taormina. It had just gone 7am and Carol phoned for room service. 'That'll save us some time not having to go for breakfast.'

'Good idea; I might squeeze in a wee session in the gym.'

When the girls were all set to leave, Katie became anxious.

'This doesn't seem so much fun in sober daylight, does it? Promise me you'll keep your phone nearby, Carol. I might need to hear your voice if I take a panic attack.'

'You'll be grand. We'll keep in touch by text. I'll probably be late back - I'm sure Alfredo will want to spend as much time as possible with his family.'

They hugged each other goodbye. 'Are we wise or otherwise?' Carol laughed. 'You have a great time, girlfriend.'

'You too,' said Katie, closing the door of their room and turning left for the gym.

Connor made his way to the fifth floor at 7.45am and sat in his usual seat by the window. He'd mentioned to Amy the night before that he may go for a coffee in the morning if he couldn't sleep. He didn't want her anywhere near the café.

There was no sign of Chris yet; his text the previous evening said he'd be there before eight. Connor sat looking out the window and was surprised to see Carol climb onto the tender boat, helped by the sommelier from the main dining room.

Leaning forward in his seat, he looked to see if his mum was there, too, but there was no sign of her. This was strange, he thought; the two were usually inseparable. He began to panic slightly, thinking she might be sick. But then why would Carol leave her alone without at least telling him to check on her? The tender took off and Connor sat uneasily watching it lightly bob across the waters to the port. He turned around to see Chris approach.

'Glad you got my message, and gladder still that you could make it,' the handsome young officer smiled. 'I guess Sleeping Beauty hasn't arisen yet?' He sat down.

'This is the middle of the night for her,' Connor deadpanned.

'Do you ever get a time on your own? Like, does Amy ever go to the spa?'

'Yeah, she talked about getting some kind of treatment, but we're getting off the ship this morning so that only leaves tomorrow - our last day. Maybe I could book a surprise for her before we go into Sorrento tomorrow.'

'That would be cool,' said Chris. 'I'd like a bit of time together… maybe I could arrange a bit of privacy.'

Connor couldn't say for certain what Chris had in mind, but, unless he was wildly off the mark, he had a fair idea. He was nervous and excited at the same time.

'I'll see what I can do; I'll text you later if I can organise a spa treatment for her.'

They chatted easily for another ten minutes. It was as if, Connor thought, they'd known each other forever. The chemistry between them was tangible. When Chris got up to leave, Connor remembered his mum was on her own.

He made his way back and knocked lightly on her door, waiting impatiently for her to open up. Nothing. He went into his own room and tried ringing the room instead. No answer. He anxiously sent her a text.

Katie came off the treadmill to discover she had two texts on her phone; one from Sam and one from Connor.

She read Sam's first:

2 hrs 45 min to go... hmmm....xxx sending U the link for hotel directions.

Excitement bubbled in her tummy... until she opened Connor's text:

Mum...ring me ... please!

Something was wrong. After dinner last night, they'd all met up at the bar and she'd told Connor she and Carol would be getting off the ship early to make a day of it in Taormina. She hurried out of the gym and ran down the stairs rather than wait for the lift. She knocked on his door.

'Mum, what's wrong?' he asked as he opened the door.

Before stepping into their room, Katie could see Amy standing by the bedside, staring at her. She looked back at Connor and saw a worried look on his face.

'What do you mean, Connor? You asked me to call you. It sounded urgent.'

'I thought maybe you were sick, or had fallen out with Carol.'

'What? Why?' Katie asked, still panting from the sprint down the stairs.

'I saw her getting on the tender earlier this morning. When I saw you weren't with her, I thought something must be wrong.'

Katie hadn't factored this scenario into her plans and had no excuse prepared. She had to think on her feet. Praying it hadn't been obvious to Connor that Carol was in the company of Alfredo for the day, she said:

'No, it's just that Carol was up early and was eager to get off. I wanted to go to the gym so we've arranged to meet around ten o'clock in the square.'

She thought that sounded plausible enough until she looked over at Amy, who stood staring at her, one eyebrow raised and a 'yeah, right' smirk on her face.

'Ah, right,' Connor said, sounding assured. 'Sorry for panicking you, Mum.'

Katie looked at her watch. 'I better get a move on, love. What time you going to shore?' She didn't want to bump into them while she was wandering around trying to find the hotel.

'We'll be another while,' said Connor. 'Enjoy your day and we'll see you tonight.'

'You too, love. See you later.' Guilt engulfed her as she walked out of the room.

When Katie was gone, Amy looked meaningfully at Connor.

'Hmm… I don't believe that for one second.'

'Amy, stop. Why do you always have to be so cynical?'

'No, Connor, why do you always have to be so fucking stupid?'

He knew there was no point in arguing with her, but he knew he was stupid, alright.

Stupid for telling Amy he'd seen Carol getting on board the tender with the wine guy.

20

Katie stepped onto the tender at 9.45am. She'd downloaded the hotel website and directions and Sam was right; it seemed straightforward enough. She wondered where Carol was now; she'd tried calling, but it wouldn't connect.

Not for the first time that morning, Katie asked herself if she was wise. Connor was curious, Amy was suspicious and Carol was uncontactable.

A shuttle bus waiting on Naxos pier took the passengers up a windy road to the beautiful old town of Taormina. Everyone stopped to admire the breathtaking views, but Katie quietly broke away from the others, her mind fully consumed by Sam and her body tingling at the thought of what they would get up to.

She checked the time on her phone and re-checked her messages; nothing. She walked along the pedestrian area, admiring the elegant boutiques and delicious pastry shops until she finally settled at a quaint little café. Two local buskers played lively music and smiled their thanks as passers-by threw spare coins into their open guitar case.

Katie checked the hotel directions again and realised she was only a five-minute walk away. Sam was probably very close by; or maybe already there. She had no intention of walking in with him - that would be too nerve-wracking - so decided she would sit tight and wait for her next instruction.

She couldn't finish the delicious pastry she'd ordered with her cappuccino; her tummy was doing somersaults.

As she took her last sip of coffee, her phone bleeped.

I'm here hon… 14th floor Rm4 xx.

Katie arrived nervously at the hotel, which sat almost on the kerb of a narrow street corner. It looked quite small from the outside; just a large, black double door framed with two black and gold marble pillars.

The reception area was quiet and, as Katie looked around, she noticed the lifts to her left. She did her best to make it look like the surroundings were familiar to her, sticking her nose in the air and making her way confidently past the glamorous dark-haired receptionist, hoping she wouldn't feel the need to come to her assistance.

As she waited for the lift to arrive, her heart was beating so fast she thought she might have a heart attack. *I certainly will if someone I know from home steps out of that lift,* she thought irrationally.

When the lift arrived and the doors opened, a fifty-something, tall, handsome 'bell boy' greeted her with a wide smile and asked which floor.

'Fourteen, please,' she answered, trying to sound chirpy even though her insides were churning like a washing machine. She silently watched the buttons light up as the lift moved up through the floors before stopping on '14'; the penthouse suites.

There were only four doors on the corridor so she found the room easily. As she rapped lightly on the door, she suddenly felt like she was having an out-of-body experience; surely this wasn't her knocking on the door of a hotel room, about to spend the afternoon with a man who wasn't her husband?

The door opened and Sam stood there, a broad smile lighting up his face. Instantly, all her fears melted - and so did her heart. He took her into his arms, walked her through the door and kicked it closed with his foot. They stood there as if glued to the spot, kissing with the passion of long-lost lovers.

When Sam finally managed to pull himself away, he stared into Katie's flushed face; she knew her lipstick must be plastered all over her face, but she didn't care.

'Come on,' he said, leading Katie into a gorgeous lounge bedroom. An enormous bed sat at the centre. A humming noise drew Katie's gaze to the corner of the room, where a curved Jacuzzi bath, raised up on four circular carpeted steps, was quietly bubbling away. On a nearby table sat a bottle of pink champagne and flute glasses.

'Sit down and relax, Katie,' said Sam, leading her by the hand to a soft, two-seater antique couch. He reached for two cut-glass tumblers and opened the fridge.

'D'ye fancy a wee gin an' tonic?' His attempt at a Northern Irish accent always made her laugh.

Sam poured the drink and, handing her the glass, planted another tender kiss on Katie's lips. 'Here's to the first of the day, honey.'

As the cool gin slipped down her throat, she began to relax… though she still felt she was somehow outside of her own body, looking in at a total stranger.

She slipped off her silver strappy sandals, which she had chosen to go with her short, peach fitted dress. The neckline, which sat just below her collarbone, was finished off with a row of small, silver rhinestones (she had a code: if the hem is short, the neckline should be high; much classier).

As she stretched out her legs, Sam took her right foot, placed it on his knee and started massaging it gently.

'Nice?' he asked. He too, was starting to relax. He'd put a lot of thought into this - not so much to seduce Katie as to spoil her - and had been really nervous. But somehow, when he was in her company, it just seemed so right. She had an easiness about her he'd always found calming.

Their personalities bounced off each other; even in a working environment they always managed a laugh when no-one else seemed to get it.

Katie lay back as Sam methodically caressed her tired feet. She watched his face, engrossed in his task, taking one toe at a time, then massaging the ball of her foot before moving on to the heel. She'd always enjoyed reflexology, but this was totally different; a more erotic experience.

And she'd never experienced such closeness… and tenderness.

Sam moved only to get them another drink and to order a delicious meal of fresh salads and a selection of cold meats from the room service menu. Before they knew it, a full hour had passed in what seemed like five minutes.

The Jacuzzi was still bubbling away in the corner. Sam looked over at it, then back at Katie.

'Fancy some bubbles?'

'I don't have my swimsuit with me,' she said, only half joking.

'I'll keep my eyes closed,' he teased.

'Well,' she said, anxious all of a sudden, 'let me get in first.'

She broke from his embrace and walked to the bathroom, taking off her clothes before wrapping a large, soft bath towel around her naked body. Although she had already made love to Sam, she knew this was going to be totally different. Their first time had been urgent; she was still half-dressed when he'd kissed her and explored her body. Today, it would be perfect. They had time and space; the excitement of it was almost more than she could bear.

When she came back to the bedroom, Sam was already standing naked, his back to her. His long limbs were so perfect she felt like she wanted to look at him forever. He turned around and walked over to her. She kept her eyes on his upper region, feeling a bit embarrassed to be seen to be looking lower. He smiled as he playfully danced his fingers over the top edge of her towel.

'Shy, are we?'

'Just a wee bit,' she giggled nervously.

He took her hand and led her to the Jacuzzi. She stepped into the inviting bubbles and dropped the towel on the steps as she lowered herself in. Sam stood behind her, taking in the curves of her beautiful body. Then he stepped in and settled down, facing her. He reached for the cold champagne bottle, popped it open and poured two glasses.

'I don't want this to end,' he said, handing Katie a glass.

'Am I dreaming?' she whispered. Then, seductively, she took a sip from her glass, leaned over and let the liquid fall from her mouth into Sam's.

'Umm… never knew champagne to taste so good,' he said, licking his lips.

They drank, talked, laughed, kissed and explored each other's bodies - above and under the bubbles.

'Let me get behind so you can lie back on my chest,' Sam said, standing up so Katie could slide forward and make room for him. He rested himself back and pulled her close as she laid her head against him.

He massaged her breasts and shoulders, then moved up to her neck and face. Reaching across to lift a creamy face wash from the basket of miniature creams and lotions at the side of the Jacuzzi, he poured some on his hands and started to massage her face.

Using his fingertips, he travelled across her forehead, moved gently over the contours of her high cheekbones, around her lips and jawline and then back up to her forehead… then did it all over again.

Katie was nearly going out of her mind at his touch; this was heaven on earth and she didn't want it to stop.

Sam checked his watch; time to move on. Picking up Katie's towel, he stood up and helped her to her feet, draping the towel over her shoulders as she stepped out of the Jacuzzi. He towelled her down as they stood on the thick cream carpet, then, planting tender kisses across her face, carried her to the beautiful white linen bed.

Sam had never experienced such heights of pleasure in his life. No woman had ever made him feel the way Katie did and this new-found feeling exhilarated him; *scared* him, almost.

Blissfully exhausted, they clung together afterwards; two happy souls in paradise.

They lay there, silent and content in each other arms, until Katie felt a bit of panic start to rise within her. She checked her phone again, hoping Carol had texted.

'She most likely has no service,' Sam said soothingly, tracing her neck and shoulders with his fingertips. 'Don't worry; it'll be fine.'

'Yeah, I know, but I'd just like to hear from her, you know… just to be sure. Anyway, we best make our way back.' She sighed.

'Today was amazing, Katie,' Sam said, struggling to contain the emotion in his voice.

'Oh, Sam, it really was,' she replied, kissing him deeply before wriggling out of his arms.

He watched her as she walked away from him towards the bathroom, taking in every inch of her naked body.

After Katie left, he showered away the evidence from his skin but knew he would never wash away the memory in his head of this vibrant, sensual women and their magical afternoon together. He left the room, went downstairs and paid the bill, then checked the time again; anxious now to get back to the ship. Jill had still been a bit cool this morning, but she'd kept her plans. If he wasn't sitting at the bar waiting for her, all hell would break loose.

Katie was lying on top of the bed in her white cotton bathrobe when Carol walked in through the state room door, not long before the ship was about to depart.

'You're back, thank God,' Katie said. 'Anyone see you coming in? Connor saw you leaving this morning; I told him I was meeting you in the town. So, we need to get our story straight.'

'No, no-one saw me; I got the lift straight here. It's all grand! I tried texting and ringing you, but I couldn't get a signal. You look relaxed and happy… how'd you get on?'

'Just fantastic,' Katie smiled. 'It was unbelievable, Carol.'

'Wow, I look forward to hearing all about it! But I need to get out of these clothes and have a nice shower first. Just hold those thoughts.'

'How about you? How did the day with Alfredo go?'

Carol sat at the edge of her bed and took off her shoes, rubbing her aching feet as she told Katie all about her wonderful Italian family experience.

'It was a real big deal; his wee mama must have been preparing for days, God love her. There were ten of us and the meal lasted for hours… don't think I've ever tasted such delicious food and wine; I'm totally stuffed!'

'That sounds like a treat. What was Alfredo's family like?'

'Aw, they were really lovely,' Katie. 'They're so passionate about their animals, their harvest and, of course, their vineyards. It's a totally different lifestyle from ours. But, here; I'm more interested in how your day went.'

Katie smiled and put her hand on her heart.

'Carol, I had the most memorable day of my life,' she said, inhaling deeply.

21

Connor and Amy had taken the 10.30am tender to Taormina. It was such a gorgeous day and it should have been a delight to be wandering around this beautiful Sicilian town. But, so far, it was anything but. The atmosphere was still frosty between them, Amy refusing to take Connor's hand as they walked around. Earlier, when she'd almost missed her step getting off the tender, she'd ignored his help and took the hand of the boatman instead.

It was like everything was Connor's fault. Amy even seemed to blame him for Carol's behaviour, even though it was none of his business what she got up to (though he had to agree with Amy that it was a bit strange her going ashore without his mum).

Mum hadn't been herself this morning; she'd seemed anxious and preoccupied. Maybe he was imagining it; hopefully they'd bump into her and Carol in the town and they could all have coffee and a chat.

Amy stopped off at a fresh herb stall. She lifted a little white linen sachet filled with crushed lavender flowers and held it to her nose, then she poured a few drops of tea tree and chamomile oil on each wrist and sniffed those, too. The young girl serving at the counter started to explain the origin and benefits of these beautiful essential oils.

Connor smiled to himself; maybe they would help calm Amy's hormones.

He stepped in: 'We'll take the chamomile and rosemary oils and the lavender sachet and eye mask. Do you want anything else, babes?' He smiled softly at her, hoping this would break the ice.

Thankfully, she smiled back. 'No, that'll be lovely. Thanks, babes.' As he took the gift bag from the young lady and they began to walk away, Amy slid her fingers through his.

After lunch in the main square, they wandered through the cobbled streets, picking up some souvenirs along the way. They chatted together contentedly, but Connor's mind kept drifting off to Chris' suggestion for a 'bit of privacy'.

Time was running out; tomorrow was their last full day. On Friday, they were off the ship early morning and straight to the airport. Connor would be back in Ireland; Chris would stay on the ship for another two months before going back to New York.

How could he make it happen?

When Connor and Amy got back on board, they decided to go straight to the pool bar for a cocktail. There was still no sign of his mum or Carol, but he knew better than to mention their names in front of her.

'I'm going to go lie down on the lounger for a while,' Amy said. 'I could be doing with a wee doze.'

Seizing the opportunity, Connor said he'd leave their bits and pieces back in the room.

That would give him a chance to go to the spa and try and book a treatment for Amy for the following morning. Chris had told Connor he was off duty until midday; a 10am appointment for her would fit in perfectly with his plans.

The receptionist at the spa, a young Korean girl, was so pleasant and helpful that Connor found himself relaxing in the midst of his panic.

'We're not too busy tomorrow morning because a lot of passengers are off on tours. I can offer you 9.30 or 10.30am?' she smiled graciously.

He knew 9.30 would be a bit too early for Amy, so he booked a luxury facial for 10.30 and was advised to tell his girlfriend to be there 15 minutes earlier for a consultation.

Connor walked out of the spa and immediately texted Chris.

I'll be free tomorrow morning from 10.30-11.30.

He was delighted with himself. He put his phone into his pocket and turned the corner from the spa, narrowly avoiding bumping into Carol, who had just come out of the nearby lift and was hurrying down the corridor towards her room. She was carrying a large beach bag and wearing the same clothes she'd had on when Connor spotted her getting onto the tender that morning.

It was obvious she was just arriving back on board. He hung back, out of sight. For some reason, he felt Carol would not want to run into him. He had an uneasy feeling about this. Where had she been all day? Who was she with? And, come to think of it, where was his mum? She'd been acting so weird… was she covering up for Carol, somehow? He hoped she hadn't to stay tucked away, alone all day, out of sight of him and Amy while Carol had a romantic day away with 'lover boy'. That wasn't fair.

He waited in the corridor until he heard Carol close the door behind her, then made his way to his room. He immediately went to the in-house phone and dialled.

'Hi, Mum,' he said, after she'd sleepily answered. 'Sorry, did I wake you?'

'No, love. Carol and I had a tiring day and we're just lying here chilling.'

'OK, I'll leave you to it - see you after dinner.'

Connor hung up, slightly dazed. His mother had just told him a big fat lie.

Sam was sitting at the sunset bar, where he'd arranged to meet Jill. The ship had filled up now that departure time was drawing near. Most of the passengers approaching the bar looked tired and bedraggled after their long day at shore, but Sam felt like a new man.

His day had been filled with fun, excitement, lust and happiness. He sipped his ice-cold beer and thought about Katie. She was amazing. He was fascinated by the spontaneity of their conversations, their humour and their intimacy.

But the bubble had to burst. The holiday would be over in two days' time and he would continue his life with Jill while Katie would go home to her husband. They'd still have to meet up for work, though. He wondered if an affair would work? No; amputation was the sensible thing to do, and, that way, the desire and obsession wouldn't spread. Best to nip this in the bud.

Jill spotted Sam at the bar and was making her way towards him. Although she'd enjoyed her day, it was tainted with annoyance at him for not joining her. But the sight of him, waiting there for her, eased her tension somewhat.

'Aw, look at you, all on your lonesome,' she said when she reached him. 'That's what you get for not coming with me.' Jill forced a smile and pecked him on the cheek.

He was so engrossed in his thoughts that he looked almost blindly at Jill before he actually saw her.

'Oh, hi, darling. You caught me unawares there; just thinking about the office. How did your trip go? Want something to drink?' Sam shot off his stool in a panic, as if she could somehow read his thoughts, and helped her onto her seat.

'Sparkling water's fine. Yes, I had a nice day - though I missed you. I saw the most amazing bright-coloured fish and the water was clear blue. And I came across an octopus; a real scary looking thing. It was camouflaged on a rock and it was only when it blinked that I realised what it was.'

Sam studied Jill as she gave him an account of her trip. She was trying her best to hide it, but he knew she was still annoyed at him.

'You must be wrecked, sweetheart. I'm exhausted just listening to you,' he laughed nervously.

'Yeah, I'm going to have a nice soak in the bath after this. How was your day?' she asked, placing the heel of her hand under her chin and staring accusingly into his face.

'Not as energetic as yours, by all accounts,' Sam replied, the vivid memory of Katie and him making love that afternoon flooding his mind.

22

Day Seven (Sorrento)

The ship docked in Sorrento at 7.30am. Connor got out of bed at eight, drew the curtains and stepped out onto the balcony. Some passengers were already stepping onto waiting shuttle buses, while others were standing on the pontoon reading information leaflets or studying maps.

When he went back inside, Amy had begun to stir; she was rubbing her eyes as the bright sunlight lit up the room.

'Nooo, babes, what's with all that sunshine? What time is it anyway?'

'C'mon, lazy bones,' he said breezily. 'It's time to get up… I've a surprise for you.'

He lifted the envelope which contained the spa treatment and handed it to her.

'Aw, nice one, a facial,' she said, pleased. 'I'd meant to organise a treatment for myself but there never seemed to be enough time. Thank you, babes.'

'We'll go for breakfast now, and then you can get yourself organised,' he said, heading to the bathroom. 'I'm just going to jump into the shower.'

After breakfast, Amy slipped on her bathrobe. Putting her appointment card into the large pocket, she asked Connor how he would pass the time while she was away being pampered.

'I'll do a few laps around the jogging track up on the top deck, but I'll be right here when you get back.' He turned to give her a parting peck on the cheek. 'Enjoy, babe!'

'Isn't life a bitch,' she sighed. 'I've to go for a luxury facial, then walk around Sorrento for the afternoon. Honestly, the things I have to do.'

With that, Amy smiled and skipped happily out the door.

Connor shifted gear the minute the door closed behind her; he'd only ten minutes to get ready. Taking off the clothes he'd worn for breakfast, he pulled on a pair of straight-legged white jeans and slipped his feet into a pair of soft navy leather loafers. He completed the look with a navy short-sleeved shirt, letting it hang casually over his jeans and leaving it open at the neck.

He hadn't felt this excited in years. In fact, he couldn't recall ever feeling this excited in his whole life. Already he was starting to sweat. He checked the air conditioner in the room, but it was down low; it was his body temperature that was on fire.

He took a deep breath as he opened the door, said a silent prayer to whatever God was up there that he wouldn't bump into his mum, then quickly made his way down the corridor to the back stairs, like a thief escaping the crime scene, to the staff quarters on deck three.

Connor checked his watch as he knocked lightly on Chris' door. He wasn't sure what to expect, even though it was more than obvious they fancied each other. All Chris had mentioned in his text the night before was that his roommate would be on duty and he'd have the place to himself.

Connor had never been in this position with a man before. Was he expected to greet him with a kiss, or shake his hand, or maybe just say 'hi'? Would Chris be feeling as awkward as he was right now? He'd often imagined what it would be like to hold another man. How strange would that be after holding a woman for the past two years?

Recently, back in Glasgow, he'd started reading the weekly edition of *GAY UK* on his laptop while Amy was at the gym. He dreamed of the day when he could be just like the men he read about: openly gay, fearless and proud.

Chris opened the door, a relaxed smile on his face. He looked much younger in his white T-shirt and denim cut-offs. He was barefoot, his hair was wet (obviously just out of the shower) and his aftershave smelt so fresh and spicy that Connor felt like closing his eyes and inhaling him. *Jesus, he looks damn good*, he thought.

Chris invited him inside, discreetly checking the corridor for any nosy neighbours before closing the door behind them.

He looked at Connor and knew immediately that the young Irishman was well out of his comfort zone. He resisted the urge to kiss him and instead offered him a seat.

'Would you like a coffee?' Chris asked. 'Bit early for alcohol, don't you think? My shift starts in two hours anyway.'

'Yeah, bit early for me, too,' Connor lied. At this minute, he could happily put a large glass of wine to his mouth and down it in one gulp. He'd never felt so nervous.

Connor sat down on a small couch and looked around the room. It was tiny, and very basic compared to the rooms the guests stayed in. There were two single beds, with a locker dividing them, and two single wardrobes fitted either side of the beds, each connected to an overhead cupboard. An average-size fridge, with a kettle on top of it, sat in the corner. A mural depicting a bright sea with green crashing waves took up the space where a window would be.

Chris handed Connor his coffee, noticing his eyes widening at the Spartan appearance of the room. 'It serves its purpose. I really only sleep here.'

'Yeah, well, I suppose the rest of the ship is like your living area', Connor said, trying to hide his shock that someone would have to live like this for months at a time.

'With my rank, I can eat in the main dining room and also get to mingle with the passengers at the bars… no alcohol intake, though.'

He continued to tell Connor he'd be another two months on the ship before getting a month off in January, when he would likely spend most of his holiday studying for his next exam.

'All being well, I'll pass and get my promotion. Then I'll have my own room… hopefully with a port hole window,' he laughed, pointing at the mural.

Still sensing Connor's vulnerability, Chris starting talking about his family back in New York; how his grandfather had come over from Cork with his parents in the 1920s and signed up to the US Navy when he'd come of age, how his son (Chris' father) had followed in his footsteps, and how it was the most natural thing in the world, growing up around all things maritime, for Chris to sign up for a life on the high seas, too.

As he listened eagerly to Chris' stories of home, Connor couldn't help noticing his deep-set blue eyes, chiselled jawline, broad shoulders and muscular body. He was a bit hesitant to talk about his own life growing up in Derry (it seemed a bit dull in comparison to Chris' privileged lifestyle), but, after some gentle persuasion, he found his rhythm and Chris seemed genuinely interested in Connor's tales of summers spent in his granny's caravan in Donegal; going fishing, jumping off high piers and staying in the wild Atlantic until the freezing waters numbed their bodies.

During a brief lull in the conversation, Chris checked his watch and Connor did likewise. It was already 11.15; time was up. Connor wished he could press a stop button that would give them an extra ten minutes. Just sitting here and chatting with Chris had somehow changed him; his heart was beating at a regular rhythm and the sweat on his palms had dried up. He had found his voice and felt listened to. He felt confident and relaxed. He'd found a friend and felt understood. And, most important of all, he'd found himself.

Should his hand never touch Chris or his lips never kiss him, he knew already that his world finally made sense. He was at peace. But it was time to go. He slapped his knees with his hands and quickly stood up.

'I suppose I'd better get back.'

Startled by his standing up so briskly, Chris did the same and they almost headbutted each other. If it wasn't so awkward, it would have been funny. But neither of them laughed.

Suddenly, the small room seemed even smaller. Here were two six-feet men facing one another, the only thing between them an invisible wall of nerves that neither of them quite knew how to break down.

It was Chris who tentatively edged his way forward; it was now or never. Connor closed his eyes and hoped for the best. Their lips touched, then Chris wrapped his arms around him in a tight embrace.

To Connor, it felt like the most natural thing in the world.

23

'Whose bright idea was this?' Carol panted, stopping halfway up the steep climb.

The ship was docked in Sorrento and Katie had suggested they take the stone steps up to the heart of the town rather than the overcrowded courtesy bus.

'Didn't look this bad from the port,' Katie laughed. 'Come on; we're nearly there.'

After catching their breath at the top, they were almost tempted to sack their planned tour of Pompeii (a 40-minute bus ride away) but they decided to get it out of the way before the heat of the day became too much.

They made their way to the local station, where they joined a bus load of tourists for the trip. On the way, the guide gave them an introduction to the famous Roman town that was simultaneously destroyed and preserved by the volcanic ash that erupted from Mount Vesuvius in 79AD. Two thousand of Pompeii's 15,000 inhabitants died that day.

As they walked around the historic ruins, Katie and Carol were fascinated, but also disturbed, by the sight of the petrified remains of some of those citizens, frozen in time where they died in the midst of their daily chores. The tour lasted two hours, at the end of which they were hot, tired and thirsty.

On the way back to Sorrento, Katie checked her phone, hoping she'd see a text from Sam. Nothing. *Too busy playing happy families to spare a thought for me*, she thought, annoyed. She knew he and Jill were off to Capri today.

She sat back and closed her eyes as the bus took the winding road along the Amalfi Coast. This time yesterday, she was lying in Sam's arms, not a care in the world. Tomorrow, she would be back in Matt's. Oh, if only he'd been able to go on the cruise she wouldn't be in this awful mess. *What type of a woman am I, anyway?* she wondered.

Her heart was racing and she wasn't sure if it was out of self-disgust or just a longing to be home again; where she belonged. All she wanted now was the security of her real life and the love of her good husband. She needed to put all this behind her.

Nice memories; chapter closed.

Sam and Jill were on the ferry to the island of Capri. Sam had got chatting to a Welsh couple sitting next to them, but Jill wasn't in the mood for idle chitchat and preferred to gaze out at the water in silence.

She'd noticed Sam checking his phone a few times; he'd pretended to be listening to the others, but Jill knew him better than that. He was clearly preoccupied and she wondered if there was maybe a problem at the bank.

When they arrived at the pier in Capri, Sam suggested hiring a private traditional 'gozzo' boat, and asked the Welsh couple if they'd like to join them.

It comfortably accommodated the four of them, and, as the skipper helped them on board, he handed them each a glass of champagne and sat a large bowl of fresh strawberries on a small wooden table in front of them. The skipper entertained them with stories of the island's celebrated caves and coves, and serenaded them as they sailed off to one of the most popular attractions, the Blue Grotto.

Back on dry land, they walked until they reached the piazzetta and sat down and ordered a bottle of local wine and some delicious tapas.

On the ferry back to Sorrento, Jill rolled her eyes as the Welsh lady pulled her phone out of her bag to take yet another picture of them all.

'I took some great photos today,' she said, looking at Jill and Sam. 'I'll WhatsApp them to you, shall I? What's your number?'

As Sam was about to call it out, Jill intervened.

'We don't exchange numbers.'

No-one knew which way to look as Jill rested back on the seat and stared, straight-faced, across the water.

Sam was cringing inside. He narrowed his eyes at Jill, then turned to the horrified-looking couple and shrugged his shoulders. No-one spoke for the rest of the journey.

He sat there, fuming. Jill could be so cold. Not like Katie, with her beautiful eyes and wide smile, her animated face and bubbly personality, her warmth and tenderness. Then he thought of their sensual kisses and passionate love-making and wished it was Katie, not Jill, who was sitting beside him right at this moment.

Amy and Connor walked hand in hand around the narrow streets of Sorrento. *Connor seems very relaxed today*, Amy thought, enjoying the comfortable silence between them as they ambled along. She squeezed his hand without looking at him, and in response he lifted her hand to his lips and kissed it. That was so nice!

She felt the holiday had actually brought them closer together; no work pressures or time schedules. Yeah, they should do this more often.

Connor's dad was very generous to pay for the trip; they could never have afforded it themselves. Matt was a good man and Amy liked him. Connor's mum was OK, too, she supposed, though she could never imagine them becoming best friends. Maybe when they got married and had a baby, Katie might want to be more involved with her. She knew Katie would love a grandchild. She'd even joked about it one night at the bar, telling them not to leave it until her bones knitted before making her a granny. That was a positive remark, Amy had thought at the time; at least Katie finally realised she and Connor were a solid item and in it for the long haul.

Amy often fantasised about her wedding day; she knew exactly what style of dress she wanted. But she also knew they were in no hurry. She was content knowing Connor loved her and that it was all ahead of them.

They sat down under a large parasol at a busy restaurant looking over the Bay of Naples and ordered two beers and a pepperoni pizza. Two guys in their early twenties sat a few tables away. One of them stretched over and kissed his companion on the lips, then leaned back against his chair and continued talking, as if nothing out of the ordinary had just happened.

'Isn't it strange how gays are more accepted in Italy?' Amy said, noticing Connor looking in their direction. 'Those guys are so openly affectionate and no-one even batted an eyelid. We could be doing with some of that back home. John, the male nurse who works with me, is gay. He and his partner would never behave like that in company. It's a totally different culture, isn't it?'

Connor stiffened slightly. *Why are we having this conversation?* he thought, wishing she would change the subject. He was quite happy thinking about Chris and the lovely time they'd had that morning. That beautiful kiss! Chris had texted him before he got off the ship with a simple *Thank you*.

How could two small words raise your spirits so high and set you heart on fire?

Connor had text back, *No - thank you. It was so good talking to someone who shares the same view of the world as me.*

There is a whole new world out there, Chris had replied.

I know, but I will have to take it one step at a time.

He also knew it would get a whole lot worse before it got better. From time to time, he found himself thinking about Amy and her doctor friend. The funny thing was, it wasn't jealousy he felt, but relief.

Amy was still babbling on about John and his partner while Connor sat there, wondering if he would ever find the courage to tell her the truth. On the up side, at least she had sympathy for the gay community. But would she have sympathy for him? Or would she feel cheated that she'd wasted two precious years of her life? Her ego would take a massive hit. Maybe it would be easier for her knowing he was leaving her for a man rather than another woman, but she would doubtless feel used and abused, like everything was a big lie. She would probably wonder if any part of their relationship was real.

'Connor, are you listening to me?' she scolded.

'Yeah, of course I am, babe,' he lied, hoping she wouldn't ask him to repeat her last sentence as she had done so many times before.

'So, what you think… should we ask them over when we get home?'

Struggling to guess who and what she was talking about, he thought he'd take his chances.

'Yeah, why not?'

She flashed him a broad smile. 'You'll love them. But don't be going all weird; just because they're gay doesn't mean they fancy every man they meet. They're good fun and they'll enjoy talking to you. They like strong, straight men, too.'

Holy fuck! That's all I need, Connor thought. But he summoned up a smile and said, 'Great. You want another beer?'

'Yeah, go on, then. It's so nice just sitting here, people-watching, isn't it?' Amy said, tilting her head to the sun. 'This is the life, babe.'

24

Back on board, as the ship made its way from Sorrento to Rome (the final destination of the cruise), passengers packed their suitcases and prepared for their onward journeys home.

Everyone's main cases were to be left outside their rooms before midnight, colour coded according to flight times, so that the disembarkation process for the 3,000 or so passengers would be as smooth and efficient as possible.

'So, what now?' Carol said, grabbing a pile of clothes from their hangers and roughly throwing them into her suitcase. She had no intention of folding them neatly away.

'What?' said Katie, knowing fine well the question she was being asked.

'You want me to spell it out? What now with you and Sexy Sam? And with you and Matt? With Sam and Jill? A lot of lives at stake, here, Katie.' Carol's tone was loaded with warning.

'A holiday romance is all it was, Carol. It's over now.' Katie tried to sound casual, but she knew her voice was betraying her.

'Did you and Sam talk about it?' Carol pressed. 'I mean, you both have to work together; it's not like you're not going to run into him again.'

'No, we didn't talk about it. Hopefully we'll just slip back into reality and it will all fizzle out.'

Katie's phoned bleeped to signal a new message.

'Well,' Carol smirked, 'what's SS saying now?'

Katie lifted her phone. Carol had guessed right; Sam.

'Yeah, it's him, just saying to enjoy our last night.' That

wasn't what the message said, but Katie didn't feel like reading out what it really *did* say.

She closed the phone without replying and wondered how she was going to be able to let him go. She loved their text messages… she loved everything about him.

As Carol attached the ship's red labels to their cases, she noticed their disembarkation time was assigned for 8.30am.

Well, that's it over, Carol thought. She was glad the only baggage she was taking home with her was her suitcase; Alfredo was really lovely and she'd had great fun with him, but she was ready to go back to the real world.

Katie, on the other hand… Carol wasn't buying her breezy, 'oh, it was just a holiday fling' chat. She knew her friend too well; Katie was in deep.

Up in room 1202, Sam lifted two matching Louis Vuitton suitcases onto the top of the bed as Jill carefully took her beautiful dresses off the padded hangers she'd brought with her from home.

'It's hard to believe it's over already,' she remarked. 'The last two days just flew by; we should book a ten-day cruise next time.'

She looked up at Sam, waiting on a reply, but he wasn't listening.

'Honey, you OK?'

'Yeah,' he said, sounding distracted. 'Just remembering I meant to ring the office today, but it's too late now.'

'Well, you'll be there on Monday morning. I'm sure they can wait.'

Sam walked into the bathroom to collect his toiletries. He

also needed space to text Katie. He hadn't contacted her all day, but he couldn't stop thinking about her.

He pushed the toilet door closed and took his phone out of his pocket. They hadn't discussed what would happen next. For his part, he hoped they would text or talk as often as possible - and hopefully see each other again soon.

He hoped Katie would want that, too, but feared she may want to move on. He typed out a text:

I missed U so much 2day. Keep reliving yesterday. I'll be at the bar after dinner. Seeing U from afar is better than nothing xxx

Sam had booked the ship's Italian restaurant for their last night. Their flight was at 10am tomorrow morning, so they had to be off the ship by 7.30. He knew Katie had a later departure so he wouldn't see her around in the morning. He guessed she'd go for an after-dinner drink in the champagne bar tonight… he needed to see her face.

His depressed look didn't go unnoticed by Jill. She walked over to him and gave him a hug.

'Come on, honey, you never let work get to you that much. It's our last night; let's have a nice bottle of champagne in the room after dinner. I'll put on my new Italian lingerie… and you can take it off,' she smiled seductively at Sam as she ran her finger down his nose and then planted a kiss on the tip of it.

That was the last thing on Sam's mind right now. Seeing a fully-dressed Katie from across the bar was way more appealing that a half-dressed Jill in his bed.

'I'll be fine after dinner, darling. Let's just take the night as it comes.'

He was feeling more depressed by the minute.

Chris had told Connor he'd be on duty on level three today. The day before disembarkation was always hectic, with passengers collecting their passports, querying their bills, making cash payments and confirming last-minute connections.

'I'll be milling around the purser's desk from 4-8pm. If you get a chance to get away, just text me,' he'd said.

Connor was trying to think of a way he could get to see him just one more time; he wanted to say goodbye face to face. Amy had finished her packing and was scanning their on-board account on their TV screen.

'Shall we just pay our bill online for handiness?' she suggested.

Connor stalled answering, pretending to be busy packing. Then he had a brainwave.

'No, you know what? I've some extra euro here; think I'd rather use them up.'

'OK, you run downstairs and settle up and I'll get my shower. Let's make our last night a good one, Connor. It's back to the grindstone next week, babes.'

'Too right,' he replied, delighted Amy was in good form and in no way suspicious.

Six separate queues had formed at the information desk on level three. Connor came out of the lift and joined the nearest line, scanning the area for Chris. He'd texted him ten minutes earlier to say he'd got a pass out. As he approached the top of the queue, he clocked Chris walking towards him. He paid his bill and left the counter, then the two of them walked away together.

'I'm so happy you made it!' Chris beamed. 'Have you time for a coffee?'

'A really quick one,' Connor replied. They headed for the stairs to level five.

Once they'd gotten their coffees and sat down, a silence fell between them.

Chris was the first to speak. 'I know it's crazy, but I'm going to miss you.'

'I know, it's crazy alright,' said Connor. Tentatively, he offered Chris a piece of paper. 'I wrote out my email address for you… and I still have your card. I'll be in touch when I'm home and settled.'

Chris put the piece of paper it into his wallet and said: 'Maybe we could Skype or FaceTime soon?'

'Yeah, I'd like that,' Connor smiled. Then his face darkened. 'But you know my situation. Come to think of it, you're the only one who knows my situation. It's been great being able to be myself, but I can't see any way out of this without hurting a lot of people.'

Chris looked at him with compassion. 'You'll know when the time is right, Connor. Just remember one thing: you've known about yourself for a long while, but Amy and your family will be hearing this for the first time.

'It may shock them and they'll need time to take it all in. They will have to readjust and try to accept you for who you really are… so give them that time.'

He placed his hand on top of Connor's, but Connor nervously pulled it away, his eyes darting around the café for fear someone had seen the intimate gesture.

'I know,' Chris said, soothingly. 'Coming out is a risky business, but it can be a positive experience, too, Connor. I can see how much your mum loves you, and, believe me, that love will get you through. You'll see. And I'll be right here to support you.'

With this, he discreetly squeezed Connor's hand under the table. Fighting to hold back the tears, Connor nodded and got up to leave. It was almost eight o'clock and he was expected for dinner; Mum and Carol would be eating with him and Amy tonight for their last hurrah.

The foursome was just about seated when Alfredo appeared out of nowhere and glided up to Carol. He greeted them all in turn, then wished them a wonderful last evening and a safe onward journey home.

Amy kicked Connor's leg under the table; it was obvious Carol and Alfredo were overly familiar with one other. Connor had enough on his mind without venturing into someone else's business. Nor was he, of all people, in a position to judge anyone. He ignored Amy's dig, but knew she wouldn't let it go so easily.

After dinner, Connor and Amy decided to try their luck again at the casino while Katie and Carol took up their seats at the champagne bar. Sam's name wasn't mentioned all evening, but Katie kept a close eye around the bar, expecting to see him. They chatted with other guests they'd become friendly with and Katie tried to keep her spirits up, but as the night went on and Sam still hadn't shown, she grew increasingly despondent.

Amy and Connor came out from the casino and sat with them for a nightcap.

'Well, any luck?' Katie asked.

'None whatsoever,' said Amy, 'so we'll just have to drown our sorrows.' She raised the glass of champagne Connor had just handed her. 'Cheers!'

Katie climbed into bed an hour or so later, feeling completely deflated. As she lay there, staring at the ceiling, her phone vibrated.

Sorry darling, I just couldn't get away xxx

She read the text and pressed 'delete', wishing she could erase the memories of the past seven days just as easily. That night, she barely slept a wink.

From 6am the following morning, the tannoy regularly

spewed out information about the disembarkation process. Guests hurried along corridors, chatting loudly and dragging their hand luggage to the breakfast room to enjoy one last meal before the journey home.

The girls got up and joined in with the chaos of it all, hugging and kissing their new best friends and swapping addresses and phone numbers, everyone knowing rightly the promises to meet up again would never be fulfilled.

Before they knew it, their plane had landed at Dublin airport.

25

Katie was back in the office early on Monday morning. The kettle was boiling when the others starting milling in, full of compliments for Katie's golden tan and fresh face - and also full of excitement as they peered into the Doherty's bakery bag, looking for their favourite bun.

Then it was back to the computer, back to meetings… and back to her first phone call from Sam. Knowing she had to keep him at arm's length, she deliberately kept her tone formal. Nervous as he was, Sam was delighted to hear her voice again. He'd missed her. Damn, he thought to himself. Katie was being so businesslike; it was obvious she was trying to distance herself from him.

The next week had been even worse for both of them. Sometimes, Katie had herself convinced she was doing ok. It was as if she could put all those beautiful memories and emotions inside a balloon, and, even though the string was attached to her heart, it was far enough away from her that she could keep a check on her emotions.

She hoped, someday soon, she could metaphorically take a pair of scissors and cut that string and let the balloon and everything inside it fly off into oblivion.

But then, when she least expected it, the balloon would float closer to her heart and all those emotions leaked out, filling her simultaneously with a desperate longing for Sam and an overwhelming feeling of guilt about Matt. She was barely in control.

Sam, for his part, knew he shouldn't push her, but he couldn't find it in him to just let her go. The bond was too strong between them... they had something special. He wanted to see her again, and, although she was acting indifferently, he wasn't totally convinced.

She was throwing herself into her work. Each time they spoke on the phone, it was more business than pleasure and she would always make excuses to finish the call. She wasn't laughing as heartily at his jokes, nor offering information on her whereabouts or any of her daily tittle tattle.

But Katie couldn't keep up the cold front, and gradually the ice started to melt. They found themselves laughing together again and Katie started sharing stories that weren't work-related. The intimacy had returned. Then, out of the blue, she told him she was going into hospital later that month to have a hysterectomy.

'Oh, I'm so sorry, sweetheart,' he said. 'The seventeenth... right, gosh, that's next Tuesday; one week away.'

'Yes, I know. Hopefully I'll not be off work for too long.'

'Don't you worry about that, darling,' he assured her. 'Take all the time you need. I'm trying to set up that meeting in Dublin; you think you could fit it in this week? Thursday, maybe?'

Sam held his breath, hoping against hope that they could mix business with pleasure.

A smirk fell across Katie's face; she knew only too well what he was thinking.

'I'm sure I can manage that. Best to get as much done now before I'm incapacitated.'

'Great,' Sam smiled into the phone. *If nothing else, I'll see her beautiful face again.*

He made a few phone calls to arrange the meeting, then booked a couple of rooms at the Westbury Hotel in Dublin's city centre. Thursday could not come quick enough.

Thursday arrived. Sam had asked Katie to meet him in the bar for a quick drink before the others gathered for their business dinner, and was already there when she walked in. The thought of seeing her had been burning in his mind all day... and now the sight of her caused his loins to stir.

As Katie approached him, his handsome smile melted away her earlier resolution to stay strong and be on her best behaviour; within minutes, they'd planned a secret rendezvous for later.

Their colleagues arrived and they had their dinner, then the party moved to the bar for a nightcap. Katie was the first to leave, complaining of a headache. Sam sat on with the others for another half hour, then made his excuses and headed to his room, where Katie was waiting.

They'd been the height of professionalism in front of their colleagues, but once they got behind closed doors their blood ran hot. There was no stopping them now, so strong was their passion and desire to touch, kiss, suck and nibble each's most erogenous zones. The night was all about them; there were no limits to their love-making, an unexplained exploration and discovery that set their hearts racing, a bonding never envisaged when they first met in Katie's office two short years ago.

After making love, they showered together. She lathered him and he lathered her, their lips never once breaking away.

In bed, he held her tight between the sheets, almost afraid to loosen his grip in case the spell would be broken. It was the first time they'd spent the whole night together.

Katie's room, two floors down, lay unoccupied until 7am, when they kissed and said goodbye with the promise to meet up again as soon as they could.

Sam returned home later that morning, feeling totally elated. Strangely, he felt having an affair made his life with Jill more bearable. She seemed oblivious as to why he often claimed to be feeling tired and seemed happy to make do with just a kiss and cuddle.

Sam would turn to his own side of the bed, happy in his thoughts of Katie. He was content, knowing no-one could see what lay beneath that exterior; his head a space no-one else could invade. His beautiful wife, who thought she knew him inside and out, hadn't a clue who lay between them each night.

26

(The present)

Matt and Connor waited down the corridor while the staff nurse was in the room with Katie.

'Dad, I'm not hanging around much longer,' Connor, whispered, unable to look him straight in the face. 'I've a few things to do.'

Katie's door opened and the nurse walked out. 'The coast is clear,' she smiled.

The two men went back into the room. Connor walked over to his mum and pecked her on the cheek.

'Do you know what time they are coming for you?' he asked, checking his watch and seeing it was already midday.

'I'm first on the list after lunch. Why don't you two go on home?'

'You sure?' Connor said, realising he'd agreed much too quickly.

'No,' said Matt, insistent. 'I'll stay until they come for you.'

Katie could hardly breathe. Her chest was tightening at the thought of the nurse coming back into the room while her husband and son were there and yelling 'Congratulations!'; she would be back any minute with the results of the pregnancy test Katie had just provided a urine sample for.

'No, Matt, you go on with Connor. You guys are making me nervous. I need to psyche myself up… I'll do a little meditation.' She forced a smile and hoped she didn't sound ungrateful. But she needed them to leave; now.

'I'll be right here when you open your eyes, my love,' Matt said, tenderly pushing a few strands of damp hair from Katie's forehead.

'I know you will, honey. I'll see you soon.'

Matt and Connor walked out of the door and down the corridor in complete silence, Matt feeling like he'd left his right arm behind him in the room and Connor feeling like he was the worst son in the whole world.

Katie tried to relax, but her mind was too busy. She checked her watch again. It had been ten minutes since the nurse had taken her sample away, and every one of those minutes had seemed like an hour.

What was keeping her?

At last, the door opened and a different nurse walked in.

Katie breathed a sigh of relief. *Thank God,* she thought. *Everything is going to plan; this must be to do with the anaesthetic.*

Walking over to where Katie lay, the nurse stretched out her hand towards Katie's, holding it a bit too long for her liking.

'Mrs Cully, I'm Paula Sheerin, the ward sister.' She gave her hand another little squeeze and her smile widened.

'There's a bit of a change of plan… I've got some very good news for you. Mrs Cully, your test is positive… you're pregnant.'

If Katie hadn't already been lying down, she would have collapsed. Staring, wide-eyed, at the ward sister, she finally managed to utter one word: 'What?'

'Yes, you're pregnant,' the sister said, smiling. 'I can see you're shocked. The staff nurse told me you've been trying for years to have another baby. Let me be the first to congratulate you.' Katie couldn't speak.

'Now, don't be worrying about your age, Mrs Cully. You'd be surprised at how many older mothers are giving birth these days.'

'Bu-but,' Katie stammered, 'I have fibroids; isn't that a problem? I mean, they can't be removed now, can they? How can I have room for a baby to grow? Won't they smother the baby?'

Tears ran down Katie's face. She couldn't believe this was happening.

'Are you sure… I mean, are you really sure I'm pregnant?'

'Yes, Mrs Cully. Your gynaecologist will be in to see you shortly. He'll explain everything to you. Do you want me to call your husband, maybe get him back here?'

'No!' Katie almost shouted.

'Well, obviously your surgery is cancelled and you'll be going home. Is there someone else I can call?'

There was a light knock on the door and Mr Lewis, Katie's consultant, walked in. She hardly recognised him in his scrubs. His black curls were well hidden under his green surgical cap.

'Mrs Cully, nice to see you again,' he said, shaking Katie's hand. 'Well, this is one for the books; isn't life full of wonderful surprises?'

'I don't know whether to laugh or cry,' said Katie, her voice shaking.

'I know,' said the sister, reassuringly squeezing Katie's hand again. 'Older mothers tend to be more anxious, but you're in safe hands here. We'll be keeping a good eye on you.' She turned to the consultant. 'Mrs Cully has a few questions for you, Mr Lewis.'

If she mentions 'older mothers' one more time, I'm going to reach for her, Katie thought, but she forced a smile and said, 'Please, just call me Katie.'

The doctor spoke. 'Don't worry, Katie. In most cases, fibroids aren't a problem. Lots of times, women don't even know they have them until well after they discover they're pregnant.'

'But what about the baby? I mean, will I miscarry or can you still remove them?' Katie asked, silently praying that the former would be the case.

'There's always a risk of miscarriage in the early stages of pregnancy, but hopefully they won't cause a problem. It really depends on the size of the fibroid and where it is within your uterus.'

Katie couldn't believe she was having this conversation.

'I'll see you in a few weeks at my outpatient clinic and we'll do an ultrasound, then we'll take it from there. In the meantime, take it easy and try not to worry.'

Fat chance of that, Katie thought bitterly.

27

Carol had just left a client's home; a gorgeous Georgian house on the outskirts of the city. She opened the back door of her jeep and threw the swatches of material, colour charts and samples of wooden flooring onto the back seat. The jeep was not only her means of transport; it was also her wardrobe and her office. Even though it was a total mess, she knew exactly what was in there and could put her hand to it when needed.

She couldn't stop thinking about Katie; she looked at her watch and wondered if she was in surgery yet. When they spoke earlier that morning, Katie told her she'd let her know what time her operation was scheduled, but she still hadn't heard from her. She'd leave it another while, she decided, and then call Matt for an update.

Carol pulled into the petrol station on the drive home and asked the pump attendant to fill her car up. As she took her wallet out of her handbag, she heard her phone bleep; a text from Katie.

Can U come to hospital asap?

Carol panicked; something was wrong. Her car was less than halfway filled, but she didn't have the patience to hang about.

'Sorry, can you just stop at £20, thank you,' she said, bundling the money into the attendant's hand once he'd finished and almost flying out of the forecourt. She did a sharp U-turn and headed in the direction of the hospital.

It was an hour or so before visiting time, so there were ample parking spaces. She thanked her lucky stars as she nabbed a spot directly in front of the entrance, then rushed through the automatic door and down the corridor to the surgical unit.

Two nurses were chatting at the reception desk and Carol interrupted them, asking if she could see Katie and be directed to her room.

Tentatively, she opened the door, peeping her head in first and not quite knowing what to expect. Someone was lying on the bed, curled up on their side with the sheet covering their head. She wondered if she was in the right room.

'Katie?' she whispered.

The sheet moved and Katie's ashen face appeared. Carol dragged over a nearby chair to the side of the bed and sat down, her mouth dry with nerves.

'Jesus, Katie, what's wrong? Have you had your surgery? Where's Matt? Is everything alright?'

Katie stared blankly at the wall; her face soaked with tears. The next two words took the wind right out of Carol's sails.

'I'm pregnant.'

Carol was reeling. 'It is Matt's… right?'

Katie's silence told her all she needed to know.

'Holy fuck!'

Katie eventually looked up and reached for her friend's hand.

'What am I going to do? They're sending me home. How am I supposed to explain this one? Matt thinks I'm on the operating table right now.'

'Hmmm,' Carol muttered under her breath. She wished she could think of something to say or, better still, that she could do something to make everything aright. This was a complete nightmare.

'You could say there was an emergency and the operation had to be postponed.'

'But I'm a private patient, does that not mean I get priority?'

'I don't know how that works; you need to talk to the sister.'

Just then, the door knocked and the ward sister popped her head in, taken aback to see Katie still in the bed.

'You OK, there? Are you feeling unwell? I thought you'd be all packed up and ready to go.'

Carol knew Katie was in no fit state to string a plausible sentence together, so she started talking out of pure panic.

'No, Katie's just wondering how to approach this with her husband. You see, he'll be so excited, but we're thinking, with Katie's past history of miscarriage, it might be best not to tell him, for now.'

Katie thanked the Lord for her friend's quick thinking, but she still wasn't sure where she was going with all this.

'Katie was wondering would it be OK to tell Matt there was an emergency and that the op was postponed? That would save another disappointment should anything go wrong with the pregnancy.'

'Well,' said the sister, staring directly at Katie as she spoke, 'what you decide to tell your husband is none of my business. But I can't be part of a deliberate lie.'

Carol pressed on. 'Well, it's only a wee white lie. And you don't have to be part of it. Katie will talk to Matt. I mean, isn't it a matter of patient confidentiality? And it is your wish, isn't it, Katie?'

Finally, Katie spoke. 'Yeah, I'm sorry, I think I'm still in shock. I'd like a bit of time.'

The sister's gaze softened. 'You're being very thoughtful, Katie, but you need support, too, so don't be keeping this to yourself too long, OK?'

'Thank you, sister. I'm sure I'll be in a better frame of mind by the time I see Mr Lewis at his clinic.'

'OK, I'll be in my office. Come and see me before you leave and I'll arrange an appointment for you.' The sister smiled and left the room.

Katie looked at Carol. 'Christ almighty, I didn't know what was going to come out of your mouth.'

'You better get dressed, get home and shag Matt's brains out… you know, just to be sure,' Carol said matter-of-factly.

Katie looked at her, puzzled.

'Well,' Carol explained, 'the baby could be Matt's. Maybe you were pregnant before you went away. And I'm sure he couldn't keep his hands off you when you got back. So what makes you so sure it's Sam's? I mean, all's not lost here, is it?'

Katie was now out of the bed and pulling on a pair of leggings. She focused on what she was doing in an attempt to avoid Carol's questioning gaze.

'It's definitely not Matt's,' she said firmly. 'We haven't had sex since I came back from the cruise… or for six months before it.'

This revelation shocked Carol to her core.

'But, why? I thought you two were at it, morning, noon and night.'

'Well, we're not!' Katie cried. Shrugging her shoulders, she added, 'It's hard to flog a dead donkey.'

Carol looked at Katie. As desperate as this situation was, all she wanted to do was laugh. She bit her lip in an attempt to stop herself, but Katie knew her too well and knew what was coming. For some reason, Carol would often burst out laughing when she should be sympathising; nerves, she supposed. Carol covered her face with her hands but couldn't control herself any longer; she threw her head back as the laughter erupted.

'Sorry, Katie, I'm so sorry, but you should see the look on your wee face… "flog a dead donkey", oh God, I know, it's not even funny, Katie, I'm so sorry,' she said, tears of mirth streaming down her face.

In spite of herself, Katie began to smile, too. She put her

arms around her best friend, their bodies shuddering together; Katie wasn't quite sure if they were laughing or crying, but the one thing she knew for certain was that she wouldn't have to go through this alone.

Carol would be with her every step of the way.

28

Katie phoned Matt before leaving the hospital. This bit had to be done on the phone; she couldn't bear to look at his face as she lied through her teeth while carrying another man's baby in her tummy.

'Aw, my poor love,' he said. 'I'm so disappointed for you. There you were, all set. What happens now?'

'They'll be in touch in the next few days. Sure, these things get cancelled all the time. I'm grand, love,' she assured him, biting her lower lip and squeezing Carol's hand much harder than she'd intended.

'Poor man,' she said after she'd hung up. 'I don't deserve him.'

Carol was having none of it. 'You stop that now, Katie. This doesn't make you a bad person. A stupid one, yes, but bad... no.'

Driving home, there were so many silences, which was very unusual for them. Katie knew there was a way out of this; everything could go back to normal if…

But could she destroy the life of this little innocent baby? She had a choice to make.

Carol eventually broke the tension.

'So, what are you thinking? The ball's in your court, Katie. As I see it, you have three options. First: tell Matt the baby is his. Second: come clean and tell him you had an affair with your boss. Then, of course, there's the third option…' her voice trailed off.

'Telling him the truth is out of the question, Carol.'

'Not even if you somehow manage to get him to perform? You're only a few weeks gone; the baby could be premature, for all Matt knows.'

'That's not going to happen. Since he started taking his blood pressure tablets, he can't get it up.'

'Not ever?'

'Well, not in a long while.'

'Could you not try and help him along? What about the wee blue pill? Apparently loads of men take that.'

'No, he won't hear of it. Anyway, it's like the less you get it, the less you look for it.'

'Jesus,' Carol shuddered. 'Sounds like a death sentence to me. OK, so you can't fool him and you can't tell him about Sam. That only leaves you one option, Katie… you're going to have to get rid of it.'

They drove along in silence again for another few minutes, each lost in the same thought. *An abortion is probably going to be the only option.* Never in their wildest dreams had they imagined a scenario like this - for either of them. Carol had always wanted a baby and Katie had always wanted another one.

Katie sat there, wondering how two topical societal issues had flagged up something about herself that she never knew. Her fear of Connor being gay… did that make her homophobic?

And wanting to get rid of her unborn baby… did that make her pro-abortion?

What is wrong with me?

'It just goes to prove,' she whispered, half under her breath, 'no-one should judge anyone until they have walked in their shoes.'

'Dare I ask,' Carol said tentatively, 'what about SS?'

'Yeah, I know; I've him to think about, too.'

'Well, he should be the least of your worries. I wouldn't go telling him anything if I were you. You need to think this through, Katie. Least said, easiest mended!'

'He thinks I'm in theatre right now. I told him I would text him before my surgery but there was too much going on. I can't afford another slip-up, to put it mildly. Anyway, nothing will change for him. He can still carry on with his perfect life, with his perfect wife. It's not fair, is it?'

'If his life is so perfect with Jill, he wouldn't be so interested in you, now, would he?'

'Oh, I don't know any more, Carol, and I'm tired of analysing this situation to death.'

'Just promise me you won't rush into anything, Katie. You don't need any more regrets.'

'Yeah, that's for sure,' Katie sighed.

Carol is right, she thought. She needed to give Sam a wide berth.

When they pulled up outside Katie's house, Matt opened the front door.

'Right, here goes,' said Katie. 'Can you come in with me, Carol? Just for a wee while… please.'

'No worries,' said Carol, switching off the engine.

Matt was his usual considerate self. He had the kettle boiled and also a bottle of white wine chilling in the fridge, guessing that would be their drink of choice. Between the two girls, their fabricated story was easily accepted by Matt; other than being genuinely disappointed for Katie, he seemed happy in his ignorance.

As Katie saw Carol out the door, she hugged her. 'Thank you,' she whispered.

'Get those sussies on, girlfriend, and get some hot blood flowing into that man of yours. Keep every option open… that's an order!' Carol winked and blew a kiss as she drove off.

Before going back to living room, Katie went into the small toilet off the hallway. She prayed there would be a little spotting.

As she sat on the loo, she thought back to the many times she'd dreaded seeing a stain; the unmistakeable sign of a miscarriage. It was always another disappointment, another dream shattered. But what she wouldn't give to see a little staining now. But there was none.

Could she go through with an abortion? What about Sam? Maybe she should tell him after all. He certainly wouldn't want her to keep it; she was sure of that. He would probably go out of his mind and do all in his power to make sure she got rid of it, terrified that Jill would find out.

No, Carol was right; don't involve Sam. For now, anyway.

One nightmare thought after another came flashing into Katie's brain, like she was being hit by sharp blades of lightning. She felt sick to the pit of her stomach. With her two hands pressing on her tummy, she studied her face in the mirror.

Oh my God, what have I done? All she wanted was to turn back the clock, but that was impossible. Taking a deep breath, she rearranged her face into something that resembled a relaxed smile and went back to sit beside her husband.

29

Chris sat at the café on level five, looking out at the rain; it didn't help his melancholy mood. He'd only known Connor for three short weeks, but felt he'd known him for years. His first thought in the morning and his last thought in the evening was of him.

He found Connor's innocence and modesty endearing. He loved talking to him on the phone - they'd spoken every day since parting ways on the ship - and loved hearing his voice; the way his accent became more pronounced when he was in the throes of a conversation.

He could actually understand what Connor was saying now, even when he spoke fast… which he did a lot. He loved the way he said 'aye' and 'naw' and 'wee', and how he talked about his 'mammy'.

Connor was so shy when they'd first met, but with each day, their conversations had grown longer and longer. They shared the same sense of humour; maybe that was Chris' Irish blood coming out.

He loved that Connor could talk to him about anything; he understood the turmoil he was in. But talking on the phone wasn't quite the same as being there with him; he longed to hold his hand and be there to reassure him.

He couldn't believe how much he was missing him - and the worst was yet to come. In two weeks, the ship would be making its transatlantic crossing from Barcelona to Miami. For 14 nights, they would be out in the middle of the ocean, and speaking to Connor would be difficult; phone calls would be very expensive, with having to use the ship's satellite.

He checked his watch. It was 5pm, Irish time. He texted Connor.

Hope your mum is feeling well after her surgery?

Connor answered immediately. *Mum's surgery cancelled.*

Sorry to hear that…can U talk?

Connor was in a taxi heading home. His dad had called him earlier to say his mum was back home again. He asked the driver to pull in at the local shop; he'd walk the last five minutes and get a chat with Chris.

'Hi,' he said when Chris picked up. 'I'm almost home, so I've only got a few minutes.'

'Just sitting at the café here, on my coffee break.'

'I can just picture you sitting there in all your white gear.' Connor felt a longing in his heart.

'Yeah, wish you were here with me. What I wouldn't give…'

Chris took a deep breath and closed his eyes, visualising Connor's face in front of him. But it didn't take his loneliness away; it only made him worse.

'So, what's your plan now that your mum is home?' he carried on.

'I took a few days off to spend some time with her, but she'll probably go back to work tomorrow. I'll just chill for a day or two, then fly back to Glasgow on Saturday.'

'Pity we're so far apart… I've a day off on Thursday.' Chris held his breath after planting the seed.

'What port will you be at?'

'Rome.'

'Um, right. So close and yet so far.' Then, after a beat, 'but it's not really *that* far, is it?'

They were on the same page. Chris interrupted Connor's thoughts.

'No, it's not far at all… only a few hours away.' His nerves shot him off his seat. He walked to the window and looked up at an aeroplane passing overhead, the prospect of seeing Connor in two days' time flooding him with excitement.

'I want to see you, Connor. Could you fly over? Please… I could book it for you.'

Connor knew this was pure madness. He really wanted to see Chris but his mind was jumping from one nightmare scenario to another. His mum, Amy… he couldn't think clearly. It seemed impossible.

But Chris was already on his iPad checking available flights.

'There's a flight to Rome at 7.30 am on Thursday from Belfast, and a late one leaving Rome at 10pm that same evening.'

Connor remained silent.

'Look, Connor, maybe it is too risky for you. It's easy for me, I know, but I'd sure love to see you again.'

'I'd love to see you too.' Connor's voice was almost a whisper; he'd reached his mum and dad's front door. He checked all the windows were closed; the last thing he needed was his parents hearing him making plans to fly off to Rome. Chris could barely breathe with excitement; it was now or never.

'I've a short shift that day - 6.30am until 10.30am. The ship has a late departure and doesn't leave Rome until 8.30pm. If you catch the early morning flight, I can meet you at 12.30 in the city centre. We could have six hours together and you could be on the 10pm flight back home.'

Chris was speaking faster than Connor could think. He tried to ignore the logical side of his brain that was screaming, 'More deceit! More lies!', but his young, carefree side urged, 'Just go for it!'

What way would he jump?

'Leave it with me, Chris. I'm at my house now. Will you text me later when your shift is over?'

'I will. And don't you go losing those thoughts… I really want to see you.'

30

Katie was flicking through the TV channels when she suddenly remembered she hadn't contacted Sam. Her phone was lying at the bottom of her bag, on silent. She got up and grabbed her handbag from the hallway floor, where she'd thrown it when she arrived home. She needed to at least let him know she was out of the hospital. She would tell Sam the same lie she'd told Matt: op cancelled.

'I'm going upstairs to change, honey,' she called to Matt, trying to sound carefree.

She purposely ran upstairs; maybe a sudden burst of energy would rattle something inside her; maybe a good shake about would bring on the miscarriage that would make everything OK. Maybe she would go out for a jog in the morning; do all the things she was advised not to each time she was pregnant before.

She closed the bedroom door and sat on the edge of the bed. Sighing, she took her phone from her handbag; there were three texts from Sam. Tentatively, she opened them, knowing she was being a bit unfair to him; he deserved to know what was going on… he just didn't deserve to know everything. His texts were clipped. Obviously, he was being over cautious in case Katie's phone got into the wrong hands.

The sudden opening of the front door startled her as she was sending off a quick reply, then she remembered: Connor was back home.

She opened the bedroom door and shouted down the stairs.

'On my way, love. Just give me a few minutes.'

Connor's head peeped around the bottom of the staircase.

'Take your time, Mum. You OK?'

'Yeah, I'm good, love.' If only.

Katie guessed Connor would be rearranging his plans and heading back to Glasgow much sooner than planned, knowing his mum was home again, her womb intact.

She had struggled with the silence in the house when Connor had moved to Glasgow. The phone didn't ring. The doorbell didn't chime. The TV didn't blare from the family room. The toilet flush didn't come between her and her sleep during the night.

As quiet as Connor always promised to be, he'd always managed to make a racket in the kitchen and close his bedroom door with a thud on returning home from a night out. But, since he'd left, she longed for all those little things which had irritated her back then. She missed him so much... her beautiful, troubled boy. She needed to lie down, just for a while. Her head was spinning.

Sam had pushed paper round his desk all day, tried unsuccessfully to answer emails and walked aimlessly towards the window looking out at nothing in particular. His head and his heart were with Katie.

'What the fuck is going on, here?' he muttered to himself, as, back home, he changed out of his Armani suit and unhinged the trouser press, meticulously ensuring his seams were aligned so as not to cause a double crease.

He'd been checking his phone all day, anxious not to miss a call or text message. One minute, he had Katie dead on the operating table; the next, he had her sitting up, eating her post-op tea and toast as Matt stroked her forehead. This uncertainty unnerved him; he was always the guy in control.

'What the hell?' he said out loud as Jill opened their bedroom door; he'd been so distracted he hadn't even heard her arrive home.

'What the hell, *what*?' she smiled sympathetically, kicking off her Christian Louboutin heels.

Snapping his phone closed and switching it to silent mode, Sam flashed her a haphazard smile.

'Oh, don't ask, honey. One of those days. How was yours?'

'Doesn't our cruise seem like light years away?' she replied, ignoring his complaint and his question as she unbuttoned her black mandarin-collared tunic. For the past two years, Jill had been the supervisor on the Mac cosmetics counter at Harvey Nic's. Looking beautiful came easily to her. Her flawless complexion sold many a product to the young and the not so young; the latter hoping this dewy lotion would miraculously make their ageing skin look as fresh and smooth as Jill's.

To his delight, Sam's phone lit up as it sat on the dressing table. He quickly covered it with the *OK!* magazine Jill had been flicking through earlier that morning and waited for his chance to read the text. His prayers were answered less than a minute later when Jill went for her shower.

Op cancelled…long story! Home now. Be in touch 2moro x

Sam couldn't believe what he'd just read; he'd had Katie dead and buried about 20 times that day.

Angrily, he punched out his reply: *Well, thanks 4 letting me know!* He hoped she would pick up on his sarcastic tone.

When Katie came downstairs, Matt was chatting with Connor, who was lying across the couch. Her son sat up, leaving room for her to sit down, then placed his head on her lap; just like old times. She brushed his hair off his forehead with her fingertips, wishing she could dig far enough inside his scalp to drag out all the fears and worries she knew were lodged deep in there.

'So, what happens now, Mum?'

'I'll have to wait and see what the consultant says; see when he can fit me in again.'

'I suppose you'll be going back to work?'

'Um, I might take tomorrow off and go back on Thursday. You fancy a jog around St. Columb's Park in the morning? We could go for a bit of lunch after. There's a lovely new coffee shop that's just changed hands on the quay - Patricia's - it's the place to go, it seems.'

'Perfect, sounds great. Patricia's it is, then.' Connor, she noticed, sounded more chirpy than usual. 'I'll have to borrow your trainers, Dad.'

'You're welcome to them,' said Matt. 'I don't have time for such luxuries as a jog followed by lunch,' he added good-naturedly.

The three of them sat there with the TV news humming in the background, Katie and Connor watching the screen while Matt lay back in his recliner, reading the paper.

Having her family all around her like this had prompted her to christen this her 'happy room'... but it didn't feel like that today. Since that day on the ship, when she blabbed to Carol about Connor possibly being gay, the subject had never been mentioned again. Katie felt by not talking about it, it would somehow make it go away... but she harboured the fear that she was right.

So many emotions were raised within her when she allowed herself to dwell on it. Some days, she was able to push the thoughts to the back of her mind; other days they tormented her. She worried that friends and family would look at him in a different light.

She felt a deep sadness that Connor would be missing out on a family life of his own (or, at least, a family life as she knew it). Maybe it was time to have this conversation with Matt. But he would probably tell her she was crazy. Would Matt and Connor still go to the pub for a few pints when he came home? Do dads hang out with their gay sons?

And so, the torture went on and on.

Maybe she should speak to Connor first. Amy was still in Glasgow; she should take advantage of getting him on his own.

She might not get another opportunity.

31

Connor couldn't think about anything other than the conversation he'd had with Chris. He would spend time with his mum tomorrow, then tell his parents he was going to get the late-afternoon bus to Belfast and stay there for a day or two, catch up with a few mates. His mum was always encouraging him to keep in touch with his friends, so he knew this wouldn't raise any suspicion.

He went to his room and called Dave, a good pal from his university days.

'Hi mate... need a favour,' Connor said.

'Hi Con, what's up? Are you home?'

'Yeah, but I was wondering if you could put me up for a night or two? I'll be in Belfast tomorrow night, heading away early on Thursday morning and back late that night. But if anyone asks... I haven't left the country.'

'Right, no problem,' Dave answered without hesitation. 'Any point asking what you're up to?'

'I'll fill you in later.'

That was the easy bit done; how to play this with Amy was a different matter. Connor thought of saying nothing to her, but if she phoned his mum looking for him, she wouldn't be too pleased hearing it second-hand. No; he needed to tell her himself.

He phoned her, saying Dave had asked him down to Belfast for a catch up. Not much point in hanging around, with his mum feeling OK and back at work, he explained. He knew Amy wasn't keen on Dave; he was a bit of a womaniser during their uni days, and, given he was still free and single, Amy would be up to high dough, imagining all sorts.

He wasn't an ideal cover story, but there was no-one else Connor could trust - and no-one else who wouldn't quiz him right, left and centre.

'I'll just get the bus and might even get the last one back home again; see how it plays out,' he tried to sound casual.

'There's no way you'll come back on the same night,' Amy said. 'Anyway, I suppose it'll be nice for you to catch up with the lads and I don't like the thought of you travelling on late-night public transport, either, because no doubt you'll be drunk. You'd be better staying up.'

'Thanks, babe.' Connor sighed inwardly; the guilt was killing him.

After they'd said their goodbyes, Connor sat with his rampant thoughts. One question after another tore through his brain. What if he was caught? Should he tell his mum? Should he just forget it and stay where he was? When would he get another opportunity? Businessmen do it all the time; fly off on early morning flights, back in their own bed that same night. If they could do it, why couldn't he?

His phone bleeped with a text from Chris telling him he was off duty. Connor called him immediately.

'Well, how are things at home? Chris asked, not even saying hello. 'Any news for me?'

'I've started the ball rolling,' said Connor. And, after a deep breath, 'All good so far.'

'Fantastic! Shall I book you on the 7.30am? I've been keeping an eye on it; there's still seats available.'

'OK, let's go for it,' Connor replied, wishing he felt even half as confident as he sounded.

Connor climbed the stairs of the double decker bus that would take him to Belfast. His mum had taken him to the station and was waving up at him as the bus took off. He'd enjoyed spending the earlier part of his day with her. They'd chatted easily; how work was going, how he and Amy were getting on. They'd had a laugh about some of the things that happened during the cruise and agreed it was a great trip.

But, every now and then, Connor got the feeling his mum was about to say something, only the words got stuck somewhere between her throat and her mouth. She'd give a sort of fake cough, then continue with a swallow as if she were drinking the words back into her gut. At one point, she'd placed her hand on top of his and squeezed it. He had a feeling she was secretly observing him… just like he was secretly observing her. Ach, maybe he was imagining things. Maybe he was just being paranoid again.

He checked the front compartment of his backpack for about the tenth time. Seeing his passport look up at him, he settled himself again.

He wondered should he tell Dave what was going on; it would be great to get a few things off his chest. Dave was the most open-minded guy he knew. Nothing shocked him. He had a few gay friends - another one would be no big deal for him. But the thought of admitting his sexuality out loud caused Connor's heart to palpitate.

The bus arrived in Belfast and Dave and Connor hugged each other like brothers when they met in the bar beside the station. Pizza and a few pints were the order of the evening. Connor had to be at the airport at 5.30am and Dave didn't want a mid-week hangover, so an early night suited them both.

Exhausted as he was, Connor found it hard to get to sleep that night. He hated all this deceit; all these lies. He'd called Amy before he left the bar, telling her they were doing a bit of a pub crawl and that he'd be having a lie-in in the morning. Connor knew Amy had an 8am start at the hospital, and, unless there was some kind of emergency, they never spoke during her always busy shifts. She wouldn't be expecting a text or phone call from him.

He eventually nodded off, woken only by Dave shouting to him that his taxi was outside; he'd slept through his alarm. The taxi driver waited impatiently as he quickly showered and dressed.

He was held up further by an accident on the motorway, which delayed him another 20 minutes, then the queue at the check-in desk was as long as a wet week. By the time he got through, his gate was flashing, calling for all remaining passengers. He sprinted to the departure gate, where one of the airline staff took his boarding pass and told him to have a pleasant flight.

As he began to set off through the gate, he thought he heard someone calling his name. But, sure, weren't there plenty of Connors around the place? He walked on without looking back, down the steps and across the tarmac to his waiting plane.

Back in the departure lounge, the man waiting for the London flight wondered why the young man hadn't heard him calling him - or why, indeed, he was going to Rome. On his own.

The man was Amy's father.

32

Amy had just hung up from speaking to Connor when John from work called her mobile.

'Andrew and I want to take you out Friday night; a wee thank you for the night at yours. Connor is still in Ireland, isn't he?'

'Oh, that would be lovely. Yeah, he's back on Saturday, so that's perfect.'

She thought back to the previous Friday night, when she and Connor had had the boys over for dinner. It could not have gone better.

The two boys had arrived at eight o' clock sharp, and, after the introductions, Amy popped open the prosecco. Connor found himself chatting mostly to Andrew (even though Amy had promised Connor she wouldn't, her and John couldn't help themselves from talking shop).

Connor felt he was trying a bit too hard. He wondered did gays spot other gays. He planned to keep himself relatively sober in case they picked up on something that even he was not aware of himself.

The evening had gone really well. Connor found John and Andrew to be very good company, but he couldn't help himself paying extra attention to the way they behaved. John was more camp than Andrew; he wondered who was the most obvious between him and Chris. When the boys spoke of places they visited on holidays, he was aware they often mentioned places that were more 'gay friendly', or had good gay bars. They also spoke of places they would never visit - even if they got it for nothing.

This was as good as a school day for Connor, though he had to remind himself not to appear too interested; he just smiled and listened to their stories.

He even gave them advice on staying safe and made them feel at ease in his home by telling them they should just be themselves. 'Stand up for who and what you are!' *Where did all that come from?* He felt like a phoney.

As the night progressed, Amy had suggested a game of charades; plenty of drink had been taken at this stage and everyone was up for a bit of fun. Before they knew it, it was one o'clock in the morning. Amy called a taxi and they'd said their goodbyes at the door, all hugs and kisses and promising to do it again soon.

What Connor and Amy weren't aware of, however, was the conversation John and Andrew had when they got back home.

'After dinner, I went to the bathroom,' John said to his partner, 'thinking Connor was in the kitchen helping Amy. But he was in the bathroom, talking on his phone. I heard him saying, "Yeah, me too", then he said "byyeee"; kinda smoochy, like. When he opened the door and saw me standing there, he looked embarrassed... but the more I think of it, it was more a look of panic or fear.'

'Maybe he was talking to his mum,' Andrew said. 'Didn't Connor say she wasn't well?'

'You don't talk to your mother like that,' barked John.

'What; you don't think he has another woman, do you?'

'No,' John said emphatically. 'I don't think he has another *woman*.' He looked meaningfully at Andrew.

'Did you not notice anything about him?' John continued.

'No... don't think so,' Andrew answered, slightly puzzled.

'Seemed like he was being on his guard, but when the guard slipped, he was very different. He was very, very comfortable with us, don't you think?'

'You think he's seeing… a man?' Andrew said, unconvinced.

'Wouldn't be surprised. You know me; I sense these things.'

'John, you think every man on the planet is gay,' Andrew said, only half joking. Then, in a sterner tone: 'Don't you be getting ahead of yourself. It's probably nothing, so just you keep out of it, do you hear me?'

John stayed silent. *I'm never far wrong*, he thought.

33

As Amy's dad settled himself on the plane, he gave his wife a quick call before take-off.

Sarah Kelly smiled to herself; Peter was so reliable. She yawned and looked at her digital bedside clock; it was 7.45am.

'Wakey-wakey,' Peter cooed into the phone.

'Good morning *again*,' Sarah replied sleepily.

'Just taking off now, love. Oh, by the way; I saw Connor getting on a flight to Rome… what's all that about?'

'Rome? I've no idea. Amy didn't mention it. Strange, I wonder why she didn't say. She told me he was home, alright, seeing his mum. That reminds me: I suppose I should give Katie a call; Amy said her surgery was cancelled. I think I have her number somewhere.'

Sarah and Katie were more acquaintances than friends. They were only ever in each other's company if it was something to do with their grown-up children. They often bumped into one another at their local Sainsbury's, where they would stop and pass a few pleasantries.

As she said goodbye to Peter, she made a mental note to dig out Katie's phone number and ring her in an hour or so. She would tell her she was sorry to hear her operation was cancelled - then casually ask why Connor was in Rome.

Then again… she could always phone Amy. She might just catch her before she went onto the ward; her nose was getting the better of her.

'Mum?' Amy answered, sounding slightly alarmed, 'is Dad OK?'

'Yes, he's fine, sweetie. I've just been talking to him, actually.'

'Jeez Mum, I don't have time for chit chat; I'm about to go on duty. What's up?'

'Sorry, sweetie, it's just... your dad saw Connor this morning, getting on a flight to Rome.'

'What? No way, Mum. Sure, Connor is in Belfast with his mates.'

'Don't think so, sweetie.' Sarah loved being the bearer of news - any news. She never stopped to think of the consequences.

'Dad must have imagined it,' Amy insisted. 'Probably still half asleep with being up so early. Look, Mum, I've got to go. Call you later, OK?'

'OK, sweetie. Hope I didn't annoy you.'

Sarah looked at the blank screen as Amy hung up.

'Hmmm,' she said, out loud to herself. 'No smoke without fire.'

She liked Connor; he was a nice fella. Truth be told, she didn't know how he put up with Amy; she could be very bossy. She smiled to herself; the apple didn't fall to far from the tree on that score, as she was quite fond of getting her own way where Peter was concerned, too. *Maybe I taught her too well,* she thought.

Then again, maybe Connor wasn't as pure as the driven snow after all. Still waters run deep. As Sarah hadn't got the information she wanted from Amy, she decided to execute plan B.

Katie was sitting at her desk at the bank, having just had a morning coffee with her colleagues. They'd fussed over her, telling her they were sorry her operation hadn't happened as planned.

When Katie's mobile rang with Sarah's name showing up on the screen, her heart almost stopped. Maybe it was her hormones, but every little thing seemed to send her adrenaline soaring these past few days. She immediately thought something was wrong.

'Hi Sarah, how are you? This is a surprise… everything alright?' She tried to keep the panic out of her voice.

'Oh, hello Katie, hope you don't mind me ringing. It's just a social call, really. Yes, everything is fine.'

Katie was still holding her breath. They didn't do social calls! She was always a bit wary of Amy's mum, for some reason. She found her very gossipy; always managing to ridicule someone during a conversation. She would never dream of telling her anything she didn't want repeated.

'I was talking to Amy last night and she told me your operation had been cancelled. I just wanted to let you know I was thinking about you and I hope you're feeling alright.'

'That's very kind of you, Sarah. Yes, it's being rescheduled; hopefully I'll get it done soon.'

'Hopefully so,' said Sarah. 'I hear Connor came home. That was good of him.' A slight pause. Then, 'Did he just stop off before going to Rome?'

Katie's antennae had already told her this had to be more than a social call, but… Connor in Rome? It didn't make sense. Sarah may have succeeded in shocking her but there was no way she was going to succeed in getting the better of her - no matter what Connor was up to!

'Yes, he had business there,' she lied. 'Some work thing.'

'Ah, I see. My Peter saw him at the airport this morning. He called after him but he was too busy rushing off… other things on his mind, obviously.'

'Listen, Sarah, I really must dash,' Katie said curtly. 'I've an office meeting. Thanks for the call; no doubt I'll see you around.'

She hung up, incredulous. *What the fuck was all that about?*

34

Connor slept through most of the flight. On arrival, he followed Chris' instructions and took the 'Leonardo Express' train to Rome's city centre. He switched his phone back on; thankfully, there were no texts or voicemails from home.

He wondered if he should text Amy, but immediately thought better of it. She was probably running around the ward, under pressure as usual. His mum would think he was still in bed, so no point texting her, either.

The train journey took 40 minutes, then he made his way outside and sat at a little coffee shop next to the station. Leaning his head back on the blue and white tiles that framed the door of the quaint little café, he enjoyed the feeling of the warmth of the midday sun on his face.

A pretty, dark-eyed girl came to take his order. If she'd been standing there naked, Connor wouldn't have noticed; only one person was filling his mind. Soon he would see his beautiful face. He placed his order and then took his phone from his pocket, texting Chris to say he'd arrived.

He decided he would switch his phone off once Chris got there; didn't want anyone back home getting an international ringtone or an Italian operator telling them his phone was out of service. Connor sipped his latte and bit into a flaky, golden croissant. He had to pinch himself to make sure he wasn't dreaming; he really was sitting here in Rome, about to meet Chris.

The ship was docked at the port in Civitavecchia, so it would take Chris over an hour by train to get to the centre of Rome.

Connor kept checking the large clock positioned above the entrance of the station and it wasn't too long before he spotted Chris emerging.

His handsome face was still tanned from the pleasant Mediterranean autumn sunshine and he was casually dressed in a long-sleeved pale grey T-shirt that hung loosely over his dark grey jeans. His blonde hair was a bit longer than Connor remembered, and he was sweeping it off his face when he eyed Connor and headed in his direction. Chris smiled with his whole face and Connor's face mirrored it. No question about it; the look was love.

Connor was startled when Chris leaned over and kissed him. 'Hey there,' he smiled. 'Fancy meeting you here.' He pulled out a chair and sat down, looking cool and easy in his own skin.

He leaned in again towards Connor. 'Thank you.'

'What for?' Connor smiled.

'For coming here to see me. For making me feel so special.'

'Well, you are special.'

'Are you happy?'

'Yes, very. You?'

'Well, if happiness is sitting here with you, listening to your gentle Irish voice and looking at that shy smile, then yes… I'm ecstatic.'

As Connor smiled back, a song he didn't recognise came through the speaker above their heads: *When you hold me, I'm alive.* The lyrics gave him instant goosebumps.

'Are you listening to that song, Chris?'

'I certainly am!'

As the song ended, the radio DJ announced the singer; Imelda May.

'Oh, she's Irish,' Connor said. 'From Dublin. I saw her in a TV show recently. I knew I'd heard that voice before.'

'Well, then, I guess we have *our song*,' Chris said, making speech marks with his fingers.

'Aye,' Connor nodded. 'Our own wee song.'

Chris suggested his favourite trattoria, a five-minute walk from the station, for dinner. As they got up to go, he reached for Connor's hand; Connor wasn't quite sure if he should take it or pull away.

It felt strange for him, a young man from Northern Ireland, to be walking openly hand-in-hand through the streets, and even more strange when he noticed other same-sex couples doing likewise. Chris squeezed his hand, gently reassuring him that all was cool. Connor thought of the saying *When in Rome…* suddenly, it had taken on a whole new meaning.

The restaurant was in middle of a busy piazza. Connor looked around, nervous that someone he knew could be nearby. He was being irrational, he told himself, but you just never knew. He suggested sitting nearer the back so he could see everything around him - and could make a quick dash to the loo if he was clocked by someone from home.

When the waiter saw Chris, he came straight to the table and greeted him with a hug and peck on each cheek. Chris introduced Connor, and the waiter, with one hand resting warmly on Connor's shoulder, took his other hand in a firm handshake.

Chris ordered two beers, and, without looking at the menu, ordered their homemade lasagne and pork meatballs in Italian sauce. The garlic bread was the nicest Connor had ever tasted and he almost wanted to run his finger around the remaining meatball sauce, it was so delicious. The pair talked non-stop in the afternoon sunshine, ordering more cold beers as the time slipped by a lot quicker than they'd hoped. It was Connor's first time in Rome - other than when he'd disembarked the cruise ship and gone straight to the airport - and Chris was keen to give him the whistle stop tour.

First up was Trevi Fountain, where they each took out a euro. 'You have to throw the coin, using your right hand, over your left shoulder,' Chris explained.

'Do we make a wish?'

'Absolutely!' Chris said, both of them laughing as they did the coin-throwing motion together. Chris took his phone from his pocket. 'Let's take a selfie,' he said, as they leaned together and smiled at the lens.

Next, they made their way to the Spanish Steps. Again, the place was packed with tourists, but there was a lovely, relaxing atmosphere about the place, with artists and musicians all around.

Making their way back down the steps, they stopped off at another piazza, knowing they only had a few hours left to sit and enjoy each other's company. They longed to be somewhere more private, but, equally, they enjoyed the easiness of spending the day walking, talking and getting to know each other a bit more.

For three weeks, they had talked on the phone, but nothing matched being able to reach out and touch one another, or the feel of their arms rubbing against each other - intentionally or otherwise. This was an important time for them to share together... and they both hoped there would be many more times ahead.

Half past six came around too quickly. They walked to the train station, Connor feeling his Adam's apple swell with the dread of parting.

'See you real soon,' Chris said when they'd reached the entrance, reaching out and hugging Connor tight... so, so tight.

Then, they walked away in separate directions to catch their respective trains, lost in the beautiful memories of the day's events.

Once Connor had settled himself on the train, he tentatively took his phone out. It was 7.30pm and it had been switched off all day. He switched it on and waited for the network to connect, then he heard a fanfare of 'bleep, bleep, bleep, bleep, bleep, bleep, bleep' as one message notification after another pinged loudly.

The noise of it on the sleepy train embarrassed him. The guy in the seat in front looked back and smiled. 'You are popular.'

'Seems like it,' Connor answered, knowing only too well popularity had nothing to do with it; he was more likely in deep shit. There were two text messages from Amy and two from his mum… and three voicemails from Amy. Connor braced himself as he read Amy's texts.

The first, at 12.30pm: *Hi babe…. at lunch. Thought I'd've heard from you before now. Give me a call or text.*

Her second, at 4 pm: *You ok?? Call me… I can't get through!*

He put his earphones in and, bracing himself, played her first voicemail.

'Connor, I'm trying you, like, forever! Call me!'

Then, the second.

'Where the fuck are you?? You better call me… and it better be good!'

The last one.

'Why is your fucking phone switched off? You are sooo dead!'

Next, he read his mum's texts.

The first one, at 11.30am: *Hi love, hope you'd a good night. Give me a buzz when you get this.*

Then, at 5pm: *Hi love, been trying to call you. Just let me know you are ok. Please. Love you!*

Connor called Dave. He wasn't happy.

'Fuck you, man; I've been avoiding calls all day. Where are you?'

'My flight's at ten and I'll be at yours by 1am,' Connor said. 'Just leave a key out for me.'

'Rather you than me, mate,' his friend replied. 'That woman of yours has left me two nasty voicemails. On your own head be it.'

'Sorry, mate. 'I'll explain all when I see you.'

As Connor sat at departures, reality started to bite. What was he going to do? He knew he had to text his mum and Amy; he was a dead man walking.

'Is that you, Con…?' a voice interrupted his panic attack.

Connor looked up to see the face of Michael, an old friend and neighbour from Derry, whom he hadn't seen in a few years.

Michael was flying to Belfast, too. He had his car parked at the airport; did Connor want a lift home to Derry? Connor was so grateful to get back home that evening; back to the safety of his bedroom. He yearned to pull the duvet over his head and block out the world. He had sent four texts before his flight.

To Amy: *Hi babe, trouble with my phone. I'll call you in the morning. Xxx*

To his mum: *Sorry mum, phone crashed. I'll be home tonight. I've a key. Don't wait up. x*

To Dave: *I got a lift to Derry. I'll call you tomorrow. Cheers mate.*

To Chris: *About to board now…talk tomorrow…loved today…miss you. Xxx*

Tomorrow, the shit would well and truly hit the fan.

35

Katie knew something was up when she heard the front door close and the fast rhythm of Connor's footsteps on the stairs. Matt slept peacefully through the rapid thuds, but Katie was out of bed in a flash.

She met Connor on the landing. 'You OK, love?' Her question was met with silence.

'Connor, please... I know something isn't right. Is it Amy? Are you two OK?'

He turned away from her, grasping at his bedroom door handle, but his mum covered his hand with hers and pleaded with him not to enter.

'There's no way I'll sleep if you don't talk to me. Please, Connor. Whatever it is, you can tell me.'

His shoulders sagged in mute acceptance and they made their way downstairs to the couch in the living room.

Katie sat there with her arm around her son, his head resting on her shoulder and his arm hooked across her tummy. She couldn't remember the last time she'd held him like this. She brushed the hair off his forehead as she held him tightly, wishing she could take this away from him... whatever 'this' was.

Had he been in Rome, and why? Why had he rushed upstairs as if a hitman was running after him? And why was he hanging onto her right now, childlike, as if the world was caving in on him?

Have I been right all along? she thought. The looks that had passed between Connor and the young officer on the ship were still fresh in her memory. She knew Connor had a story to tell...

was the 'closet door' about to open?

Katie pulled back slightly and placed her hand on his handsome face. He raised his head to her, his beautiful brown eyes swimming with sadness. She wanted to tell him everything would be OK and that there was nothing they couldn't get through together.

She willed herself to stay quiet and give him space. As she waited, she thought of the irony of the situation. She, too, had a secret, yet she expected Connor to come clean and tell her all about his; to do something she couldn't do herself. Was this a lesson for her? Was someone up there trying to tell her to do the right thing?

Not able to bear the silence a moment longer, she spoke.

'Were you in Rome today, Connor?' she whispered, hoping Amy's mum had been wrong.

Connor lifted himself off his mother. Silently, he reached into his pocket for his phone, swiped it into life and handed it to her. Katie tentatively took it from him; a text from Amy. She could see at a glance that the text was peppered with foul language. She looked back at Connor.

'Read it, Mum,' he urged.

She sat up straight and started reading.

YOU FUCKIN LIAR. DON'T COME BACK HERE. GO FUCK YOURSELF.

The instinct to defend her son rose to the fore. 'How dare she! I don't care what you've done - or who you've done it with; she has absolutely no right.'

Connor stared at the ground, deep in his own thoughts. Katie's heart was coming out through her chest. She wanted to break glass; break anything that would shatter the silence in the room. But she sat there, waiting. Eventually, he spoke. His voice was barely audible but she was afraid to ask him to speak louder in case he would clam up.

'I'm not in love with Amy, Mum. I have to tell her it's over.'

'She'll get over it,' Katie said angrily, still reeling from what she had just read. But she knew that would get her nowhere. She tried again - more gently this time.

'It's not the end of the world, love. These things happen; it's better to be honest with her.'

'I've met someone else, Mum.'

For a split second, Katie doubted her motherly intuition; maybe Connor had met another girl.

'Who?' she asked, hope raising her voice an octave higher.

'You've already met,' he whispered.

'Really? Who is she?' Katie swallowed hard in anticipation, wanting to kick herself for using 'she'.

For the next few moments, silence filled the room again.

'It's okay, Connor. Just say what you have to say.'

Katie looked at his sad profile as he stared down at the floor. She loved this boy more than words could express. She placed her hand over his, and Connor laced his fingers around hers. Another minute passed; it felt more like an hour.

'It… it's not a *she*, Mum.'

Connor slowly raised his head and looked into his mum's face; she tightened her grip on his hand.

'It's a *he*.'

'Ri-right,' Katie spoke slowly in an effort to let the words sink in. 'A *he*.'

'Yes, Mum. I'm gay.'

At this, their hands loosened and their arms went around each other, holding on tightly as if trying to draw strength from one another. Katie eventually pulled away.

'I wish I could take this weight off your shoulders, but I will always be here for you, my darling boy. And I promise you, Connor: everything will be OK.'

Connor sighed deeply.

'How come one minute I feel like I'm floating on a cloud and the next like I'm in the gutter?'

'You'll never be in the gutter while I'm around, love. Over my dead body!'

She felt like a protective tigress; almost feeling her nails lengthening at the thought of someone harming her little cub. *Just let them try!*

'Were you in Rome today, Connor?'

'Ho-how, why are you asking that?'

'Because I was told this morning.'

'By who?'

'You were seen at the airport by Amy's dad, who told his wife, who couldn't wait to tell me.'

Connor closed his eyes and exhaled.

'I guess that explains a few things,' he sighed. 'Why didn't you tell me they all knew, Mum?'

'Connor, I tried to get you, but your stupid phone was off all day.'

'Yes, it was off. And yes; I went to Rome to meet my friend Chris. You remember him, Mum; the American guy who worked on the ship.'

In the midst of her shock, Katie felt a smile forming. *Fair play to him!*

He was braver than she'd given him credit for.

36

Matt had been sleeping peacefully upstairs, totally oblivious to the goings-on in the living room below. He woke at 3am, feeling the coolness of the empty space beside him where his wife should be. He glanced at the en suite, but it was in darkness. Calling Katie's name, he got out of bed, pulled on his dressing gown and made his way downstairs. As he about to open the living room door, he heard them talking; they didn't notice him as he stepped quietly inside the room.

'What about Dad?'

'Your dad will be fine. Trust me; he will be just fine.'

'I don't want to be around when he finds out, Mum. Will you tell him when I go back to Glasgow?'

Matt spoke. 'Tell me what?'

Startled, his wife and son looked over at him, neither of them uttering a word.

Matt sat down in the armchair next to the couch. 'Did you have an accident, son? What's going on? Somebody say something, for God's sake!'

Katie swallowed hard. This wasn't how Connor wanted his dad to find out, but things were out of their control now.

'It's okay, Connor. Just tell your dad.'

'Tell me what?' Matt repeated, more insistently this time.

'You're not going to like it, Dad.'

'Let me be the judge of that.' Matt was trying to stay calm but his patience was running thin.

Connor looked at his mum and she nodded sympathetically at him. He then turned to his father, knowing what he had to do.

'Dad, I'm...' Connor stopped and swallowed hard, dropping his eyes to the ground before continuing.

'I'm gay, Dad.'

'You're what?' Matt's eyebrows furrowed. 'Is this a joke, Con?'

He looked at the two people sitting in front of him and realised no-one was laughing.

Katie wanted so much to cry, but she wasn't going to do that in front of Connor. She wasn't even sure who she'd be crying for: Connor, because she knew his life would be a lot more difficult now, or Matt, who sat looking at his son with a mixture of disbelief, worry and love written across his face.

Or was it herself she pitied? Her own life was just as turmoil-filled at the minute, too. Her ruminations were suddenly interrupted by Connor's voice.

'I'm sorry, Dad. I only ever wanted to make you proud of me; be even half the man you are.

'I never wanted you to be ashamed of me. But now I've let you down. I was willing to live a lie just to make you, Mum and Amy happy, but I've met someone. And, for the first time, I know who I am.'

Matt stood up from the chair and started pacing around the room, his face unreadable.

'I had no idea. Jesus, how could I have had no idea?' He looked directly at his wife. 'Did you know, Katie? Why didn't you tell me?'

'Matt, no... I didn't know; Connor has just told me.' Katie patted the couch. 'Come and sit here; you're in shock, love.'

Connor, seeing his dad struggling to take it all in, said: 'I'm sorry to be a disappointment to you, Dad.'

'No, son; you're not a disappointment to me. Don't you ever think that. It's just a bit of a shock, that's all.'

Then, summoning up a smile, Matt reached his arms out to

his son. 'All that matters to me,' he said, hugging him tightly, 'is that you're happy.'

After a few moments, Matt broke off the embrace. 'Listen, it's late. Let's all get some sleep and we'll talk more in the morning. I love you, son.'

With that, he headed upstairs, Katie and Connor following silently behind him.

After bidding her son goodnight, Katie climbed into bed beside Matt. As she cuddled up to him, the floodgates opened; she started sobbing into his chest.

'I know, love,' he comforted her. 'It will change Con's life, alright… but it won't change how we feel about him.'

Katie lifted her head and kissed him on the lips. He held her tightly, then caressed her tenderly, nuzzling at her neck and shoulders. He hadn't done that in a long time. She felt little shivers run through her and encouraged his foreplay with a few groans of pleasure; she had missed their intimacy.

And then, it happened; so unexpectedly, yet so naturally. When Matt rolled over on top of her, Katie could feel him getting more excited and she eagerly responded to his needs. Here, in the wee hours of the morning, they actually managed to make love. Afterwards, Katie sank into Matt's chest, a contented smile on her face as she drifted off to sleep.

Though drained by the weight of Connor's revelation, sleep was the last thing on Matt's mind. There he'd been, sailing through his daily routine, thinking Con was well settled with a good job and in a loving relationship.

How wrong he had been. Connor would now, presumably, be living a gay lifestyle; he would have a same-sex partner. Matt could only imagine how difficult it must have been for Connor to come out, but he was glad he was man enough to stand up and say it.

That was good enough for him, but he knew how Katie would

handle this. She would be a pillar of strength in front of Connor but flop like a rag doll when he wasn't around. He needed to be strong now; he had a broken wife to fix and an anxious son to reassure. But his family would be OK; he would see to that.

He kissed Katie's forehead, turned on his side and finally surrendered himself to sleep.

37

Katie woke up that morning feeling totally exhausted. Matt was already out of bed; she could hear him pottering about in the kitchen. She usually didn't mind Fridays at work, but it was the last place she wanted to be today. She would go in for a while but take the afternoon off.

As she lay there, she relived the previous night over and over again: Connor's late-night news confirming her deepest fears; making love to Matt for the first time in months. *And as for you*, she thought, pressing her hand to her tummy.

She lifted her phone and sent Carol a message.

Can you do a long lunch?

The phone pinged with an immediate response: *Where? When? Why?*

She typed. *One o'clock at McNamara's.*

Carol was lost in thought. The only time they picked this restaurant was when one of them had something on their mind and needed a private place to talk. It was a popular place, but it was designed in such a way that no-one was on top of each other.

She couldn't help wondering what was going on this time. Could it be about Katie thinking Connor might be gay? Her friend hadn't mentioned it since that time on the ship, and Carol had thought it best to let sleeping dogs lie. Katie was already sitting at the back booth in the restaurant when Carol walked in and spotted her.

'Am I going to need something stronger than that?' she asked, pointing to the water jug as she pecked Katie on the cheek and sat down.

'Maybe.' Katie replied, not quite knowing where to begin. 'A lot has happened since I was last talking to you.'

'Go on, I'm all ears.' Carol sat back and silently braced herself; she didn't like the sound of this.

Katie, her face the colour of death, started filling her in; from the phone call from Amy's mum first thing on Thursday morning right up to Connor arriving home distraught in the early hours of the morning.

'And was he in Rome?' Carol asked, struggling to understand.

Katie stopped and swallowed hard, her eyes starting to fill up.

'Believe it or not, Connor had indeed gone to Rome... to meet his *friend*. Only... he's more than a friend. Carol, he came out to me and Matt.'

'Jesus, Katie,' Carol said, putting her hand over her mouth. 'He came out! Oh, God, you were right. When you hadn't brought it up with me since that time on the ship, I thought maybe you'd dropped that idea.'

'No, I didn't drop it. I just tried to deny it... but there's no denying it now.'

'Is Con alright? What about Matt... what about you?' Carol reached across and took hold of Katie's shaking hand.

Katie sat there in silence. It was as if the penny had just dropped; saying it out loud made it all so real. Carol sat quietly, waiting for Katie to find her voice again. Then, the words came tumbling out as she told Carol about the awful text Amy sent to

Connor and how wonderful Matt was when Connor told him he was gay. Katie blurted it all out without pausing for breath, then finished her monologue with, 'And, to crown it all off, me and Matt did it last night!'

Carol's jaw was hanging open. '*Did it?* You mean you two had sex? Fuck me pink!' She called to a passing waitress and asked for a large bottle of their house wine.

'We're both driving,' said Katie.

'We can leave the cars and get them in the morning. I can't believe all of this. Where is Connor now?'

'He's at home, probably still in his bed. He was shattered last night, God love him. He has to go back to Glasgow tomorrow. I feel so sorry for him, Carol. And, to tell you the truth, I feel sorry for Amy, too. It's a total mess.'

'I know it won't be easy, but they will sort it out between themselves, Katie. Amy is young; she has her whole life ahead of her.'

Carol looked at Katie's worried face; she could see her friend was crumbling in front of her.

'Well,' they say every cloud has a silver lining,' she continued brightly.

Katie looked at her, puzzled.

'You can tell Matt the baby is his.'

'I can't think about that right now, Carol. I have to sort Con out first. He's not in a good place. I always hoped he and Amy would outgrow each other and that no-one would get hurt, but it looks like it's not going to go all that smoothly.'

The waitress came back with the wine and the girls ordered a light lunch.

'I shouldn't be drinking, Carol. I'm an emotional wreck. Not to mention the fact I'm pregnant.'

'One wee glass will do you no harm. It'll help you relax.'

Katie put her glass to her mouth, but the taste turned her

stomach. She sat the glass back down on the table and took a sip of water.

'I'm just so worried for the things Connor may have to face now, Carol. How come gay people are still having to justify themselves? They've won the right to marry, they've earned the same legal rights as everyone else, but still there are people who refuse to accept them for who they are. There was a debate on the radio this morning; some religious crackpot arguing against gay couples' right to adopt - 'a child should have a mother and a father' etc - and I swear I felt like bursting through the speakers and grabbing the guy by the throat and throttling him. Why don't they just give over? How must a gay person feel, listening to those bigots? Why are they like this?'

'Because gay people have a voice now,' Carol replied. 'They have rights, and the politicians and bible thumpers who preferred it when they were treated like second-class citizens don't like it one bit. Society has moved on and it's only the Neanderthals who can't accept it. Gay people have great lives nowadays; they're just getting on with it.'

Carol took Katie's two hands in hers.

'Fuck all those naysayers. You and Matt should feel proud that Con was able to open up to you. He knows you're both there for him.'

'Aye, I hope he knows that,' said Katie, blowing hard into her tissue.

'You can't live his life for him, Katie... and you can't control who he loves.'

'You're probably right, Carol. But there's still a lot of hatred in the world and I am so worried for him. My poor wee Connor.'

'There's nothing wee about him,' Carol chided. 'He's six foot and gorgeous, and he's just about to blossom. You'll see a change in him now that all that pressure is lifted from him; just you wait and see. If I had a son, I wouldn't mind him being gay. It's a whole new world out there - think of the craic we're going to have at the next Gay Pride parade! I can't wait!' Carol smiled and punched the air with her fist.

For the first time in days, Katie's heart felt lighter. She knew Carol was right... they just needed a bit of time to let it all sink in.

'Will you come to mine tonight and we'll all get a Chinese together?'

'Of course I will,' said Carol, corking the bottle of wine and smiling across at Katie.

'Connor is feeling a bit awkward, so give him the biggest hug when you see him, will you, Carol?'

'Don't you worry Katie...I've got this.'

38

Connor stayed in his room that morning, well out of his parents' path. When they'd left the house for the day, he texted Chris to say he was home alone. Chris called him immediately.

'Hey, how you doing?'

'I'm fine,' Connor answered, hearing the tremor in his own voice.

'You don't sound good. What's going on, buddy?'

Connor took a deep breath and told him everything that had happened.

'Mum and Dad were great. My biggest problem right now is Amy.'

'I'm so proud of you, Connor,' said Chris. 'Amy needs to hear the truth from you, too… it's the only way,' he added gently.

'Would it be easier for her if I told her I'm bisexual? Like, lighten the blow a wee bit?'

'If it makes you feel better, then say that. But the truth will come out eventually, Connor. Get your mum's take on it. Or your auntie Carol's. They seem to be women of the world.'

'Yeah, I could bounce it off them. I'm sure Mum will tell Carol today.'

'Go back to Glasgow and face the music, buddy.'

'I will. We need to talk. She doesn't want me back but I need to get my things and look for new digs.'

'That's the spirit. You'll feel better once it's done.'

Connor hung up, then fell asleep for a few hours. He eventually moved from his bed to his recliner in the living room, spending the afternoon in front of the TV, flicking aimlessly through the channels.

Just after three o'clock, his phone pinged. A text from Amy.

Very hurt that U lied 2 me…I know I over reacted. We need to talk… call me after 5.

Connor didn't reply. He didn't know what to say.

He closed his phone and placed it under a newspaper on the coffee table. He'd be back in Glasgow tomorrow; he'd face her then. He was back at work on Monday. He could use a few more days off, but he'd have to pull a sickie and that wouldn't sit right with him. Then again, it wouldn't be a lie; he was feeling sick to the pit of his stomach.

That evening, Carol arrived at Katie's, calling hello as she let herself in and stepped into the front hallway.

'In the kitchen,' Katie shouted. 'I'm trying to do ten things at once.'

Carol walked towards the kitchen but changed direction when she spotted Connor in the family room.

'Hi, Con, you look cosy,' she said.

He stood up. 'Here, let me take that,' he said, reaching out for the bottle of wine Carol was carrying.

She stood on her tiptoes and gave Connor a peck on the cheek, noticing how tense he was.

'Love you,' she murmured, squeezing his arm.

'Love you back,' he replied with a shy smile.

Just then, Matt came downstairs and they all made their way into the kitchen, where Katie was folding the laundry she'd just taken from the tumble dryer.

'That's your clothes all ready now, Connor.'

'Thanks, Mum. You didn't have to do that.'

'Well, sure, you'll be back doing your own washing next week.'

Sensing the tension in the room, Matt said, 'Right, what are we having? Chicken fried rice, salt and chilli prawns, beef curry, chips?'

'Yeah,' said Katie, 'but throw in a wee surprise.'

'I'll go with you, Dad,' Connor said, grabbing his coat.

After the boys left, Katie began clearing the table as Carol lifted out the cutlery and glasses.

'A great big elephant is sitting right here, Katie. Might be a good idea to tell Con that I know - though I'd say he's guessed that already. He gave me that wee quiet, sad look of his. His eyes always give him away, don't they?'

'Yeah, you're right, Carol. Here, pour me a small glass; my nerves are getting the better of me.'

They set the table together in companionable silence.

When the two men arrived back, the Chinese food was placed on heated serving dishes. Everyone was starving at this point and their taste buds were heightened with the delicious aroma and flavours. They filled their plates as the talk of food and wine changed the conversation and lightened the atmosphere, and the awkwardness and dread finally began to dissolve.

Katie's glass of wine gave her a bit of Dutch courage.

'I was telling Carol you were in Rome, Connor.'

Carol almost choked on her food; she hadn't expected the introduction to Connor's new sex life to be so direct.

'Yes, good for you, Connor,' Carol answered. 'And I hear you met that lovely lad from the ship?' There was no point in pretending she didn't know. She raised her glass.

'I propose a toast to Connor. Life is too short, so we have to give it our all. Here's to you, pet, you're the best and you deserve the best.'

They all clinked their glasses together.

'So, tell me,' she continued. 'How was Rome? Did you climb the Spanish Steps? What's the guy's name, anyway? He's American, isn't he? I remember he was gorgeous!'

Connor laughed at all the questions being fired at him. It felt strange talking openly about Chris, but he loved being given the opportunity. He happily told them all about Chris and how great a day they'd had. Katie was proud of him and told him so. Connor looked back at his mum; the look of relief on his handsome face warmed her heart.

Matt added his penny's worth, too. 'That place is far too expensive; what did a beer cost you?'

'Well, we were in the tourist area so it wasn't cheap. You'd never stick it, Dad!'

When they'd finished eating, Matt left them to it and went off to meet the lads for a few much-needed pints. Connor stretched out again on his recliner and the two girls took up the opposite corners of the couch, their feet tucked up under them.

'Amy sent me another text a while ago and she also tried calling me. I didn't answer either of them.'

'You can't run away, love,' Katie insisted. 'Does she want you back again?'

'I think she might. She kind of apologised and said she wants to talk. She probably just thinks we'll both say our bit, I'll apologise and then it will all blow over; back to square one. But those days are gone, Mum.'

'I know, love. That's why you have to do the right thing.'

Connor took a deep breath and sat up, running his fingers through his hair. Katie felt so helpless. If only she could go to Amy and tell her how hard this was for Connor, how distraught it was making him. She wished she could spare him all this anguish. But she couldn't do that; this was one thing he had to do for himself.

'Right,' Carol announced, uncurling her feet and placing them firmly on the ground. 'The bottom line is that you're out now and you're not going back in, right, Con? And you don't have to face anything on your own... right, Katie?' Carol looked from one to the other.

Katie nodded as Connor stared blankly at Carol. All he could think about was how to tell Amy. His head started running riot again. He knew how much she loved him. She was most likely waiting for him to pop the question: engagements rings, wedding bands, the full works. Their friends often remarked they were like Posh and Becks. What would they all think now? Connor felt so selfish. He wondered if it would be easier to just stay with Amy, then he wouldn't have to hurt her. But could he lead a life of dishonesty and sadness just everyone else got to be happy?

'You can't pretend to be straight and end up marrying Amy,' Carol said, as if reading his thoughts. 'You'll both be miserable. Listen, Amy is young; she'll recover.'

'But where do I start?' Connor sighed. 'Which would be easiest for her: that I don't love her any more, or that I'm confused about my sexuality? Do I just say, "Amy, I've met someone else, and, by the way... it's a *man*".'

He dropped his face into his hands. 'I just don't know what to do and how to do it.'

'Look, Con,' said Carol. 'Just be yourself and treat Amy with respect and love. Let her see this is the hardest thing you've ever had to do. You'll know what to say when the time comes.'

'Yeah,' Connor sniffed, 'as the cliché goes, *it's not you... it's me.*'

Katie intervened. 'You're dropping a bombshell on her, Connor, but let her be shocked. Let her be angry and let her break a few glasses if she needs to. Just be there for her. Do it now, before any real harm is done. One day, love, she'll thank you for it.'

39

That same Friday, Sam, on a call with Paul, the manager of the Derry branch, had casually asked if Katie was back at work. He hadn't heard from her since her surgery was cancelled three days ago. She hadn't answered any of his texts and he was going crazy, wondering why she was giving him the cold shoulder.

'Yeah,' said Paul. 'Katie came back to work yesterday, and it's well she's looking, too, thank God.'

Sam thought better of ringing Katie's mobile. Only one thought stuck in his mind: he needed to see her, and if she wouldn't come to him, then he would go to her.

Sam and Jill usually met up after work on a Friday evening. They had one drink in their favourite bar in Canary Wharf before going on to a delicious Italian restaurant around the corner.

Sam picked his moment when Jill was relaxing over dinner.

'I've to go to Derry next week, honey.'

'Really? I've a few days to take off… I might go with you.'

Adopting a poker face, Sam answered, 'Great; can you take Monday and Tuesday off?'

'Oh,' she said, deflated. 'I thought maybe you were talking later in the week.'

'No honey, I need to be there Monday - midday at the latest. I'll try to get back Tuesday. But, come over next time. We'll organise it better and take a few days in Dublin, too.'

'Yeah, I'll save my leave and maybe we'll do a Thursday and Friday.'

You're a jammy bastard, Sam thought to himself as he sipped his merlot and smiled lovingly at Jill. Maybe he was confusing 'jammy' with 'crazy', but right now he didn't care. He had a plan and he needed to see it through.

'What's Derry like, anyway? You rarely talk about it.'

'It's actually very nice. I always stay in the City Hotel. It looks across at a beautiful footbridge over the River Foyle; it's called the Peace Bridge, to mark the end of the Troubles.

It links the Cityside to the waterside; in other words, the Protestants to the Catholics. I must admit, at the start I was afraid to open my mouth, you know, with my English accent, but Derry people are so warm and friendly.'

Jill seemed genuinely interested. 'Is there much to do there? I mean, could you spend a few days there without getting bored?'

'Oh, yeah, it's a walled city, loads of history. They have a great museum and walking tours. It was City of Culture a few years ago and it has hosted the round-the-world clipper race a few times. It's a real foodie place, too; some great restaurants.'

Sam continued, warming to his theme. 'They know how to enjoy themselves, these Derry people. There's a jazz festival every summer and a carnival every Halloween that has become world-famous. And the nightlife is brilliant; any night of the week, you can hear live music in one of the many bars in Waterloo Street. Great for drawing in the tourists.'

'How come you never told me all this before? Sounds very quaint,' Jill said, surprised at how fondly Sam spoke of Derry. For some reason, she thought he preferred Belfast.

'Yeah, it is quaint. And they have a cute accent too...' Katie's voice lilted through his head.

As Jill drank in each word, her mind worked overtime. She knew very little about this city in the north of Ireland other than that its name popped up on the news from time to time - usually with some reference to its troubled past. But, listening to Sam speak of it like this, she was intrigued. Perhaps it was time for a visit.

40

'Good morning... or should I say bad night?' John looked at Amy with a worried look on his face. 'You look awful, hen.'

'Gee, thanks, John' she replied sarcastically, pulling off her fleecy pink hoody and throwing it into her locker.

'Thank God it's Friday; I've been up all night. But I don't want to talk about it.'

'Well, you just get your wee self over to ours tonight. Andrew has taken the day off and the kitchen - the whole apartment, in fact - is his. Clean it 'til it shines, cook it 'til its edible!'

'Good for you, John,' she said ruefully. 'Must be great to trust your partner implicitly.'

'What's up? Murder in paradise? I thought Connor was still in Ireland.'

'Aye, me too. He was in Rome yesterday, by all accounts. Still there, for all I know. Probably Dave's idea; he's always up to no good. I never liked him.'

'Who's Dave?' John asked, wondering if maybe this was the person Connor had been speaking to on the phone that night of the dinner party at Amy's.

'He's our friend from, like, forever. But he's a total tramp; would shag his granny if there was no-one else around.'

'Look, I'm sure there's a good explanation. Try to put it out of your pretty wee head for now, hen. We'll have a good night tonight, I promise.'

Amy decided to keep her phone in her uniform pocket during her shift, taking it out each time she moved between wards. Each time, a blank screen started back at her. She couldn't believe

Connor hadn't even acknowledged her text. She knew the text she'd sent last night was over the top, but he would know that was just her way.

She still felt she was owed an apology; or an explanation, at least. Was she such a bad girlfriend that he couldn't be honest with her? All he'd had to say was he was going away with the lads. She hated the lies.

But maybe she needed to look at herself, too. She re-read her text to Connor; it certainly was nasty! She sent another text, keeping it more civilised this time.

Before she left work, she called him. He didn't answer.

The madness in the ward took the edge off things, but the fact that Connor hadn't attempted to make amends still niggled at her. He knew she was going to John and Andrew's place tonight. Maybe later, after a few drinks, she would get John to ring him with a bit of banter. He might pick up for him, and then she could get a chat, too. Yeah, that would be a good icebreaker, she reckoned.

Amy arrived at 7pm sharp. She'd never been to John and Andrews's apartment before. She buzzed their number on the intercom outside the main door.

'If you're young, beautiful and Irish, push the door,' John answered in his best telephone voice.

'All of the above,' Amy laughed, shoving the heavy door and making her way to the lift.

Truth be told, it was the last place she wanted to be, but she couldn't cancel, knowing the bother the boys had gone to. She couldn't believe Connor had ignored her all day. Even her backhanded apology hadn't worked. His silence and rejection totally unnerved her. The thought that her dad might be mistaken had haunted her and she'd called him the night before, needing to hear it from his own lips. *Was he sure it was Connor he saw at the airport?* Her dad had no qualms about it; it was definitely him.

As the lift carried her to the fifth floor, a large lump formed in her throat and tears were making her eyes glaze over. The only good thing about this evening was it was just the three of them, and she knew, before the night was over, she'd get to blurt everything out and have a good cry on their shoulders. The boys loved hearing all the gossip - but they also gave very good counsel.

When the lift doors parted, John was standing there, waiting. He gave her a tight squeeze and she handed over a large M&S bag filled with wine and goodies.

'Come on,' he said, linking his arm through hers, 'Andrew's speciality cocktail is waiting on you.'

'Hi, gorgeous,' Andrew greeted her, taking her coat and replacing it with a cocktail.'

'Thanks, Andrew. Something smells good.'

He went back to the kitchen, leaving John and Amy to enjoy their drinks on the couch. When dinner was ready, they sat at the table. Amy, in spite of things, found she was actually enjoying herself. The boys were good company and the food and wine were going down nicely.

She'd managed to keep a lid on things, but when they made their way back to the couch, one look from John was all it took; the waterworks started.

'Ach, Amy, hen,' said John. 'What's happened?'

Amy sat there between them on the couch and gave them the sequence of events from the day before.

'What was he doing in Rome? What had he to say for himself?' John asked.

'Well, that's the whole thing: he won't talk to me. I sent a terrible text last night because I was so annoyed at him for not telling me he was going away.'

'Too right,' Andrew murmured, even though he'd vowed to stay well out of Amy's domestic.

'Anyway,' she went on, 'he didn't answer, so I sent him another one this afternoon, kind of apologising. And I phoned him after work, too. Nothing.' She sniffed loudly into her tissue.

'He's not being fair on you, Amy,' John said, reaching for her hand. 'He should have taken your call.'

'Do you think he might be seeing someone else? I mean, he can't be; he never goes out the door.'

'Well, for someone who never goes out of the door he wasn't long in going out of the fucking country,' John replied. 'Something is definitely up.'

Andrew's stare warned John to keep his mouth shut.

'Isn't he back here tomorrow?' Andrew said, quickly filling in the gap to prevent John saying something he might later regret.

She hesitated. 'I'm not sure. You see… I told him in my first text not to come back…then later I said we needed to talk. Do you think he wants to break up with…' she swallowed the rest of her sentence as her body started to shudder and tears streamed down her face.

'C'mere, you,' said John, putting his arm around her shoulders and hugging her to him.

'Everything will be fine; just you wait and see.'

He furrowed his eyebrows over at Andrew while silently mouthing 'Poor Amy'.

41

Connor's phone vibrated on the coffee table. Anxiously, he leaned over and lifted it. No Caller ID. He tentatively answered and a loud 'hello!' bellowed from the other end. It was Amy's friend John.

Then, Amy's voice: 'Hi, babe. You OK?' John obviously had his phone on speaker. The phone trembled in Connor's hand. His mum, sitting across from him, could hear the shouting coming down the phone. She nodded encouragement.

'Aye, I'm sitting here with Mum and Carol. Yes, I'm fine.'

'Can't wait to see you tomorrow, babe. Let's do something nice, OK?' She sounded tipsy.

'Um, yeah. How's it going there?' he asked, not really knowing what else to say.

'They've eaten me out of house and home,' Andrew's voice boomed out.

'Come over for a drink tomorrow night, Connor,' John invited.

Caught on the hop, Connor agreed. 'I'll call you from the airport tomorrow, Amy. Should be in around lunchtime.'

'I've a hair appointment in town,' Amy said.

'I can pick you, up if you like,' John intervened.

It was settled. John would collect him from the airport at one o'clock.

Katie was the first to speak once Connor had hung up.

'Will John be alone when he collects you?'

'I guess so. Amy is going to get her hair done.'

'Why don't you talk to him when you have the chance? See

what advice he has to offer… maybe he's been in your shoes.'

'Yeah, but John is more Amy's friend than mine.'

'Exactly, so he'll have Amy's best interests at heart, then, won't he?'

'I'll see how I feel tomorrow,' Connor yawned. 'Think I'll call it a night.'

'Yeah, sleep well, Con,' Carol said, getting up and giving him a tight hug. 'I must get going myself; it's been a long day. You stay positive, pet. I'll be thinking of you.'

When Carol's taxi arrived, Katie left her to the door.

'Thanks for today, Carol. I couldn't have done it without you.' She could feel her eyes welling up.

'No crying. Get some rest; you know where I am if you need me.'

Katie woke early the next morning with imaginary cramps in her tummy. Sending up an unspoken prayer, she crossed her fingers as she made her way to the bathroom. These toilet trips were becoming a habit; she was constantly checking for some sign she was miscarrying. One bit of spotting and she would have her life back… but there was nothing.

She crawled back into bed. She reckoned she was about 24 days pregnant by now. As Matt lay beside her, snoring lightly, she Googled what a foetus looked like at three or four weeks. The internet informed her that the baby's neural tube - the building block of the spine, brain and backbone - had already formed.

The thought of getting rid of it still haunted her as much as the thought of keeping it and having to lie to Matt that the baby was his. Or, worse still, having to tell him it wasn't. She was sick with worry. She still had a few weeks to think about it. A few more weeks of agonising trips to the loo and a few more weeks of lying awake, dementing herself.

Matt stirred beside her and asked what she was looking at on her phone. She quickly closed down her search and clicked her photos icon.

'Just a few photos I took last night.'

At least that was partly true. They'd taken photos at the dinner table and a few more after Matt had left for the pub.

'Many in the bar last night?' she asked, trying to take her mind off herself.

'Busy enough. Alan and I just sat by ourselves... I told him about Connor. I got a bit flustered. Suddenly, I felt embarrassed, or something; don't even know why. Maybe it was just actually hearing myself say it. To be fair, Alan was very honest. He said he could understand how I would be a bit cut up about being told that. Said he'd be the same if his Gary told him he was gay.'

'It's strange,' Katie replied. 'It's kinda like we have to go through the coming out thing, too.'

Matt looked at her. 'What do you mean?'

'Well,' she explained, 'you told Alan and I told Carol, but we have others to tell. I find myself wondering how, and when, I should do that... and how will they take it. The girls in the office are always asking if Connor's getting married soon. Suppose I'll just have to pick my moment and tell them.'

'I guess you're right,' Matt said, 'but I don't give two hoots about anyone else. If they have a problem with it, it's *their* problem. Con could have told us a helluva lot worse, couldn't he? He's our boy, and we'll be here for him.'

Katie felt a surge of love for him as he lay there, admitting his fears and worries but determined, in the middle of it all, to put the wellbeing of his son first.

'I would do time for him if I had to,' she said quietly.

'Hopefully it won't come to that, my love,' he joked. 'Right, we'd better get up and give him a shout… he has to get on that plane and go sort his life out.'

42

John and Connor chatted amiably enough on the drive home to Glasgow from the airport. After 15 minutes of small talk, the conversation moved to Amy; she was really the only thing they had in common.

'Amy speaks very highly of you, John. You're a good friend to her.'

'Aye, I love that wee lass,' John said, pausing briefly before adding, 'But the question is: do you?'

Connor didn't answer straight away; he needed to work out his options. Should he stay in denial and laugh it off? Maybe John had a strange sense of humour and meant it as a weird joke; he didn't know him that well, after all. Did he know about Rome?

John drove in silence, letting the question hang in the air. Connor felt like he was walking into a trap, but he had to say something.

'I'm guessing Amy told you I was in Rome,' he said. 'Probably not the wisest thing I've ever done.'

'Aye, she did. She was quite upset. She's hoping you'll explain, and you two can make amends.' Another silence fell between them.

John spoke again. 'Look, Connor, feel free to tell me this is none of my business, but if you don't want to be with Amy, you need to be honest with her; she deserves that.'

'Have you time for a coffee?' Connor asked. He needed to bite the bullet.

They pulled off the main road and walked into a Starbucks

without saying a word. John pointed to an empty table at the side of the café. 'You grab that seat and I'll get the coffees in; Americano OK?'

'Great,' said Connor. He steeled himself; there was no turning back now.

When John sat down with the coffees, it was Connor who spoke first.

'I know there will be a lot more questions than I can answer…' he trailed off.

He knew he was being cryptic, but there it was: the flicker of recognition in John's eyes.

'Am I that obvious, John?'

'Not really,' John replied with a lopsided smile. 'It just takes one to know one.'

Connor half laughed, then turned serious again.

'Has Amy said anything to you? She doesn't know, does she?'

'No, I'd say she hasn't a clue. But she loves you… that much I *do* know.'

'What am I going to do? Hurting Amy is the last thing I want.'

'You and me both,' said John. 'But the sooner she knows, the better. Do your parents know?'

'Aye, I told them on Thursday night. They were cool with it… I think.'

'That's good. You're halfway there already. Once the family know and you tell the girlfriend, you're all sorted.'

'Sounds like you're talking from experience.'

'I am,' said John. 'I survived and so will you. It's out now and you have to deal with it. Drink up; it's time to face the music.' They walked along in silence to the car.

'How come you knew about me?' Connor asked as they drove along. 'Did I do something, or say something? What was it?'

'There were a few things. I heard you talking on the phone in the bathroom, and then there was the look of guilt on your face when you opened the door and saw me standing there. And also; you seemed very fond of Kylie. But it was when you did your Freddie Mercury impression during charades that I knew for sure!'

Connor burst out laughing at this last bit and John joined in. As the car approached Connor's house, however, the mood sobered up.

'So, you're going to tell her straight away, then?' John said, more telling than asking.

'Don't know what to do,' Connor muttered. 'You know the temper Amy's got, John. She's going to crack up.'

'Best to pull the plaster off, Connor,' John said, then started tapping the steering wheel, obviously mulling something over. Eventually, he spoke.

'If you want, I can drop in after fifteen minutes or so. Not quite sure who will need me more; you or Amy. There's room at ours, by the way, if she throws you out. Or, if she walks out, we'll look after her.'

'Thanks, John,' Connor said, relieved. 'It's cowardly of me, but I think I'd like that.'

'Right, then, off you go. Best of luck mate,' said John, leaning across and opening the car door.

Connor put his key in the front door, took a deep breath and shouted out that he was home.

Amy came through from the kitchen with a big smile on her face, wearing a lovely red top he hadn't seen before and her favourite black skinny jeans. She flicked her hair, showing off a new style as she did a twirl. She looked stunning.

Connor smiled at her as she came closer to him, but it was like he was greeting a younger sister or a close friend. That warm, caring feeling was there, for sure, but there was absolutely nothing sexual about it. His heart didn't skip a beat and sweat didn't break out on his forehead; he didn't want to grab her and devour her with loving kisses, his loins on fire. Not like he did with Chris.

'You look beautiful, Amy.' He smiled, but his eyes remained sad.

'What's up, babes? You not feeling well?' Amy said, placing the back of her hand against his forehead. Connor reached up and removed her hand, and, holding onto it, asked her to sit down.

'You're scaring me, Con. You're not ill, are you?'

She didn't take her eyes off him as he led her towards the couch, the colour draining from her beautiful face.

'What is it, Connor?' she urged. 'Tell me.'

'I-I don't know how to tell you, Amy. It's the hardest thing I've ever had to do.'

'Whatever it is, it can't be that bad.'

He took a deep breath and looked straight into her lovely brown eyes. She looked terrified as she looked up at him and placed her two hands on either side of his face.

'Just say it, Connor.'

He took her hands and held them, tight, in his.

'Amy, I've been very confused for a while now.'

'Confused? About what? About *me*?'

Here we go, thought Connor, bracing himself for the torrent of rage he knew was coming his way.

'What the fuck are you trying to say?' she fumed. 'Are you seeing someone else behind my back? Is that why you went to fucking Rome?'

She jumped off the couch and turned to face him.

'You bastard. Who is she?'

'No, it's not like that, Amy. Please, let me speak.'

'Oh, you'll be telling me now that you didn't mean it, that

you're really sorry…'

'No; you don't understand. *Please* listen…'

'Yeah, I can't wait to hear how you're going to get out of this one, you lying cunt…'

She lifted her hand to slap his face, but he caught it before it struck.

'Stop it, Amy!' he shouted, angry now too. He got off the couch and stood in front of her, willing the words to come out.

'Amy, I'm so, so sorry, but… I-I'm gay.'

She stood there, frozen to the spot, not uttering a sound. Connor had never seen her like this before; he almost preferred her shouting at him. Even slapping the face off him would be good right now.

He put his arm around her and walked her to the couch, then knelt down in front of her and took her hands. Her face was blank; she was obviously in shock. He wondered if he should get her a brandy; he could certainly do with one himself.

He hunkered down onto his heels and lowered his head so it lay between their hands. Still, she didn't speak. They stayed like that for what seemed like an eternity, then the tension was broken by a loud knock on the door. Amy startled back to life and Connor almost threw up; it had to be John.

Amy watched him, still unable to speak, but her face was telling him not to open the door. But he didn't really have a choice. And, selfishly, he felt he could be doing with a bit of support; Amy might benefit from John's wisdom, too.

He went to the front door and opened it; it was John. Connor ushered him into the living room, and, when Amy saw who it was, a look of realisation came over her face.

'You… you knew all along, didn't you?' she said, staring accusingly at John.

'No, Amy…' the two men said together.

'Con just told me today…' John continued.

'Go fuck yourself!' she interrupted. 'I thought you were my friend. I confided in you, I sat and cried with you. You told me everything would be alright…. you are as fake as fuck.'

She dragged the words from the pit of her stomach and spat them out of her mouth, one at a time, as tears streamed down her face.

Before John got a chance to say his peace, Amy was up off the couch, her face red with anger.

'You two were in cahoots all along,' she screamed. How stupid was I? Get out of my fucking sight, the pair of you. Now!'

John headed towards the door, but Connor didn't have it in him to walk away from someone he cared so much about. Just because he wanted to end their courtship didn't mean he could just switch off other feelings. He loved her in his own way; just a different way to what Amy wanted and needed. He couldn't leave her in this state.

'Amy, I feel so awful,' he said, as John lingered at the living room door.

'Regardless of what you think right now, I would never, ever deliberately hurt you. I just couldn't… I had to be honest with you.' He reached out to touch her arm.

'Don't you *dare* touch me,' she said, shrugging away from him. 'Oh, it's all about *you*, isn't it?'

She walked to the TV unit, lifted a framed photo of the two of them on holidays and fired it at him. It bounced off his shoulder and landed on the rug; he knew better than to pick it up.

'You didn't just wake up this morning and decide to be gay. How long have you known? Am I not woman enough for you? Or you want the best of both worlds… is that it? You greedy bastard!'

'Amy, please,' he pleaded, but she came towards him and began thumping his chest as hard as she could. With each blow, she roared all sorts of abuse and obscenities at him.

He stood there and took it. It was no more than he deserved and it was better she took her anger out on him rather than doing something stupid when he left.

It was John who intervened. Walking over to Amy, he pulled her off and held her as tight as he could without getting battered himself.

'Calm down, hen,' he soothed. 'Come on, now, Amy. It's not the end of the world.'

As she began crying uncontrollably on his chest, John nodded for Connor to leave them to it. Reluctantly, he walked into the hall, picked up his overnight bag and quietly let himself out of the flat, the tears blinding him. Once the door had closed, Amy disentangled herself from John's embrace.

'I want you to go, too, John,' she said.

'I don't want to leave you like this, Amy.'

'Why didn't you tell me, John? Everyone will be laughing at me. Like, how do you not know your boyfriend is gay? What am I going to do now?'

'Why don't you sit down and I'll make us a nice wee cup of tea.'

'No,' she said insistently. 'Please, John, I'd like you to leave.'

'OK, if that's what you want. I'll call you later, OK?'

John leaned in to give Amy a hug, but she turned away; he walked out of the flat without saying another word.

Sarah Kelly was in the hairdressers for her weekly blow-dry, casually flicking through *Hello!* magazine when her phone rang. It was Amy. 'I need to take this,' she mouthed to the stylist.

She hit 'accept' and said, 'Can I get back to you, sweetie? I'm just at the hairdressers, here…'

When there was no immediate reply, Sarah thought they'd been cut off… until she heard wailing coming down the line.

'Amy, darling, what is it? Are you alright?'

'Mum… me and Connor… it's over.'

Sarah put her hand over the mouthpiece and rolled her eyes in apology to the stylist, who was standing impatiently behind her.

'Look, it's probably just a wee tiff, sweetie. Give me five minutes and I'll ring you back.'

Amy stabbed the off button. Lifting the nearest cushion, she buried her face in it and began crying even harder. Nobody cared about her - not even her own mother.

But, ten minutes later, when her mother rang back and she told her everything, Amy was no longer the only one who was angry… Sarah Kelly was livid.

43

Connor sat on the kerb outside Amy's flat, distraught. He'd just texted Chris, who was on day shift, to let him know he'd spoken to Amy and would call him later. He wished Chris were here now. He could be doing with his strength and his comfort; the guilt was killing him and he didn't know what to do next.

He felt a hand on his shoulder... it was John.

'Come on, let's get you out of here.'

Connor wiped his nose with the back of his hand as he stood up and they made their way to the car.

'I appreciate all this, John,' he said as they drove along. 'But Amy is your friend; you should be with her. I'll book into the Travelodge tonight.'

'Amy kicked me out; wants to be on her own. Don't worry. She has other friends and she'll call someone when she gathers herself. I'll check in with her later. For now, you're staying at ours... no arguments.'

John parked up and phoned Andrew, telling him Connor was with him and that he'd be staying in the spare room.

'I'm putting you guys out; I feel really bad about this,' Connor sighed as he followed John into the lounge. He gazed out the large bay window at the other apartments across the way, wondering what was going on behind all those closed doors. Were other people's lives falling apart, too?

'You have a great set-up, here,' he said, turning back and looking around the impeccably-decorated space.

Andrew met him with a brandy. 'Take this, it'll help settle you.' Then, taking his bag and smirking, he said, 'Shall I show sir to his room?'

Connor followed Andrew as he pushed open the door of the spare bedroom and started lifting all sorts of bags, boxes and clothing off the futon bed.

For a second, Connor thought he'd walked into the *Strictly Come Dancing* dressing room: a metal clothes rail that took up the length of the wall was filled with sequenced dresses in all sorts of bright colours, the shoe rack below crammed with ridiculously high stiletto-heeled shoes and knee-length boots with thick platform souls. Andrew was still shifting things around while Connor sat tentatively at the edge of the futon.

'Look, I don't want to get in your hair - ' he stopped abruptly when the boys started to laugh.

'Bit late for that,' John said, pointing to the shelf behind him: it was filled with an array of coloured wigs, most of them on mannequin heads, the hair highly backcombed and curled. Connor's mouth fell open.

John smiled. 'Those are for our drag shows.'

Connor awkwardly sipped his brandy.

'Right... not my thing,' was all he could venture.

'Aye, I remember me saying that, too,' John laughed. 'Never say never.'

They went back into the lounge and ordered a pizza. Connor said he needed to call his mum and did so from the privacy of his room. She sounded so relieved to hear from him and told him she was glad the boys were looking after him.

Andrew suggested a movie from Netflix but none of them could concentrate on it. John had tried to call Amy at least four times throughout the evening but she didn't answer or return his calls.

'She'll probably have to move somewhere more affordable now,' Connor said, thinking out loud. 'We've only just done the place up... she loves it there.'

'I'm sure she'll get a flatmate,' said John. 'There's always nurses looking for digs.'

Realising he sounded flippant, he went on, 'Look, I love Amy to bits, but the bottom line here is her happiness. Couples can sometimes fall in and out of love and patch things up again… but you can't fall in and out of being gay.'

Just before midnight, they decided to call it a night. Connor lay down on the futon, glad of the quiet space. He called Chris, who was only too happy to listen to him as he unburdened himself about his distressing day.

He was still talking when he heard what sounded like a doorbell. He stopped for a second and checked his watch: it was 12.15am. Then, the sound of footsteps passing his door. Making his excuses to Chris, he hung up and lay there, his stomach in knots. His ears perked up as a conversation started up in the hallway.

'Aw, hen, look at the state of you,' he heard John say.

Next, Andrew's voice: 'Let me grab a towel; you're soaking wet.'

And then… Amy's. 'Can I stay here tonight, John? I can't bear to be on my own. I had to get out of that apartment… I've been walking around this past hour.'

'Course you can, pet,' said John. 'Go to the bathroom and dry yourself off; there's a bathrobe behind the door. I'll put the kettle on.'

Once he was sure she'd gone to the bathroom, Connor got up and opened his bedroom door. He peeped his head out and saw John and Andrew standing there.

'It's Amy, right?' he whispered. 'I can be out of here in two minutes.'

John walked over to him and gently pushed him back inside.

'You're going nowhere. When Amy settles, I'll tell her you're here. Just leave it to me, OK?'

Connor closed the door and rubbed his forehead. In pure panic, he reached for his jeans and sweater; he would do a runner and slip out the door without her seeing him. But, in the short time between pulling his jeans up and struggling to get into his sweater, he knew running away was not the answer. He couldn't let the boys do his dirty work for him. He hastily packed his bag and left it at the front door. There was no way he could stay here now that Amy was here, but he had to speak to her before he went.

Bracing himself, he walked up the hallway and into the living room, where Amy sat in an armchair while John and Andrew took up the couch. All three looked up him, but nobody spoke. Connor pulled a kitchen chair away from the table, placed it next to Amy and sat down. He took a deep breath.

'Amy, John kindly offered to let me stay tonight, but I'll leave now. I know I'm the last person you want to see.'

Amy just sat there in silence, staring at the ground. The day had drained her of every emotion: shock, anger, hurt, disgust, sadness and fear. And now, the very person who'd caused all that was sitting right in front of her.

'We'll leave you to it,' John interrupted, nudging Andrew, who was only too glad to get away.

Once the boys had closed the door behind them, Connor slowly began to talk, picking his words with care.

'A-Amy, I…' he stopped, not able to finish the sentence.

'You *what?*' she demanded. 'Just say it!'

'I'm just… I'm just so sorry.' It was now Connor's turn to be overwhelmed. Tears ran down his face. He brushed them away with the back of his hand, but more followed. Amy had never seen him this upset; she felt a pull in her heart.

'I've always loved you, Amy, and I will never stop loving you and never stop caring for you. But we all need a love that has no limits… and there is a limit to how much I can love you.'

'Oh, so it wasn't "to the moon and back" like you always claimed?' she snapped.

'You did make me very happy for a long time, Amy. I wasn't lying back then.'

'So, who's the lucky man, then?' she smirked bitterly. 'Is that what Rome was all about?'

'Yes, I went to see someone. Actually, it was the guy from the ship; the blonde American officer we played volleyball with.'

Her eyes widened. 'Did you... oh my God, did you and him? Aw, the very thought of it...' she clasped her hand across her mouth.

'No, Amy. I... we... we didn't.' Connor looked straight at her, then covered his face with his hands and shook his head. 'I'm so sorry to be putting you through this.'

The sight of him sitting there in so much pain stirred something in her, and for the first time since he'd dropped his bombshell, she actually felt sorry for him.

'Listen, Connor,' she said, her tone softer now. 'It's late, and we're both exhausted. Why don't you sleep on the couch and I'll take the spare room.'

'OK,' he said. 'I'll be gone by the time you wake up in the morning.'

Rising from her chair with a sigh, she walked to the spare bedroom and closed the door quietly behind her.

Connor lay down on the couch but couldn't sleep. Amy was a complete mess and he just didn't know how to make things right; what he'd done had destroyed her. As he ran his fingers distractedly through his hair, he noticed a desk at the far side of the room. He got up and walked over to it. Suddenly, he knew what he would do. Picking up a note pad and pen, he sat down at the desk and started writing.

My dearest Amy,

I hope you don't mind me calling you that, but you will always be very dear to me. I can't imagine what you are going through right now. But I know I have caused you so much pain. And for that I am truly sorry.

I fell in love with you the minute I saw you two years ago in the students' union bar…

I remember that night so well. You were stunning! I couldn't believe you were interested in me. My love for you was real, Amy, and I never want you to doubt that. We built a lovely life together …all those memories I will treasure forever.

Our recent troubles have all been my fault. And you were right when you said you didn't know me anymore. I don't even know myself. I have been living with these confused feelings for a while, now, and I hoped by ignoring them they would go away. But they didn't.

You asked me were you not woman enough for me. Amy, you are women enough for any man and he would be very lucky to have you. But I could never be that man, nor give you the life you deserve. This is the hardest thing I've ever had to do… but I know it's the right thing.

I could never complete you… and you could never complete me.

I will call to the apartment during the week while you are at work and collect my personal belongings. I want you to have everything else.

I'll push my key through the letterbox when I leave.

Amy, you have been my best friend for the past two years and I can't imagine my life without you in it. I will always be here for you and I hope we can somehow find a way to remain friends.

All my love,
Connor x

Through a blur of tears, he re-read the letter, then folded the page in half and wrote Amy's name on the blank side. He didn't have an envelope but it didn't matter; he knew she would share it with the lads anyway. He was glad she had them.

Connor got up and left that morning while the others still slept. He walked along the docks, then took a window seat at the Quayside Café. Early-morning walkers were booted, hatted and scarved, some holding hands with their partners, others holding the leads of their four-legged friends. People just going about their daily lives. But, for Connor, the world was standing still.

What now? he thought.

44

Amy was sitting on the couch with Connor's note in her hand. She'd heard the front door close gently about half an hour ago as she lay in bed and knew it was Connor leaving the apartment; in that moment, she'd realised he was leaving *her*, too.

A deep sob had shaken her small body as she'd gripped the top of the duvet and pressed it against her mouth, not believing this was happening to her. Connor should be lying here beside her, she'd thought. He should be kissing her sleepy head and telling her to lie on while he made his Sunday speciality: bacon butties, lightly toasted on both sides, plenty of butter and brown sauce.

He knew what she liked - and what she didn't. In fact, he knew everything about her. She was part of him. Who was going to take care of her now? Who would worry about her when she was feeling unwell and make her laugh when she was upset? Who would calm her down when she had a hissy fit, and who would be there to make all the wrongs right?

She'd found herself thinking, for a split second, that maybe she'd had a bad dream and Connor would bounce in any minute and playfully tease her for still being in bed. But the thought fled as quickly as it arrived; she felt so empty inside.

She'd got up, dressed herself and made her way into the lounge, where she'd spotted the piece of paper with her name on it sitting on the desk. She had just finished reading it when she heard the sound of the lounge door opening; it was John.

'You up and dressed already, hen?' he said gently.

'I suggested for Connor to take the couch and I'd take the

bedroom, and when I got up, he was already gone... but he left me this,' she said, holding up the sheet of paper and gesturing for John to take it and read it. He did.

'Aw, c'mere, you,' he said, sitting down beside her and hugging her tight.

'He's left,' she said, starting to sob. 'He's really left me.'

Her friend rocked her back and forth, tears springing from his own eyes, too.

'Why don't we get out of here and grab a bit of brekkie?' he said after a few minutes, lifting a tissue and tenderly patting Amy's wet eyes.

'Aye, OK,' she sighed. 'Thanks, John. And I'm sorry for throwing you out yesterday.'

'Don't be silly; you were upset, naturally.' He stood up, pulling her up with him.

'Look, Amy, this is huge, but time will make it smaller and you will eventually get over it. As my maw always says, 'there's nothing worse than a bad marriage', and she's dead right!'

He chuckled softly and pecked her cheek. 'It may not seem like it at the minute, but someone up there is looking after you, hen.'

Connor was on his third cup of coffee when his phone bleeped. It was a message from Gerry, his pal from work, confirming the arrangement they'd made to go to the pub that afternoon to watch Man United v Liverpool.

Gerry was sound. He'd started at Google HQ in Glasgow at the same time as Connor, but he'd worked at the Apple store for five years before that and had been very good about keeping

Connor, who was fresh out of university, up to speed. He still lived at home with his mother, who was rapidly progressing through the various stages of dementia.

Connor was just about to text him back when a sudden sniff of stale body odour reminded him that he badly needed a shower; he decided to phone him instead.

'Hi Ger, just got your text, there. Listen, would it be OK if I called over before the game? It's just that… me and Amy had a falling out and I packed a few things and left,' he sniggered nervously down the phone.

'Sure, pal,' Gerry said immediately. 'Mum's still in bed; she's been up most of the night. So have I, trying to stop her from going out shopping at four this morning,' he yawned.

'Don't know how you do it, Gerry. That's a hard one. I'll jump in a taxi and see you soon.'

Ten minutes later, Gerry opened the front door, and, taking in the sight of Connor, comically raised one eyebrow and said, 'And I thought *I* had a rough night.'

'Aye, it's a long story,' he sighed. 'Do you mind if I have a shower? I'll tell you all about it after.'

Connor held his face up towards the shower head and let the steamy water run into his pores, steeling himself for the conversation he was about to have with Gerry.

Then he thought about meeting his friends in the pub later; should he tell them, too? What would they think? They played indoor soccer together once a week; how would they feel about having a gay man in the changing room? And what about his co-workers? How would they react to him?

He thought about keeping his business to himself, but knew that would be virtually impossible. Amy would have told somebody by now - probably her mum. Definitely her mum.

He shuddered. *Sarah Kelly will have a field day with this.*

45

Jill cut short her Saturday morning shopping so she could get home and arrange her flights before Sam came back from the gym. She was feeling like a giddy teenager as she booked the midday flight on Monday, returning with Sam on Tuesday. She was looking forward to surprising him in Derry on Monday evening.

Their weekend routine, like their working week, ran like clockwork. Saturday afternoons were fairly relaxed; catching up on household chores or pottering around the garden, weather permitting. Sam liked to cook on a Saturday night and then they'd pick a movie and finish off with a nice bottle of wine.

On Sundays, they headed out for brunch followed by a cuddle and a nap in the afternoon. They read newspapers in the evening and flicked the remote control until something of interest came on the telly. Then it was bedtime and the lazy weekend put to rest; all to be repeated the following week.

This Sunday, however, Jill found Sam in a strange mood. As she was getting ready to go out, he said he might have to give brunch a miss; he'd a lot of work to catch up on.

'Why don't you go visit your mother?' he suggested. 'You haven't seen her in a while.'

'Only if you're sure you'd rather work. Shall we do an early tea, then?'

'Not *rather*, Jill,' he said, somewhat tetchily. 'I *have* to work. Yeah, maybe we'll do tea later.'

She hated seeing him under pressure with work and was on the verge of telling him about her plan to join him in Derry, but she didn't want to spoil the surprise; he'd be thrilled to see her walk in to the hotel dining room.

When Jill came back from her mother's, she headed upstairs, where Sam was in the bedroom, packing for his trip. As she walked into the room, he was taking a new white shirt out of its cellophane bag.

'Why are you taking that with you?' she asked. 'What's wrong with the one I ironed for you?'

Walking over to the wardrobe, she lifted a white shirt from its hanger and threw it on the bed, snapping the new one from Sam's hand.

'You're only going into the office, aren't you?' She eyed him suspiciously. 'Or have you plans for later?'

'This one will do fine, Jill,' he said, exasperated, lifting the shirt she'd ironed, folding it and putting it in his bag. He didn't have the energy for a fight.

'Why are you so touchy?'

'I'm not,' he said, in as neutral a tone as he could muster. 'Just getting myself organised. How was your mum?'

'How is she ever? I'm sorry I went over there; she was in one of her moods.'

Your mum's not the only one, thought Sam.

She went downstairs, wondering why Sam wanted to wear a new shirt into work. Who was he trying to impress? Something about that shirt didn't sit easy with her… but then, not much about Sam being away on his own sat easy. She stood at the kitchen sink and stared out the window. She was never sure if he was trustworthy or just a very good liar.

Sam stayed upstairs, leaving Jill to cool off; he'd take her out for dinner and hopefully lift her spirits. Sitting on the edge of the bed, he wondered what Katie was doing.

The next morning, Sam was up and away by 7am in order to make his morning flight to Belfast. Jill lay in bed for an hour after he'd gone, then got showered and dressed before packing a small overnight bag.

She had a nine o'clock hair appointment… then she would take a taxi to the airport.

46

Katie left for work on Monday morning, determined to focus on the 'now'. Skipping out of the car, she bounced into the office, inwardly repeating her favourite mantra to herself: *I am complete. I am perfect. I am peace.*

'Morning, Katie,' Paul greeted. 'Just got a call from Sam; he's on his way here. Wasn't expecting him for another week or two.'

At this news, Katie's *I am peace* flew out the window and was replaced with sheer panic. Sam was the last person she wanted to see. She wasn't ready to speak to him just now. How could someone who brought her so much pleasure before be causing her so much distress now?

She wondered how she should handle this. Should she be straight with him and tell him what had been going on? Explain why she'd been ignoring him, share her fears and ask for his help? But, would that be wise? She was choked with indecision.

The office was filling up and Katie had no choice but to pull herself together and concentrate on her work... she would have to face it soon enough.

Sam arrived at the office just before lunch. Sauntering in with his usual confidence, he greeted everyone in turn by their first names and with a chirpy remark. He stopped at Katie's desk, happy to see her looking so fit and well. Was he imagining it, or had she put on a pound or two? Something was different about her. Maybe she'd had her hair cut?

He couldn't take his eyes off her. Lowering his gaze, he caught a glimpse of the lace camisole underneath her cream silk blouse and his pulse quickened.

'Hi, there,' he said, steadying himself. 'How are you?'

'I'm fine, Sam,' Katie said. Stealing a quick glance at her colleague at the desk nearest her and noticing she was busy on the phone, she continued. 'Sorry for not getting back to you. I've a lot going on right now… you really have no idea,' she said in a whisper, shaking her head.

'I think we need to talk, Katie,' he said, his voice also lowered.

'About what?'

'Well, *us*, for a start.'

'There is no *us*, Sam. We had a fling. It was nice, but it's over. The whole thing was stupid.'

She glanced furtively around the office. 'We shouldn't be having this conversation here.'

'I know that,' he said. 'Look, I'm staying in Derry tonight. Please meet me - even for an hour. I need to talk to you properly. You're the main reason I'm here.' His eyes pleaded with her.

'I-I don't know, Sam. I'm so busy. Look, leave it with me and I'll see what I can do… I'll text you in an hour or so.'

Sam slapped her desk twice with the flat side of his right hand. 'Thanks, Katie, that all sounds great,' he said, as if they'd been discussing the quarterly projections. He walked off in the direction of Paul's office.

Katie went back to her computer screen. Her insides were shaking but there was no way she would let herself down. Sam looked so handsome in his navy suit; his white open-necked shirt showing off what remained of his tan. The smell of his aftershave still lingered.

When Katie looked up, she watched him through the glass panelling of Paul's office. He looked so serious and businesslike; she couldn't quite believe that, only a few weeks ago, she'd been holed up with this man in a loved-up hideaway. Couldn't quite believe that they'd talked and laughed together. Got slightly intoxicated together. Kissed passionately and explored each other's naked bodies with so much desire and ease, legs wrapped around each other and connected in every way possible.

But, above all else, she couldn't believe she was carrying his baby.

She decided she would meet up with him. It was only fair. Matt was out of town on business and wouldn't be home until 7pm; she would meet Sam and tie up any loose ends, and that would be that. She texted him mid-afternoon, saying she would meet him after work. He phoned her in response.

'Why don't you just come to my hotel, Katie? I'm in room 404. It makes more sense. We can talk in peace there. No distractions or worries about being seen.'

'OK. I'll be there at 5.15.'

'Great, I'll be waiting.'

She called Carol as she walked across the hotel car park.

'No kissing and telling, you hear me?' Carol warned.

'I've absolutely no intention of doing either,' Katie assured her.

And she meant it… until he opened the door and stood there in a pair of jeans and white T-shirt, head tilted slightly and giving her that 'little boy lost' smile. As she walked into the room, he placed his hands on her face and kissed her softly.

'Thank you for seeing me. Katie. I've been going crazy.'

Katie gently pulled herself away and walked over and sat on the edge of the bed, dusting invisible fluff off her black trousers. Butterflies were gathering in the pit of her stomach.

Was it Sam's kiss… or Sam's baby causing the movement inside her? She wasn't quite sure.

'We need to talk, Sam…'

'Shush, my darling,' he interrupted, sitting beside her and tucking a stray lock of hair behind her ear before stroking her face.

'You are so beautiful, Katie.'

He started to kiss her. Softly. Slowly. Sensually. And, with that, her resolve melted away.

He gently slid her back on the pillows, tracing each of her high cheek bones delicately with his fingers before placing a kiss on them. Brushing his lips lightly on top of hers, he began to unbutton her blouse. She wrapped her legs around him, pulling him closer. Before she even realised it, they were in the throes of making love.

Afterwards, they lay silent, her face buried into his chest. With his eyes closed, Sam gently traced her lower back and rounded hips with his fingertips, marvelling at the dips and curves.

But as Katie lay there, relishing Sam's tender touch, reality started to bite. As much as she wanted to lie there with him forever, she couldn't ignore things. What about the baby? *Their* baby. At that moment, she felt so close to him; telling him felt like the most natural thing in the world.

Then Carol's voice disturbed her thoughts; she knew her friend would go mad if she blurted it out. But maybe Sam could help her. Then again, maybe he would cause her even more problems.

She decided she'd better get dressed and get out of there before doing something else she'd live to regret.

47

Jill took the train from Belfast airport. She was puzzled each time she heard 'Derry-Londonderry' being announced over the tannoy or when she saw it flashed up on the information board. She found herself humming *New York, New York, so good they named it twice…*

Yeah, maybe that's the reason, she thought. This little town in the North of Ireland was so special and unique, they had to name it twice. She smiled to herself, sat back and enjoyed the beautiful scenery on either side of the train.

When she reached her destination, a bus waiting at the train station took her and the other passengers across the bridge to the Cityside. Under the bridge, the River Foyle flowed steadily downstream. To her right, she could see a beautiful footbridge; *that must be the Peace Bridge,* she thought.

Jill had dressed wisely in black skinny jeans and a pair of Skechers. She wore a red padded jacket and a red and black woollen scarf. After pulling into the bus station, she'd made her way to the tourist office to pick up a visitors' map and get directions to the City Hotel; it was only a five-minute walk away. It had been too early to head to the hotel to surprise Sam, so she'd passed an hour in the Tower Museum, nestled within Derry's historic walls, before making her way there.

She arrived outside the hotel at 5.30pm. Walking inside, she scanned around to ensure he wasn't about, then took up a seat in the foyer and ordered a cup of coffee from the waiter. When Sam was away on business, he usually rang her around this time to check in with her before having dinner in whatever hotel he was staying in. She would answer the call as normal as if she were in London; it would enhance the surprise when he made his way to the restaurant and found her sitting there in the foyer.

Excitement bubbled inside her as she kept one eye on the reception and the other on the front entrance. Guests were coming and going and she sat there for half an hour enjoying people-watching as she waited on Sam to call her.

Glancing at her phone to check she had service, Jill wondered why he hadn't called yet. She thought about ringing him, but decided against it; she would wait.

Then, the lift opened. Was this him now? No, it was a woman. As she made her way towards the exit, Jill studied her, thinking she looked vaguely familiar. The woman seemed to look her way for a split second, then turned her face away and walked purposefully to the exit.

Do I know her? Jill thought. But that was impossible; she didn't know anyone from here. It took another few seconds for the penny to drop: it was the Irish girl from the ship.

Katie kept on walking; her eyes fixed on the exit. She couldn't believe Jill was sitting there in the foyer. What was she doing here? Obviously, Sam didn't know! She couldn't get through the revolving door quick enough - Jill had definitely recognised her.

Emerging into the cool evening air, she picked up her phone and rang Sam as soon as she'd turned the corner outside the hotel entrance. No answer. She tried again, but it just rang out. When she got to her car, she sent him a text.

Jill is downstairs in the hotel foyer. She saw me. Ring me back. Please!!!

Back in the hotel, Jill approached the reception desk and explained as nicely as possible that her husband was staying there and she had come to surprise him. The girl behind the desk smiled happily at this lovely gesture and very willingly told

Jill her husband was in room 404.

Upstairs in his room, Sam was finishing his shower, feeling elated from what had just happened between him and Katie. Wrapping a large fluffy towel around himself, he walked into the bedroom. He spotted something shiny on the floor and picked it up; it was one of Katie's earrings. She rarely wore long earrings and it was one of the first things he'd noticed that morning when he arrived at her desk.

There was a sudden rap. He smiled to himself as he opened the door.

'You forget this, darling?' he said, his smile instantly disappearing as he realised that he was dangling Katie's earring right in front of Jill's pale, shocked face.

48

Katie kept glancing at her phone as she drove home. Why hadn't Sam got back to her? Jill was bound to be with him by now. She hoped against hope that Sam's wife would think it was just a coincidence that Katie had been in the hotel.

Well, it is a public place, she thought, trying to calm herself down. She was glad Matt wasn't home when she arrived back. Her heart was pounding but she couldn't phone Carol as Ciaran would be home for his dinner.

She had a quick shower, got dressed in fresh clothes and came downstairs to the kitchen. She checked her phone again; still no messages or missed calls. The lights in the driveway caught her attention; that must be Matt arriving home. As she gathered herself, she heard the car door slam, followed by three persistent rings of the doorbell. She opened the front door, assuming Matt had forgotten his key, but it wasn't her husband... it was Amy's mother.

Sarah Kelly didn't wait to be invited inside, instead pushing her way past Katie and then turning back to face her in the hallway. Katie was dumbfounded; she could hardly believe anyone could be so bold and rude. But, then again, Sarah Kelly had the nerve of Nelson. *She knows,* Katie thought.

'To what do I owe the pleasure?' Katie demanded, standing with her arms folded.

She was in her own territory and had no intentions of being bullied by this hateful old bag.

'I need to talk to you about that son of yours,' Sarah replied, her face like thunder. 'I always knew there was something about him.'

'Now you just hold on one minute,' Katie said, unfolding her arms. 'If you've come over here to judge and criticise my Connor then I suggest you leave right now.' She pointed forcefully at the door.

Sarah didn't move an inch. 'And what about my Amy? She's devastated! She has given that boy of yours two years of her life.'

Her voice was getting louder and her two arms were in full flight as they waved above her head like some kind of lunatic. Katie was glad Matt wasn't at home to witness this, but he was due any minute. She knew she'd have to bring her into the lounge and settle her down a bit. Sarah had come for a battle and Katie needed to defuse it before Matt came home.

'There's no point in us two fighting over this,' Katie said, her tone less bullish now.

'Come in and sit down. I'm expecting Matt home for his dinner shortly and I don't want him coming in to us squealing at one another like a pair of banshees.'

Sarah sniffed loudly and followed Katie into the lounge and sat on the couch. Taking a white cotton handkerchief from her handbag, she dabbed her eyes with it, then spread it across her knee before folding it and pushing it up her sleeve.

'I can see I'm wasting my time here,' she sobbed.

'What exactly do you want me to say, Sarah? Should I tell Connor to waste more of Amy's life? Waste more of his *own* life? On something that's never going to work?'

'Oh, it's all right for you, Katie. Your Connor decides he's queer, and he's all loved-up with some other queer, and my poor Amy is left heartbroken and alone.'

'All right for *me*? Believe it or not, Sarah, it's going to change my life a helluv a lot more than it will change yours.'

'Really? How's that, then?' Sarah Kelly's nostrils were

flaring in anger.

'I was expecting my son to walk his beautiful bride down the aisle. I was expecting a lovely daughter-in-law and a beautiful grandchild. But now there will be no white wedding, will there? My son will have a husband; not a wife. And as for me having any grandchildren; they won't come easily now… if at all.'

Sarah seemed to consider this for a few seconds but was still too wrapped up in her own crisis. She pulled the hanky back down from her sleeve and blew noisily into it.

'Why don't you get your head out of your ass, Sarah?' Katie went on. 'Look at the bigger picture. Do you not think I wouldn't love my Connor to be straight? Of course I would. But I can't change him and he can't change himself. He's never going to make Amy happy and Amy is never going to make him happy. So, believe me when I tell you that I've cried, too.'

The two women sat for another moment in silence before Sarah spoke.

'What's my Amy supposed to do now? She feels like her life is over. She loved that boy of yours.'

'I know it's hard to see your child in pain, Sarah,' Katie said, softer now. 'We're both mothers and only want what's best for them. But they are not compatible. Amy might not see it now, but one day she'll find another man who can make her happy.'

'Yes, well,' Sarah said, checking her watch and rising to her feet. 'I need to go.'

Katie saw her to the door and wished her good luck, glad she'd never have to be in this woman's company again.

She closed her front door, walked back into the living room and picked up her phone. Still no word from Sam. Sick with worry, she rang Carol.

'Well, how did it go?' Carol answered, bright and breezy and relaxing with a glass of wine after her dinner.

'Not good. Oh God, Carol, you're never going to believe it…

when I got out of the lift, Jill was sitting in the foyer.'

'What the fuck?' Carol said, taking a big a gulp of wine.

'She must have wanted to surprise him. Or do you think she was checking up on him? I almost ran out of the building, but I know she saw me. I tried to warn him, but he didn't pick up and I still haven't heard from him.'

'Right. Jesus,' Carol said, searching for something to say. She could hear Katie's panic and fear down the phone and knew she needed reassurance.

'Wait a second, Katie; there's umpteen reasons why you'd have been in that hotel this evening, and - let's face it - that boy could worm his way out of anything. He's probably wining and dining her right now.'

'Maybe,' Katie replied, unconvinced.

'Just let them get on with it. Anyway, I'm more interested in what you said to him. Did you tell him it's over? Hope you held it together and didn't go getting all emotional.'

'Aye, I did what I had to do,' Katie replied. As she spoke, she heard a key turn in the front door.

'Listen, that's Matt home now. I'll chat to you tomorrow, Carol.'

Katie clicked off, wondering how being dishonest was somehow easier than telling the truth.

That's what her life had become… a big bundle of lies.

49

Sam still held Katie's earring in mid-air; but not for long. Jill swiped it from him, and, using the same hand, clenched her fist in rage and swung at him. He just about ducked in time but wasn't quick enough to dodge her second punch, which caught him squarely on the bridge of his nose. He could taste the blood that had dripped onto his upper lip as he staggered backwards.

'What are you up to, you cheating bastard?' Jill screamed, consumed with rage.

Another slap landed on the side of his head as she followed him into the bedroom.

'For Christ's sake, Jill, settle down,' he said, reeling from shock but trying to get his head straight. 'You've got it all wrong. What... why are you even here?'

Whack!

'Stop, please... she's a colleague...she works for me,' Sam shouted, reaching for a tissue from the dresser to wipe his blood-soaked face.

Jill was running around in small circles and squealing, as if she was doing a war dance. Which, he supposed, she kinda was. Suddenly, she stopped and ran to the bed and began pulling at the sheets.

'Why is that pillow flattened?' she demanded, examining it for traces of make-up and sniffing it for traces of perfume. Then, punching the life out of it, she roared, 'I can't believe this! And I know this woman!'

'Jill, stop, you don't understand. She was just... she had to leave some documents for...'

'Hang on,' she interrupted. 'Did you just say she works for you? She fucking *works* for you? I knew it! On the ship... I knew there was something between you two. You made me out to be crazy and paranoid.'

She stood up from the bed, her face ghostly white and her red-rimmed eyes bulging. Her arms fell straight against the sides of her body but her fingers continuously clenched and opened, her eyes darting around the room as if wondering what else she could destroy or hit him with.

Sam was reeling; he had never witnessed her go this ballistic.

'Jill, please,' he pleaded. 'Let me explain. It's not what you think.'

She went to speak, but her tongue stuck to the roof of her mouth. She was starting to wither in front of him. He had to try again.

'Jill, look... I-I didn't want to tell you she was a colleague when we were on the ship. I didn't know she was booked on that trip...' he tried to make it sound plausible but Jill wasn't having it. Her eyes glared at him with a look of disdain and disgust.

'Why couldn't you tell me? What did you have to hide?' Her voice was slow and trembling.

'Nothing. Absolutely nothing. I just... I didn't want to spoil our trip. I knew you'd get upset - you know how your mind plays tricks on you. Jill... *please*.'

'Stop patronising me!' she screamed at him. 'You two are at it, aren't you?'

She leaned over and picked up the earring that was now lying on the bed and threw it at him. 'How do you explain this?'

'I don't know. I-I just saw it lying on the floor,' he stammered. 'Maybe the cleaners missed it.'

Sam quickly scanned the room, hoping nothing else was lying around.

'She was just leaving documents in for me; I'd to sign off on them this evening.'

She looked at him sceptically. 'When you opened the door, you said 'darling'... why would you call her that?'

'It was just a casual expression. I call most women I know 'love' or 'darling'... it doesn't mean anything.'

Spotting his phone on top of the bedside locker, Jill reached for it and pushed it towards him.

'Unlock this!' she barked.

'What? There's nothing on it, Jill.'

'Fucking open it. Now!'

Panicked, he took the phone from her, trying to remember what Katie had said in her last message. There were two missed calls and the message icon was lit up; a new message from 'Work' - his alias for Katie.

'It's just a message from the office,' Sam said, trying his best to sound unfazed.

Snatching the phone from him, she opened the message and started reading it out loud.

'Jill is downstairs in the hotel foyer. She saw me. Ring me back. Please!!!'

She scrolled up the screen to the previous message that Katie had sent and read that one out loud, too. 'I'll meet you after work.'

Sam had deleted all her other messages. He remembered Katie hadn't signed off with xxx; something that had annoyed him at the time but for which he was now extremely grateful.

'Jill, you're reading too much into this. Please, darling, this is all innocent stuff,' he pleaded.

'Why was she worried I saw her? Why didn't she just say hello to me? It doesn't make sense,' Jill persisted. But she was starting to doubt herself. *Maybe it was only a business meeting*, she thought.

'Well, you two didn't exactly get off on the right foot, did you? She was probably shocked to see you because I didn't say you were coming to Derry. I didn't know, did I?'

'Where are the documents she brought you?'

'I put them in the safe,' he said, feeling on slightly firmer ground now. He always carried files with him when he was away on business, so at least this part of his story would stand up. He went over to the safe, punched in the code and lifted out a large folder. 'Here,' he said, handing it to her.

She desperately wanted to believe him… because she desperately loved him. Sam, sensing she was beginning to mellow, cocked his head to one side and smiled lovingly at her.

'That's all this was, Jill. Business, plain and simple. Maybe we can go and have dinner now… what do you think?'

'I'm going for a shower,' she muttered, and began walking towards the bathroom. Suddenly, she stopped, looked straight at him and said, 'This conversation is not over.'

Sam got dressed while Jill showered. When she came back into the bedroom, he did what he normally did after a row and chatted away as if nothing had happened.

'I've a table booked downstairs in half an hour, then we could go and listen to some live music. What you think?'

Jill shrugged a shoulder in answer as she got dressed. *At least she didn't say no*, he thought.

After an awkward dinner together, they walked over to Waterloo Street, the epicentre of Derry's vibrant pub scene.

'That's our bank,' Sam announced proudly as they passed his work's Derry branch, which was on the way. Jill said nothing, but the seed of an idea formed in her brain.

A few minutes later, they were walking into Peadar O'Donnell's, a pub popular with tourists and locals alike. Traditional musicians were doing a live set and, even though it was a Monday night, they were lucky to get a seat.

Before long, Sam was pleased to note, Jill started to loosen up. In contrast to the strained conversation at dinner, she was chatting easily with him now, tapping her foot to the music and swaying along as she sipped her G&T.

The evening went quite well, but Sam knew he wasn't out of the woods yet. When they got back to the hotel, Jill silently got into bed and faced away from him. He placed his arm around her waist and tummy, but she just lay there, motionless, in his embrace.

He lightly kissed her shoulder before turning back to his own space. She hadn't thawed completely yet, but he knew the worst was over. Somehow, he'd managed to get away with it, which was unbelievable, really, given that he'd been pretty much caught red-handed. *God*, he thought, *she really does love me.*

He thought back to Katie telling him they needed to get on with their own lives. He knew she was right but the thought of saying goodbye to her was more than he could bear. He would talk to her again and try to convince her to continue with their relationship; they would just have to be more careful in future.

He knew he was playing with fire, but he just had to be with her.

50

Katie had seen every hour on the clock - from 11pm until 7am - and it hadn't been the wind and rain that had kept her awake. Her phone was charging on the dressing table. As much as she was tempted to get up and check it, fear glued her to the bed. Sam had made no attempt to contact her. No news was good news, she supposed.

She arrived at the bank at 8.30am and was surprised to see Sam and Paul already in the office, deep in conversation.

'Morning,' she smiled falsely, slipping her damp coat off her shoulders.

'Morning, Katie,' they both replied, before Sam continued, 'Good; you're here early. Let me get you a coffee and we'll look over a few things.'

She followed him into the kitchen.

'Sam?' she hissed under her breath, glancing over her shoulder to check Paul was occupied in the main office.

He snapped on the kettle and turned to face her. 'I know, Katie, I know. Look, everything is OK… I just didn't get a chance to get back to you.'

'Have you any idea what you put me through, Sam? You left me totally in the dark; I've been worried sick. *This is not on,* Sam.'

Before he could open his mouth to explain, the door swung open and Ruth walked in, fighting with her umbrella.

'Wow, that's some morning out there. Put my name in the pot,' she called to Katie, not realising Sam was standing nearby.

'Oh, morning, Sam, didn't see you there,' she added, blushing.

The moment to talk having passed them by, Sam exchanged formalities with Ruth before heading back into the office.

Katie had an appointment with a client at 10am and was at her desk, busy collating information and getting forms ready to be signed. The bank's main door opening didn't distract her, but the whiff of Coco Mademoiselle perfume did. Ruth, who was sitting at the first desk, asked the lady who had just walked in if she could help.

'Yes, thank you, I'm just looking for... oh, there she is,' the lady replied, looking directly at Katie.

It was Jill... walking towards her desk. A bolt of fear shot through Katie's stomach and she felt like she may throw up at any second. She was standing in front of her, an unreadable expression on her face. Katie swallowed hard. Her heart was racing but she managed a weak smile.

'Hi, Jill.'

'Oh, so you *do* remember me,' Jill replied, her tone dripping with sarcasm as she dug her hand into a small bag that was slung across the front of her body.

'Just thought you might want this back. What good is one earring to anyone?'

She dropped the earring onto the keypad of Katie's computer and stood there, eyebrow arched. Katie could feel a flush of heat rising under her skin and prayed it wouldn't reach her face. She had to act cool. *Deny, deny, deny!*

Katie lifted the earring and said, casually, 'Nice earring, but it's not mine, I'm afraid. Shall I just bin it... or do you want to ask around?'

Jill remained silent. Katie, confidence returning now, pressed on.

'I'm actually just off to a meeting,' she said, pushing her chair back and standing up, staring defiantly at Jill.

The sound of Paul's office door opening prompted both women to turn their heads; Sam was standing there, looking at them, his hands deep in his trouser pockets and a stony look on his face. Stepping into the main office, he forced a smile.

'Hi, Jill, I'll be another hour or so. Shall I see you back at the hotel at 11.30, say?'

'Fine, I was just passing,' Jill nodded shyly, knowing she had crossed the line.

Katie walked her to the door and held it open for her, aware of the atmosphere in the room. She knew the girls would be dying to know what had just happened but she was confident they hadn't heard their conversation. She would deal with the questions later.

She went into the meeting room and decided she would stay in there until Sam had left. She was seething. While she waited for her client to arrive, she angrily punched out a text to Sam.

You could have warned me... I will never allow myself to be in this position again. We are done.

51

The silence had been deafening on the drive to the airport. Jill had made an attempt to apologise to Sam earlier in the hotel, but he had turned to her and flatly answered,

'That is my place of work and you embarrassed me. You were totally out of order, Jill.'

He was still furious and had no intention of humouring her. And he knew he had blown any chance of keeping his relationship with Katie alive. If Jill hadn't confronted her, he could have passed everything off with a few white lies.

He was also annoyed he hadn't gotten a chance to talk to Katie. Her text had been very blunt… and final. He blamed Jill for that, too. When they got back home that evening, he sent a text to Katie.

I'm so sorry I couldn't text U last night Katie. Yes…Jill saw U… I told her U were leaving off files. She saw the earring but I said it wasn't yours… took a bit of convincing but I thought in the end she believed me…. I had no idea she would show up this morning. Regardless of what U think of me, I did try to protect U, Katie.

Katie's first thought on reading Sam's message was to answer it, but she was still rattling from her earlier encounter with Jill so decided against it. *It's over*, she thought. A relief, of sorts, washed over her.

She lifted her phone and rang Connor. He'd already told her he was staying with a friend from work until he found somewhere to rent and that he'd had a chance to speak with Amy again in an attempt to explain things.

Connor sounded upbeat when he answered his phone, but any time Katie mentioned his friends and colleagues, she could hear panic in his voice.

'I don't know how to tell them, Mum. I don't even know where to start.'

'Once you ring a bell, you can't un-ring it, Con,' Katie answered softly. Connor didn't respond but she could picture his mouth puckering.

'Start by telling the ones you trust. The people who care about you, Con, will accept you for who you are. Remember that old saying: *Those who matter don't mind, and those who mind don't matter.*'

'Aye, hopefully you're right, Mum,' he said, taking a deep breath.

After they said their goodbyes, Katie searched for Amy's number. Though she sounded surprised to be hearing from Connor's mum, she let her speak.

Katie asked how she was feeling and told her she'd been thinking about her a lot and was so sorry for the heartache she was going through.

'Don't beat yourself up, Amy. This is not your fault,' she'd said comfortingly when Amy started to break down and blame herself.

'It's no-one's fault… it just is what it is. You are a strong young woman, Amy, so pull on all that strength now, love. I'm here if you ever want to talk.'

Katie felt drained when she came off the phone, but she wasn't done with the calls yet; next, she had to talk to Carol.

She told her friend about Sarah Kelly calling in with her the night before, then about Jill showing up at work that morning and dropping the earring on her desk - omitting the bit about the lovemaking with Sam.

Carol listened, stunned. She wanted to ask Katie who the owner of the earring was, but thought better of it.

'Jesus, Katie, that makes my day sound like wee buns. Are you alright?'

'Well, the only good thing that has come out of all of this is that I ended it with Sam and he knows it's over... once and for all.'

'You know what?' Carol said, deciding all the gory details could wait, 'I saw a flyer for the Sligo Arms today; they're doing a really good deal on two nights B&B, an evening meal and a spa treatment. It's running until the first weekend of December. Will I book it? Just the two of us... what do you think?'

'I'd love it, Carol. I could do with a nice relaxing time away. The first Friday in December sounds perfect.'

'Right, hon... leave it with me.'

Katie threw herself into her work and the next week flew by. There were no personal calls or texts from Sam, and Paul seemed to be answering most work queries.

Katie signed off the following Friday and Carol picked her up at midday and they set off for Sligo. They drove through a typical Irish winter day of sunshine and blizzards, so the warm and welcoming fire in the hotel foyer that greeted them on their arrival was heartening. The smell of eucalyptus oil unblocked their sinuses and already the girls felt relaxed. Carol had pre-booked their treatments - full body massages at 4 pm - which gave them time to settle in and have a light lunch.

This was just what I needed, Katie thought as the two lounged later that evening in their room, still in the dressing gowns and slippers they'd worn for their luxurious massages. They'd ordered room service for dinner and were now both lying on top of their beds watching TV.

'This was a great idea, Carol,' said Katie, getting up and grabbing a bar of chocolate from the mini-bar fridge and pouring some sparkling Ballygowan water into her white wine to dilute the alcohol.

She pulled back the duvet, puffed up the pillow and climbed under the covers. Carol filled her wine glass and lifted a packed of cheese and onion crisps, then pulled the pillow off her own bed and walked over to Katie's.

'Shove over,' she laughed, as Katie made room in the bed and they both giggled like schoolgirls.

'Don't care what anyone says,' said Carol, licking her fingers, 'it's hard to beat Donegal Tayto crisps and Dairy Milk chocolate. Umm, perfect!'

Then, in a more serious tone: 'So, tell me, hon… what are you thinking?' She gently patted Katie's tummy.

'Aw, I don't know, Carol. My first scan is on the seventeenth; that's less than two weeks away. To be honest, I just pray it'll be like before and I'll lose it, but I've a feeling this wee person is not going to let go.'

'So,' said Carol, 'you're leaving it to the Gods, then?'

'I think so, Carol. My pregnancy is on record at the hospital and I don't know if I can face telling them I want an abortion. This is my home town and you know how word gets out. Even if I got the procedure done elsewhere, they'd still have to be informed.' Katie's voice was shaking.

'Well,' said Carol, 'it would be a lot worse if you and Matt hadn't had sex. You'd have had a lot more explaining to do.'

'Poor Matt.' Katie said, feeling a lump rise in her throat.

Carol took her hand in hers and held it tight. 'I know, Katie. But, for now, let's just enjoy the rest of our time here and we'll worry about all that when we get back to Derry.'

Gripping her hand even tighter, she added: 'Everything will work out… just you wait and see.'

52

Gerry had gotten used to having Connor around this past two weeks. Apart from being good company, he was great with Josie, his mum. She was only 72 and should have been looking forward to many good years ahead, but she was diagnosed with dementia two years ago - a year after Gerry's dad had died - and, almost overnight, this vibrant, healthy woman had become confused, agitated and vulnerable. There were times when Josie would appear completely lucid in her thoughts and actions; then, out of nowhere, she would become forgetful, angry, frustrated and tearful.

When Connor listened to Gerry and witnessed his daily struggles, he felt nothing but admiration for this hard-nosed Scottish man. Gerry talked openly about his fear of not being able to manage and having to put his mum into a care home.

Josie had always told him she didn't want to end up 'in one of those places', but Connor could see he was struggling and the day was probably coming soon; his heart went out to him.

Connor got on great with her. He was very patient with her even though she repeated the same sentences or stories over and over again. He actually enjoyed sitting with her, because, when he encouraged her to tell him stories from her past, that blank stare was replaced by a bright sparkle.

When Connor had told Gerry he and Amy had broken up for good and he was looking for an apartment, Gerry had insisted he stay with him until he got a place.

'Take your time; that room is yours until you get somewhere suitable. I'm sorry you and that wee Amy girl didn't work out, though. You seemed really good together.'

Connor had said nothing more at the time, but now, two weeks on and having grown more comfortable here, he decided tonight was a good time for full disclosure. He looked at Gerry, and then at Josie, who was dozing in her armchair. Gerry was a good friend and he felt he should be honest with him, so he sat down and told Gerry everything.

'Aw, for goodness' sake… I'm coming down with gays!' Gerry laughed out loud.

Connor didn't know what way to take him. 'Sorry?'

'I've a gay brother, a gay uncle and a gay cousin, so, as you can imagine, there were a lot of happy people in our family,' he said, his tone sarcastic but tinged with good humour.

'But you know what, Connor? Everybody got over it. It makes no difference to me what you are,' he said, slapping Connor on the back.

'They say it runs in the family,' Gerry went on. 'Ran past me, though!'

'What ran past you.?' Josie asked, slowly coming around after her nap.

'I'm talking about Uncle Robbie, Mum. He's a sound man, isn't he?'

'Aye, poor Robbie. Sure, he wouldn't say boo to a goose.'

'You've a real soft spot for Robbie, haven't you, Mum?'

'As long as our Robbie is happy, that's all I care about,' Josie said with a soft smile.

Connor could see the love in her eyes as she spoke of her brother; it was the same look of love and concern that radiated from his mum's eyes when he talked about his future. He wondered about Gerry's gay brother: how had Josie reacted to him? Does she even know he's gay? Does she remember? When he got a quiet moment, he asked Gerry.

'Stuart's a few years older than me. Moved up to Aberdeen

about six years ago. He came out to me at Dad's funeral, but we both thought it best not to tell mum at that particular time. Then, there never seemed to be a good time. And now... there's no point. Stuart still comes to see her very six weeks or so. He's a great lad and has a good life up there.'

Connor was glad he'd come out to Gerry. He'd been dreading it but all he'd been met with was acceptance and respect. *If everyone else reacts like this,* he thought, *then maybe this won't be so bad after all.*

Connor had collected his stuff from Amy's and left his key as promised. She'd been out at work when he came. Before leaving, he took one last look at the place. It had been very sparse when they'd moved in a year ago, but all their little touches had turned an empty shell into a comfy home.

He'd looked at their little loveseat; Amy had been crazy for it the minute she'd seen it in the store and it was the first piece of furniture they'd bought together. He remembered how she'd rushed in, full of excitement, with two matching cushions the following week.

He'd walked around the small sitting room, looking at the large collage of photos from their years at uni, and smiled at the memories of those mad nights of loud music and endless shots... but what he had done to her weighed heavy on his chest.

He'd phoned her and, when she hadn't answered, left a message telling her he'd collected his stuff and that he was staying with Gerry for a while. 'I hope you're OK, Amy' he'd said before hanging up.

A few days later, when she'd still not responded to any of his calls or texts, he'd contacted John to see if she was alright.

'Just give her some space, Con,' John had said gently. 'Look, call me any time... I know you're worried about her. I'm keeping a good eye on her; she'll be grand.'

Connor hoped John was right.

53

Katie had left the office at 11am. She'd lied and said she had a dentist's appointment and would be back after lunch. She and Carol were now sitting in the consultant's office in the hospital. Mr Lewis sat across from Katie and asked her how she'd been feeling over the past four weeks.

'I'm keeping well; no problems at all,' she said, placing her hand on Carol's arm and squeezing it lightly. 'This is my friend, Carol. I'd like her to be here for the scan.'

'Of course,' he said reassuringly. 'Now, you think you're about seven weeks pregnant, so today we'll be doing a transvaginal scan; we'll do the abdominal one when you're eleven weeks along.'

The sonographer arrived and invited Katie to pop up on the bed while she set up the monitor.

'This might be a wee bit uncomfortable,' she said, 'but you just keep your eyes on the screen.'

'I can't make anything out… should I be seeing something?' Katie said, anxiously staring at the monitor.

'Well, we're not counting fingers and toes just yet,' the sonographer smiled, 'but look, see right there?' She pointed at the screen.

Katie had to squint to make it out; there was a flickering motion and then she heard a faint beating noise.

'Is that… my baby's heart?' Katie asked, completely awestruck. Carol, who was sitting beside her, squeezed her hand tightly.

'It sure is,' the sonographer beamed. 'Now I'm going to take a crown-to-rump measurement.'

Katie's eyes remained locked on the monitor. Any doubts she'd had about keeping this baby had been instantly swept away by the sight of that tiny heart beating.

'When is my baby due?' she asked.

'Let's see, eight millimetres, which would make you seven weeks... so your due date will be August 4th.'

Afterwards, the girls walked arm in arm down the corridor, Katie still riding on a wave of euphoria. She was having a baby; what she'd always wanted... the rest would work itself out.

'So,' said Carol, once they were sat in the car, 'when are you going to give Matt the good news?'

'I don't know. We're going out tomorrow night but I think I'll leave it another while, you know, just in case. Maybe in the new year, all being well.'

'Aye, maybe so. He'll be over the moon for sure.'

'I know, God help him. Oh, Carol, I hope I'm doing the right thing.'

She inhaled deeply as reality crashed in on her again. She turned to her friend and shook her head.

'All this secrecy... all this lying.'

'Come on, now,' said Carol, taking her hand. 'No fretting. What Matt doesn't know won't harm him.'

Carol started up the car and they drove back into town in silence.

54

Traditionally, Katie and Matt had their own Christmas night out before all the madness of their respective office do's. As they both liked to have a few glasses of wine, they usually stayed local and took a taxi home, but Katie suggested they go across the border into Donegal; to the Railway Tavern in Fahan.

'I just fancy a nice steak from their Firebox grill,' she said as she pulled her black faux leather leggings over her tummy, grateful for the stretch in the fabric and the elastic waistband. Furtively patting her little bump, she added casually, 'so I don't mind driving.'

Matt looked at her somewhat surprised, but said, 'OK, if you don't mind; the tavern it is.'

They sat at the bar near the open fire while they waited on their table, the expensive bottle of Muga Gran Reserva Matt had ordered breathing nicely in a decanter. Once at their table, he started pouring Katie a glass but she held her hand up to stop him.

'I'll just have water for now. I'll keep my wine for my steak; remember I'm driving, honey.'

'Oh, right,' he answered, eyebrow slightly raised as he poured himself a large glass.

It seemed as if work and other commitments had been eating into their days and nights recently, so this was the first time in a while where they could sit down and really talk. As always, the conversation got around to Connor: Matt, ever the pragmatist, focussing on how he was doing at work and if he was on top of his finances; Katie more preoccupied with his emotional wellbeing and how he was coping with all the recent upheaval in his personal life and whether the long-distance romance with Chris would work out.

Matt was chatting away about Connor's current living arrangements, and how his friend Gerry seemed to be a good influence on him, when Katie felt a pair of eyes on her. She lifted her head and saw a pretty girl walking towards her from across the room, all dolled up with grey smoky eyes and bright red lipstick and hair curled loosely around her face.

Matt, who was spreading his chicken liver pate on another piece of delicious sourdough bread, looked up, mid-sentence, and followed her gaze.

'Gosh, she looks different,' he whispered. 'Isn't she that wee nurse who was taking care of you in the hospital?'

Katie shoved her last piece of bread into her mouth and stood up; she needed to head her off at the pass before she reached the table and started congratulating them on the pregnancy.

'Oh, yes,' Katie said to Matt. 'That's Megan, I think her name is. I must go say hello and thank her for looking after me.'

Leaving Matt with a puzzled expression as she strode off to meet the young nurse. She barely got a few steps away from the table, however, before Megan was upon her. Katie could tell by the glassiness of her eyes that she'd already had a few drinks; she tried to pull a 'say nothing' face but knew the signal would be missed in her current intoxicated state.

Placing her hand on Katie's arm, she squealed, 'I couldn't believe it when I heard…' Katie was cringing inside; there was no way Matt wouldn't hear.

'Oh, so nice to see you again… how are you doing?' Katie said, desperately trying to redirect the conversation. It was a waste of time.

'No, how are *you*? You're looking great. Are you keeping well?

'I am *so* happy for you…'

Matt hadn't been paying too much attention to the pleasantries being passed between the two women but his ears perked up when he heard this last line.

'You're not really showing yet, are you?' Megan went on. *Now* he was paying attention.

Katie shot round towards him in trepidation. He was afraid to jump to wild conclusions, but he looked at Katie's full wine glass and then at her almost empty water glass… and suddenly the penny dropped.

His mind was now like a projector flashing back over the last few weeks: Katie looking pale; Katie not sleeping; Katie crying at nothing; Katie always seeming preoccupied. He had tried to put it down to Connor's disclosure and the worry it was causing her - causing them both - but he'd sensed there was something else going on. And here it was: Katie was obviously pregnant.

A lump formed at the back of his throat as he looked up at her. Here was this amazing woman, in the middle of everything else, trying to keep it a secret from him; trying to protect him from the pain and sadness should she suffer yet another miscarriage.

Noticing Matt's surprised expression, realisation finally dawned on the young nurse.

'Oh dear… I'm so… oh God… I didn't know it was a secret…'

Matt rose to his feet, his eyes glistening with emotion. Placing his large hand tenderly on Katie's tummy, he said, 'Is this right? We're pregnant?'

'I just wanted to be sure, honey,' Katie said, half squirming.

But Matt pulled her to him forcefully.

'I have big broad shoulders. You should have told me… you didn't have to carry this by yourself, my love.'

Wishing Megan a very happy Christmas, he turned to Katie and kissed her forehead, then led her back to the table.

'Come on, we better get you fed,' he said, beaming. 'I feel like the happiest man alive. Happy Christmas, my darling… please God, it will be OK this time.'

Katie's clinked her glass to his and smiled… and said a silent prayer of her own that he would never, ever find out the truth.

55

It was Christmas Eve. Connor had arrived back in Derry earlier that day and, after checking in with his mum and dad and grabbing a quick shower and change, was out having a few drinks with his mates.

He was enjoying the relaxed and festive atmosphere in the pub. John had told him Amy couldn't face going home to Derry for Christmas, so her parents were spending it with her in Glasgow. Although Connor was loaded with guilt, he also felt relief knowing he wouldn't be bumping into her. They'd spoken a few times on the phone - outstanding bills and the like - but the conversations were to the point and never strayed into pleasantries. He hoped and prayed that time would make things easier between them.

He glanced at his watch; it was 11.30pm. Finishing off his pint, he stood up and pulled his coat off the back of his barstool.

'Hey, where are you going?' his mate Rory shouted over to him. 'I'm just about to get another round in.'

'Told my mum I'd be home for midnight,' Connor lied.

'For fuck's sake, lad, we haven't seen you in a year. Tell your ma you got into bad company. Same again,' Rory said, nodding to the barman.

'No, seriously,' Connor said, slipping on his coat. 'You boys stay and enjoy the craic and sure I'll see you all on Boxing Day. Happy Christmas.'

He made it home just before midnight and grabbed his mum at the front door in a playful hug. He thought her very drawn and tired when he'd arrived home earlier that day, but when he'd mentioned it to his dad, he'd just shrugged his shoulders and muttered something about it being down to the usual stresses of Christmas.

With his mum still in his embrace, his phone rang; he instantly let her go and dug his hand into his jeans pocket. When she saw his face light up, Katie had no need to ask who was calling him at this time of night.

'Go on - give Chris my love,' she smiled, before going back to curl up on the couch beside Matt; they were watching *It's a Wonderful Life*. Looking at the clock on the mantelpiece, Matt put his arm around her.

'Happy Christmas, my love. Life *is* wonderful, isn't it?' he said, lightly patting her tummy.

'It is. Happy Christmas, honey,' Katie replied, swallowing hard and burying her face into Matt's chest.

Connor was already halfway up the stairs when he answered Chris' call. 'Hello, you,' he said, unable to keep the smile from spreading across his face.

'Hey, man, you home? I'm in my room.'

'Yeah, just heading into my bedroom now.'

'Can we FaceTime?'

'Absolutely.' Connor took a quick glance in the mirror and ran his fingers through his hair before accepting the FaceTime request.

'There you are,' Chris said appreciatively. 'Happy Christmas, buddy. You look like a little Irish Rudolph with your *wee* red nose.'

'Well, I rushed home hoping to speak to you,' Connor said, rubbing the end of his nose with the palm of his hand. 'It's bloody freezing here!'

'It's hot as hell here but I'd swap that in a heartbeat to be there with you. Listen, Connor,' Chris said, his tone slightly nervous now, 'I've an idea…'

'Sounds dangerous,' Connor interrupted. 'The last idea you had got me into a lot of trouble.'

Chris smiled at the memory of the two of them in Rome, then went on. 'I'll be in New York in eight days' time. Could you come over? Even for a long weekend? You could meet my family.'

Connor's heart soared, then immediately sank; he'd be due back at work by then and couldn't possibly ask for more time off.

Unless… Gerry was due to work December 28th through to January 2nd. He'd tried to swap with someone so he could have an extra-long Christmas with his mum, but he'd had no joy with his workmates. Connor had offered to work it for him but Gerry knew he'd already booked his flights to Derry and wouldn't hear of it.

'If I go back to Glasgow early and cover Gerry's shifts,' he excitedly said to Chris, 'I should be able to get away the following week.' Connor stopped momentarily and wondered if his mum would be annoyed at him cutting his visit short but he quickly decided she wouldn't mind at all; his happiness meant everything to her.

It was decided: he would phone Gerry in the morning.

56

Connor walked through the arrivals hall at JKF airport and felt his heart skip a beat when he spotted Chris there waiting for him. He was wearing a New York Yankees baseball cap and holding up a sign up that read *Mr Connor Cully*. Laughing, Connor strode quickly towards him and Chris let the sign fall to the floor as the two men hugged each other tightly.

'Hey, man, you look amazing,' Chris said with a broad smile. 'Can't believe you're finally here.'

'I can't quite believe it myself,' Connor said, reaching for Chris' hand and squeezing it. 'My nerves are all over the place.'

'Come on, let's get you out of here,' said Chris, leading him towards the car park. 'Betsy is waiting for us.'

Betsy? Connor thought, confused. He was pretty sure Chris' sister was called Grace.

'Who's Betsy? Is someone picking us up?'

'No... here she is,' said Chris, tapping the roof of a sporty black jeep which had a silver italic decal on the windscreen that read *Betsy*.

'I always name my cars,' he laughed.

'Oh, right,' Connor said, smiling. 'Thought you were going to drop a bombshell on me, there.' Was he imagining it, or did Chris stiffen slightly when he said that?

They pulled out of the airport and made their way towards the city. At first, Connor was slightly disappointed by how suburban the landscape looked, but as soon as they approached the 59th St Bridge, the New York he knew from the movies unfurled before him.

Chris smiled to himself as he watched Connor's eyes widen with excitement at New York's trademark sights: the yellow taxis - horns blasting - darting between lanes, the impressive Chrysler and Empire State buildings, the hustle and bustle of Central Park with people jogging and roller-skating, or grabbing hotdogs and pretzels from the food carts that stood on every street corner. Connor was buzzing. *New York definitely lives up to the hype*, he thought.

Chris pulled into an underground car park and they took the elevator to the fifth floor Airbnb apartment he had booked especially for Connor's visit. After they'd both freshened up, they walked the short distance to Tao, an Asian fusion restaurant on East 58th St.

After enjoying a cocktail at the bar, their waiter led them into the dining room whose main feature was a massive gold Buddha who sat majestically against the back wall, as if inviting everyone into his home.

The staff were so friendly and articulate as they explained the delicious dishes before taking their order. A waiter carried a bottle of champagne Chris had ordered previously and they got a cheer from a nearby table when the cork was popped. As they clinked glasses, Connor thought how lucky he was to be sitting here in this amazing place, with this wonderful man; he had never felt happier.

As the next few hours flew by, jetlag began to set in. Chris had booked a show for them for later that evening but one look at Connor's heavy eyelids told him it would be best to take a rain check.

Back at the apartment, Connor nodded off to sleep, fully dressed, on the large double bed. He looked exhausted, Chris thought. Realising he would probably sleep right through, Chris switched off the lamp and quietly slipped into bed beside him.

During the night, the rain battered the windows and Connor's deep breathing gradually changed to a light snore, then a bolt of lightning followed by a roar of thunder woke him out of his sleep. He momentarily forgot where he was until he felt the light pressure of Chris' lips on his; gentle, at first, then intensifying as both men responded to each other's growing desire. In that moment, time stopped and there was only the present: two hearts beating, naked flesh touching, mind and body in total harmony.

When they woke early next morning, their fingers were still entwined.

57

That morning, as they enjoyed coffee and toast at the marble breakfast bar, Chris rambled on about what he had planned for the day.

He seems a bit on edge, Connor thought. *I hope he isn't getting cold feet about us.* Last night had been amazing - at least, it had been for him... but what if Chris didn't feel the same?

No, he was being silly; Chris was just eager to make sure Connor had a good time in New York and that's why he was a bit nervy this morning.

'Hey, it's all good,' he smiled, rubbing Chris' forearm. 'I'm happy doing whatever. Even just walking around is good; this whole city is amazing.'

Chris didn't respond. Instead, he placed his coffee cup on the counter and ran his finger around the rim, deep in thought.

Connor observed him silently. He hadn't seen this side of Chris before; he was always so calm, so positive, so confident, but whatever his brain was processing right now, he seemed anything but.

Chris put his elbows on the counter and, lowering his head, rubbed his forehead with his fingertips, then continued to draw his fingers over the hollow of his cheekbones down to the corners of his mouth. He stopped and looked up at Connor.

'Con,' he said, his voice trembling slightly, 'there's someone I want... I *need* you to meet.'

'Only one?' Connor teased, though his stomach was doing summersaults. 'And there's me thinking I was meeting your whole clan.'

But Chris didn't smile. 'Look, it's a long story, Connor, and please don't be angry at me for not telling you sooner… it's just… I wanted to tell you in person.'

'Tell me what, Chris? Who do I need to meet?' Connor said, terrified about what the answer might be.

Chris straightened up and took Connor's hand in his. After a deep breath, he looked him straight in the eye and continued.

'Con, the person I want you to meet is… is my three-year-old daughter.'

Connor's eyebrows furrowed in confusion.

'What? Sorry, did you just say you have… a daughter?' Connor pulled his hand away from Chris in total disbelief.

'And you're only telling me this now?' He got up and walked over to the window, then stopped and looked back at Chris, who sat with his head in his hands.

'I bared my soul to you over these past few months, Chris. Don't you think this is something you should have told me? What the fuck?'

He turned back towards the window but his eyes were in a trance. Then, the worst-case scenario came flooding into his mind and he angrily turned back to his lover.

'After you convinced me to do the right thing and break up with Amy, now you're telling me you have a family?'

Chris just sat there, wanting to speak but no words came out.

'Aw, Jesus,' Connor went on, 'don't tell me you still have a girlfriend… or a wife? Why did you even bring me here, for fuck's sake?'

'No, Connor,' Chris said firmly. 'I absolutely do not have a girlfriend or a wife. I have a daughter from a one-night stand with an old college girlfriend; I didn't even know about her until she was three months old.'

When Connor didn't respond, he went on. 'What started off

as a complete nightmare turned out to be a wonderful blessing. Carrie is the best thing that has ever happened to me... and I was blessed again the day you walked into my life.'

He got up and walked slowly towards him, but Connor didn't turn around, so he just stood behind him and put his forehead on his upper back.

'Please, Connor.'

'I had dreams of why you asked me here,' Connor said tonelessly, still facing the window. 'I thought it was to move things along. I thought that... that maybe we had a future together. And now you're telling me you have another life.'

'No, Connor, you're not hearing me. I love you, man. You are a part of my life... but so is my little girl.'

Chris placed both hands on Connor's shoulders and turned him round to face him.

'I've plenty of room in here for the both of you,' he said, placing the palm of his hand against his chest. 'Connor, please let me explain.'

Weak with shock and disbelief, he meekly let Chris walk him to the couch, where he sat and listened.

Chris had befriended a girl called Debbie halfway through his second year at college. She was a loner and rarely spoke to anyone, but he sat beside her in the canteen one day and things grew from there: she eventually started opening up about her mother dying when she was young and how she, an only child, was stuck at home with a drunk for a father.

The more he got to know her, the more he got to like her; before long, they were hanging out at her run-down apartment most weekends when her dad was off on a bender somewhere. Debbie introduced him to vodka, weed - and sex (Chris was only 18 and still working out who he was).

The relationship petered out after they finished college. Chris moved on to the Maritime Academy and he didn't see her again for four years, when he bumped into her on a night out in Manhattan with his fellow graduates from the academy.

He could see that drink and drugs had really taken hold of Debbie in the years they'd been apart, but he went off with her that night to a house party, in a dingy basement apartment in Queen's, for old times' sake. At some point, in the middle of all the joints being smoked and liquor being drunk, Debbie reached out to him; though he had long since worked out he was gay, he gave her the physical comfort she sought.

They went their separate ways the next morning, but a year later, while he was out at sea, his sister Grace called to say social services had been in touch: a woman called Deborah Knox had died after taking a heroin overdose. Chris was shocked and saddened to hear of Debbie's death... but more shocked still when Grace went on to say social services were trying to locate the father of Debbie's three-month-old baby girl and that her flatmate had given them Chris' details.

Chris was granted leave to return to New York, where he underwent a paternity test that confirmed he was the father. It was arranged that he would have a visit with little Carrie - in a playroom in the social services department; the minute he set eyes on her, Chris knew right there and then that he wanted to be a proper father to his child.

Over the next few weeks, and with the promise of support from his parents and sister, he underwent a series of evaluations which resulted in the social worker submitting a report to the family court recommending that the state transfer care of Carrie to her biological father.

Their lives had been turned upside down, but Chris' family rallied round and came to the rescue. Grace and her husband Ted were not blessed with children and they adored little Carrie, while his mum, unable to believe she had a grandchild, eagerly helped out, too.

Chris went back to his career on the ocean while continuing to build a bond with his baby girl through FaceTime; when he came home on leave, he spent every second with his beautiful daughter so that they could strengthen that bond in person.

'And that's my story, Con,' said Chris. 'I understand it's a lot to take in, but when you meet my little Carrie she'll melt your heart - they *all* will. Mum, Dad, Grace; they're all dying to meet you.'

'Yeah,' said Connor, 'I'm sure they are.' He rose from the couch. 'I need to take a shower; clear my head a bit.'

'Sure. I'll phone Mom, shall I? Tell her we're good for Sunday lunch tomorrow?'

'I guess so,' said Connor, walking into the bathroom and locking the door behind him. He sat on the edge of the toilet and ran through everything Chris had said.

He knew deep down that Chris would never purposely hurt him; his reasons for not telling him were valid enough. Some things are better being told face to face. He realised he'd reacted that way because he loved this man and was terrified of losing him. He stood up and opened the bathroom door.

'You OK?' Chris asked softly.

'I'm sorry for shouting at you, Chris,' Connor replied. 'And I'm sorry for being so selfish. I had no right.'

Connor bowed his head for a second, then lifted it before continuing.

'Of *course* you had a life before me. For sure, it's a shock to hear about Carrie, and I wish you'd told me earlier, but I understand why you waited until now. The bottom line is that I don't want to lose you.'

Relief flooded Chris' face. 'I don't want to lose you either, Con. I'm sorry; I should have told you from the start. But, we're good, man…*right?*'

'Yeah,' said Connor. 'We're good. I must get that shower.'

'Want some company?' Chris asked with a glint in his eye.

Connor walked through the bathroom door and left it invitingly ajar.

58

Connor and Chris spent the perfect Saturday together in New York, taking in the sights before enjoying a romantic boat ride in Central Park followed by a late lunch at the park's legendary Boat House restaurant. They'd taken in so much of the city that, by five o'clock, Connor thought he was going to collapse - but Chris was having none of it.

'A quick power nap, then we're right back out again,' he said when they'd got back to the apartment.

'This city is going to kill me,' Connor joked. 'I'm almost afraid to waste time sleeping in case I miss anything.'

That evening, they went to the Duplex Piano Bar in Greenwich Village.

Connor had never enjoyed nor experienced a night like it; though it was a gay bar, there were just as many straight people there enjoying the talented singers, who would unexpectedly sprout out from any corner of the bar - most of them in drag - and burst into song or dance.

Everyone, no matter what persuasion, laughed and sang along. It was such a welcoming and accepting environment; as he sat there, he thought about how far he'd come since that night in the living room of his parents' house when he thought his whole world was about to come crashing down around him.

Connor woke up at 5.30am on Sunday and couldn't get back

to sleep. He was anxious about meeting Chris' family and wondered what they would think of him. What if Carrie didn't take to him? He was embarrassed, too, about having to sleep with Chris in his parents' home.

Quietly, he slid out of bed and went into the kitchen to make himself a cup of tea, then turned to observe Chris through the bedroom door. He lay there, face down, his broad shoulders bare and the white bedsheet tucked around his narrow waist, outlining his perfect buttocks and strong legs. He began to stir and sleepily spread his arm across the bed. Realising Connor wasn't there, he looked up in surprise.

'Hey, you're up early,' he said, checking his watch. 'You OK?'

'Yeah, fine,' Connor sighed deeply. 'Well, to tell you the truth, I'm feeling pretty anxious about meeting everyone for the first time.'

'No way, Connor. You have absolutely no worries there. My family are the most easy-going people I know. They're awesome and they're going to love you.'

'OK,' said Connor. 'Do you think I should get Carrie a wee present?'

'She's mad about those LOL dolls,' said Chris. 'We'll grab one at the toy store on the way and she'll be your friend for life! Now, come back to bed; it's lonely in here.'

A few hours later, Chris pulled his jeep into the driveway of a beautiful grey-cladded range-style house. Chris' mum, already on the doorstep, slung her tea towel over her shoulder and walked down the steps to greet them.

She hugged Chris first, then turned to Connor, who was standing with his hands in his jeans pockets, looking awkward. She linked her arm through his and kissed his cheek.

'It's really nice to meet you, Connor. I've heard so much about you that I feel I know you already.'

'It's lovely to meet you too, Mrs O'Malley.'

'Oh no; call me Beth,' she smiled. 'Come on inside and meet Joe before the others arrive.'

As they made their way down the hallway, Chris' dad came out of the kitchen to greet them. He was chewing on a piece of turkey and holding another slice in his hand.

'Just finished carving,' he shouted in a jolly voice. 'Hey, son, how's it going?' He hugged Chris to him and slapped his back.

'And this must be Connor,' he said, pulling him into a bear hug as if he'd known him all his life. 'Come on into the living room and get those heavy coats off; the fire's blazing in here.'

Ten minutes later, as Chris was putting more logs on the fire, the door burst open and a high-pitched yell filled the room. 'Daddy!'

The little girl ran over to Chris just as he turned around to meet her.

'Hey, baby girl!' Chris' face lit up brighter than Connor had ever seen before. Her grandparents fussed over her, too, kissing her face and leaning in for a hug as Chris held her in his arms.

The door opened again and Grace walked in.

'I didn't dare tell her you were here,' she said, walking over to her brother and giving him a hug, 'cos she would have driven me crazy to get here sooner.'

Connor stood up and offered her his hand. 'Lovely to meet you, Grace.'

Ignoring his hand, she pulled him into a tight squeeze and kissed his cheek. 'Lovely to meet you, at last.'

By now, Carrie had wriggled her way out of her dad's arms and was studying Connor with a child's curiosity.

'Daddy's friend Connor has a nice present for you, Carrie,' said Chris in encouragement.

Connor picked up the bag that held the LOL doll and knelt down to Carrie's level as she cautiously approached him.

'Hello, Carrie,' he smiled. 'Aren't you just beautiful?'

But Carrie was more interested in what was inside the bag; she pulled it out of Connor's hand and ripped it open.

'Oh, Mama Grace, look!' she ran to her aunt, waving the doll at her.

'You better give Connor a big hug for that lovely gift,' Grace said, smiling.

Carrie turned back to Connor, looking at him with her head slightly bowed. In a shy, soft voice, she said, 'Thank you, Connor.'

Then she leaned her little face against his shoulder and Connor thought his heart was going to burst.

Grace's husband Ted joined the gathering and they all settled down to eat. Everyone clinked glasses and welcomed Connor to their home, but it was little Carrie who stole the show at the dinner table. She gave everyone their full title: Grandma Beth and Grandpa Joe, Mama Grace and Papa Ted. *There is so much love around this table,* Connor thought in awe.

When it came to Carrie's bedtime, Chris lovingly picked her up, enjoying every minute of being the proud, doting daddy. Everyone in turn got their goodnight kiss from her, and, when it came to Connor, she kissed him and immediately turned to Chris and said, 'I like your friend, Daddy.'

Everyone looked at each other and laughter broke out.

'What can I say?' said Chris, gazing straight at Connor, 'My baby girl is the smartest kid in the world and she's got great taste, too!'

For the second time that evening, Connor felt his heart would burst.

59

It was early February. Connor had settled into a routine since coming back to Glasgow from New York: work during the day, a bite to eat with Gerry in the evening (usually off of trays in the living room) then upstairs to his room for a lengthy phone call or FaceTime, if Chris' work schedule allowed it. He missed him terribly but accepted this was the way it had to be for now.

Life had changed dramatically for Gerry over the last few weeks. Connor had arrived home from New York to be told by his friend that his mum had fallen down the stairs the night after Connor had left for America. By chance, Amy had been in the house at the time - dropping off post for Connor - and she went straight into nurse mode, ringing the ambulance and making sure Josie was in the recovery position and as comfortable as possible until the ambulance arrived. She'd even gone to A&E with them.

Although she'd not broken any bones, the fall had had a severe impact on Josie's overall health, and the medical care team, along with her social worker, urged Gerry to strongly consider moving her into a care home.

It was a devastating thing to hear, but Gerry had known in his heart that he had reached the stage where he could not provide adequate care for his mum at home. Within a matter of days, a spot became available at a facility not too far out of the city and Josie had been transferred there directly from the hospital.

The house wasn't the same without her, Connor thought - and Gerry definitely wasn't the same without her. Even though he was forthright in telling others that his mum was in the best place, Connor knew he was struggling with the fact he couldn't look after her any more. All he seemed to do these days was to go to work and then to the care home. Connor thought a change of scene might do him good and suggested Gerry go with him to Ireland for his mum's birthday celebration that weekend.

'Aw, why don't you come home with me, Gerry?' he pleaded. 'It's just two days. We can get the 7pm flight to Derry after work on Friday and back Sunday night. It'll be good craic; Mum is dying to meet you.'

But Gerry made every excuse under the sun as to why he couldn't go.

'And anyway, I can't; Amy's coming to the care home with me on Saturday afternoon to see Mum.'

Connor was slightly taken aback at this. He'd often asked if he could visit Josie but Gerry never seemed too keen, saying it was best to wait until she was more settled. He was a bit thrown by the introduction of his ex-girlfriend into this scenario and Gerry noticed his reaction.

'Amy keeps in touch, you know,' he said evenly. 'She's always asking about Mum. I owe her big time. If it wasn't for her, on the night that mum fell… God only knows what would've happened.'

'Aw, no problem,' said Connor. 'I just didn't know you guys were so friendly.'

'Aye, she's a nice girl, is Amy.'

Connor looked over at Gerry with a quizzical expression.

'Now, don't be getting the wrong end of the stick, Con,' Gerry said. 'Me and Amy are just friends. To tell you the truth, my biggest plan right now is trying to get you two back on good speaking terms again.'

'I'd like that, too,' Connor replied. 'What I did… the pain I caused her… I know I can't undo any of it, but I really want her to be OK, you know?'

'Aw, I know, man,' Gerry said. 'And she is doing better. She has a flatmate now; a girl called Hannah who works as a nurse in the hospital; moved here from Aberdeen last month and was needing a room. Really lovely girl, actually.'

He hesitated for a few seconds before continuing: 'And... Amy's started seeing someone... a doctor from her work... Greg, his name is.'

'Oh, right,' said Connor. 'I'm pleased.'

And he genuinely was.

60

When Connor arrived back in Derry that Friday night, Carol was in the house watching a movie with his mum. Katie pressed pause the minute she heard the door opening and the two women got up to hug him, firing questions at him as if they hadn't seen him in a lifetime.

Ten minutes later, Matt returned from the pub and the living room was a hive of chatter as he welcomed his son back and they all discussed the plans for Katie's birthday the following day. In the middle of it all, Katie felt a strong kick in her tummy; she immediately put her hand on the exact spot and her eyes lit up. Matt looked over at her.

'Is that what I think it is?' he asked, all smiles. She turned to look at Connor, and Carol, sensing what was about to happen, said, 'This feels like a special family moment; maybe I should go.'

'You will not,' said Katie, taking her arm with her spare hand.

Connor looked at all three of them. 'What's up?'

'Go on,' Matt nodded to Katie, 'tell him our good news.'

Connor could see the excitement and joy in all their faces and guessed what was coming, but he also thought, *no way*; his mum was just about to celebrate her 44th birthday, after all, and he'd been an only child this last 20-odd years.

'Connor,' said his mum, 'you're getting a new wee brother or sister.'

His mouth fell open in shock and all he could say was, 'Wow!' He'd actually planned on telling his parents about Chris having a daughter, never thinking for one second that he'd be hearing this news from them.

'So, when is the baby due?' Connor asked, still feeling a bit weird about this new arrival.

'Not until August,' Katie answered quickly, purposely not saying if it was the start, middle or end of that month.

Matt had gone to the kitchen and came back with a beer for himself and Connor.

'Here, son,' he said, handing him the bottle. 'What do you think of that news?' He couldn't keep the smile off his face.

'Great,' Connor replied, secretly thinking his parents were a bit too old for an addition to the family. 'It'll keep you guys on your toes, that's for sure.'

'Aye, sure it will keep us young, too,' his dad answered.

Katie, desperate to steer the chat away from the pregnancy in case Connor honed in on specific dates, changed the subject.

'How's things in Glasgow?'

'Yeah, all good. Couldn't get Gerry to come over, but he promised next time. He's not ready to leave his mum right now.'

'That must be so hard for him but he is best sticking to his routine,' said Katie. 'Things can change very quickly with dementia patients. And how's Chris doing? How's the studying going?' she continued, grass-hopping from one subject to another.

'He's sounding a bit stressed, alright, but we had a few great days together so he has his work head on him now.'

'I'm sure you'll be back over there the first chance you get,' Carol said. She looked at her godson with a mixture of love and pride and said, 'Ach, Katie, our own wee Derry Yank!'

'Stop, Auntie Carol,' Connor said with mock embarrassment.

'So, where're we off to tomorrow? The Red Door?'

'Absolutely,' said Matt, looking adoringly at Katie. 'A special place for a special lady.'

61

It had been almost three months since Sam had visited the Derry branch. There was nothing unusual about that, but because of what had happened between him and Katie the last time they'd met, it had felt like an eternity for Sam.

He had purposely kept his distance in an effort to keep on Katie's good side. She had been adamant it was over between them and he had respected her wishes; their phone conversations remained formal and he'd resisted the temptation to send her any texts.

But he had stayed away long enough and it was time to show his face; he'd been at a meeting in the Belfast branch this morning and had then driven to Derry.

Sam steered his hire car into the small car park at the rear of the bank. It was a typically wintry, February day, and morning fog had caused his flight from London to be delayed by two hours. A light dusting of snow was beginning to fall as he zipped up his Ted Baker overcoat and hurried to the entrance. Opening the office door, he noticed that Katie's work station lay empty, her chair pushed up tight against the desk. His shoulders sagged with disappointment.

'Hi, Sam, you made it,' Paul said, walking out of his office to greet him. 'Hardly worth your while at this stage.'

'Yeah, bloody weather,' Sam replied. 'Anyway, I'll get caught up here after you all leave.' He unzipped his coat and welcomed the blast of heat.

'It's freezing out there… is there a coffee going?'

'Sure, on its way,' Ruth said, pushing her chair back from her computer and walking into the small kitchen.

'Katie still off? Not like her.' Sam tried to sound casual as he placed his briefcase down.

'Poor Katie,' Ruth shouted from the kitchen. 'It's not looking good - especially with her past history.'

'Past history?' Sam tried to conceal the worry in his voice.

'Aw, you know, just with what happened with her previous pregnancies…' Ruth said, stirring instant coffee into a mug of boiling water.

Sam looked at her, clueless, so Ruth explained further.

'Katie's in hospital; taken in this morning. They did a wee procedure today. Aw, I hope it works and she doesn't lose the wee baby. She's not even four months yet; we're all keeping the prayers going.'

Katie's pregnant? He was reeling inside, but when he looked back at Ruth, he noticed she was watching him intently. He needed to gather himself.

'Has someone organised flowers?' It was the first thing that came into his head as he tried to camouflage his anxiety.

'No, well, it all happened very quickly,' Ruth replied. Katie phoned on Monday to say she wasn't feeling too well and needed to stay in bed. And then she was taken to Altnagelvin Hospital this morning. She's on a drip and they're monitoring her. Please God, it will be OK.'

Sam gripped the cup tightly as he took a sip of coffee. All he wanted to do was run out of the place and go straight to Katie's bedside. He looked at his watch; it was only 4.30. He composed himself and walked towards his office.

'Poor girl,' he muttered. 'I've a few calls to make, so if you all want to shoot off early, feel free.' The staff, Paul included, didn't have to be told twice. They switched off their computers, gathered their belongings and wrapped themselves up against the flurry of snow that was starting to land outside.

When everyone had left, Sam took his last gulp of coffee and thought about his next course of action. He had to see her. But if he rang through to the hospital, they'd hardly give him information on Katie's condition, never mind what ward she was on. They were really strict about those sorts of things these days.

Screw it, he thought. *I'll drive over there and work it out when I get there.*

He ran out the door of the bank, hastily locked the main door with the spare keys Paul had left him, then jumped into his car. It was approaching rush hour and traffic was slowing up; it seemed like every traffic light was against him. After what seemed like an eternity, he pulled into the hospital car park and took the first available parking spot, then jumped out of the car and ran towards the entrance.

Once inside the foyer, he scanned the large board listing the names of all the various wards and departments. *Ward 5... Antenatal unit... she could be in that one,* he thought. He followed the signs for the lifts, jumped in and pressed 5. It hadn't dawned on him until that very moment that her husband might be there with her. A wave of panic hit him. Sam knew he would recognise Matt from the family photo Katie kept on her desk at the bank, but he hoped Matt didn't know what he looked like. The lift stopped and he got out. The door to the ward was closed; a buzzer and intercom were fixed to the adjoining wall. As luck would have it, a nurse came out of the ward as he was about to press the buzzer.

'Can I help you?' she asked him.

'Yeah, I was hoping to see a close friend before I get my flight back to London,' he said, using the authoritative but friendly tone that had served him so well his entire adult life.

'Hmm, well, visiting isn't until seven,' she answered, checking the upside-down watch on her uniform. But he knew by her sympathetic tone that he had won her over.

'Who are you visiting?'

'Katie Cully.'

'I think she's in Room E... fifth door down... make it quick,' she smiled, buzzing him in.

'You're a star,' he said, flashing her his best smile.

'Safe flight home,' she added, in a tone that was unmistakeably flirtatious.

Sam walked down the corridor, slowing down as he approached Room E. Inside, a man with his back to him was sitting on a chair, blocking the view of the person in the bed. As he hovered in the corridor, he saw the man get up and lean over to kiss the patient. Whoever he was, he looked as if he was about to leave.

Sam walked a few metres beyond the open door and then stopped, pretending to be taking a phone call. Even if the man was Matt, he would only see Sam's back as he left the room. A few seconds later, he heard steps. He waited a beat or two, then stole a furtive look up the corridor, where the man who had just left Room E was going out through the main ward door.

Sam put his phone away and walked back to the room. He looked through the window... and there she was. Katie was lying on the bed, her eyes closed and her hands placed across her tummy. Sam walked slowly into the room. He was shaking.

'Katie,' he whispered.

Her eyes flew open and a look of panic flashed across her face.

'Sam! What are you doing here?'

'I had to see you. I... I need to talk to you.'

Now that he was here, he didn't know how to approach this. He didn't really have the right to ask the question he was about to ask, yet he had to know the answer.

He rolled his fingers one at a time into a clenched fist and slowly released them again until he got the nerve up. He had to bite the bullet.

'I've just found out that you're pregnant. Is… is the baby mine?'

'You can't be here, Sam,' Katie said. 'Matt's gone to get me something to eat; he'll be back any minute.' She closed her eyes and flung her head back onto her pillow in despair.

'Please, Sam, just leave me alone.'

But Sam was going nowhere. He sat on the edge of the bed and unzipped his coat; the sweat was pouring down his back at this point.

Katie felt his eyes boring into her and she looked up at him. Part of her wanted to tell him the truth, but the consequences would be too severe. She needed to protect Matt… and her baby.

'Sam, the baby is not yours,' she lied. 'I'm three months pregnant and I'm most likely going to lose it; I have before - *loads* of times. They've put stitches around my cervix to try and prevent a miscarriage but there are no guarantees it will work.'

But Sam had stopped listening after 'I'm three months pregnant'. It *had* to be his. The timing was too much of a coincidence. He looked at her, disbelief written all over his face.

Katie could tell what he was thinking but she didn't have a choice: no good would come out of the truth.

'You need to leave, Sam. *Now*,' she said, with as much force as she could summon. 'I'm not supposed to have any stress. Please, forget about me and forget about what happened between us. It was a big mistake.' Then, her voice breaking, 'Oh, God, I wish I could turn back time!'

She fixed her eyes on the ceiling, unable to look at this beautiful man sitting on the edge of her hospital bed. The father of her baby… a baby that was just about clinging on to life.

'Please, Sam, just go home.'

He stood up and began zipping up his coat.

'OK, Katie, I'm going,' he said, resigned. 'But, for what's it worth, I don't believe you.' Tears filled his eyes. 'I understand your reasons for not wanting to tell me the truth, but please: find it in your heart to be honest with me.'

When she didn't respond, Sam turned and walked out of the room, down the corridor and out of the ward. He pressed for the lift and stood waiting, the tears running down his face.

After about 30 seconds, the lift door opened and a man walked out, carrying a large brown paper bag. Sam recognised him immediately. Matt, totally preoccupied, bumped into Sam and almost spilled the potato and leek soup he was carrying.

'Sorry, mate,' he apologised. 'Here's me, can't even hold a bag together and I'm hoping my wife can hold onto our baby.'

Sam found it hard to wish him good luck, but Matt seemed so genuine he felt had to say something.

'I hope the baby is OK,' he replied.

My baby, he said to himself as the lift doors closed.

Sam left the hospital in a daze. He couldn't even remember where he'd parked and had to press the ignition key to get his car to flash its headlights. Once he'd located it, he climbed in and slumped into the driver's seat. He couldn't shake the feeling that Katie was lying to him. This could be his only chance of fatherhood and she was going to take it away from him. But he knew he had no choice right now but to leave things as they were. He took a few deep breaths before driving slowly out of the car park.

When he was on the main road, his phone started to ring. His spirits lifted; maybe Katie had had a change of heart. In his haste to retrieve it from his coat pocket, the phone flew from his hand and landed in the passenger side footwell. He leaned over to pick it up; just a split second was all it took. When he looked up again, he had veered over to the other side of the road and the lights of an articulated lorry were blinding him.

The loud blast of a horn was the last thing he heard.

62

It was the lorry driver who called 999. A small crowd had gathered around Sam's mangled car and a woman - a doctor - had approached the scene, but she, too, stood helpless; nobody could get to him.

An ambulance and fire engine arrived within five minutes of each other and Sam was cut from the car, but, though the paramedics did all they could, he remained unresponsive. His phone rang several times as they worked on him but the medics were too busy trying to keep him alive to be bothering about it.

When the police arrived, two officers took statements from the onlookers while two others carried out a search of the vehicle; they found Sam's driving licence and details of the car hire firm. One of the officers found the phone under the passenger seat. As he was about to bag it, it started ringing. The name *Jill* lit up the screen. Taking his lead from his nodding sergeant, the officer hit 'accept' and said 'hello?' in a grave tone.

'Who is this and why are you answering Sam's phone?' Jill demanded.

'This is PC James O'Donnell. Who am I speaking to?'

'This is Jill Taggart. Is there something… is my husband alright?'

The officer looked at the scene in front of him. The paramedics had moved Sam onto a stretcher. One of them looked up at the officer and slowly shook his head while the other pulled a white cotton sheet up over Sam's lifeless body.

'Mrs Taggart,' he said, 'have you someone with you?'

The blood drained from Jill's face. 'No, I'm on my own.

What's going on? I need to know.'

Then she was screaming. 'What's happened to my husband? Tell me!'

'I am so sorry, Mrs Taggart, but your husband has been in an accident. The paramedics have...' he trailed off when the screeching from the other end of the line became unbearable. He waved over his colleague, PC Anne Doherty, and held the phone out to her.

'You might be better at this,' he said in a low voice. 'Woman to woman. It's his wife - her name is Jill.'

The woman officer took a long sigh to centre herself, then put the phone to her ear and began speaking.

'Jill, this is PC Anne Doherty...'

'Is he dead? Is Sam dead?' Jill interrupted. 'Please, I need to know: is my husband alive or dead?'

'Mrs Taggart - Jill - your husband was involved in a collision with an articulated lorry. The paramedics were on the scene within minutes and they did all they could...'

There was only a deathly silence from the other end of the phone.

'I have your address here,' the PC continued sympathetically. 'We've contacted your local police station and an officer will be with you in the next five minutes.'

There was a click and the phone went dead. PC Doherty put her hand over her eyes and lowered her head; all the training in the world could never prepare her for having to deliver this type of devastating news to a loved one.

Jill sat on the bed and stared at the colourful wallpaper in the bedroom she shared with Sam. She could see his face - such a handsome face - looking back at her through the pattern: full of life, full of smiles, full of devilment, full of mischief, full of love. Then the images disappeared and she sat there, paralysed by grief.

She could hear roars and screams in the room, but didn't realise for the longest time that they were actually coming from her.

63

Paul arrived at the bank at 8.30 on Friday morning. He was expecting to see Sam already there, but there was no sign of anyone. He put the kettle on and switched on his computer, feeling glad it was almost the weekend; it had been a tough week without Katie at his right hand.

The office began to fill up but still there was no sign of Sam. *Not like him to be so late,* Paul thought.

The phone on his desk bleeped. 'Call for you, Paul,' Ruth's voice said on the other end. 'I'll just put you through.'

'Paul McFadden here.'

'Good morning, Paul. This is George Taggart; Sam's brother…'

Ruth couldn't help but glance over every now and then to the glass panelled office. She watched Paul as he dipped his head and put his left hand across his brow. He was shaking his head as he listened to the caller, then, after a few more minutes, he hung up and walked into the main office. He looked like he'd just seen a ghost. Ruth stared at him as he lumbered towards the middle of the floor.

'Everything all right, Paul?'

'It's Sam,' he said. 'He's been in an accident.'

Everyone in the office looked at one another, but no-one spoke. They waited for Paul to go on.

'He's dead.'

Shocked gasps filled the office and everyone started talking at once. Some of the girls, unable to take it in, were crying.

'That was Sam's brother, George, on the phone,' said Paul,

still in a daze. 'They need someone to go and identify him.'

'I'll come with you,' Ruth said immediately.

'No, Ruth, I'll be fine by myself. But thank you.'

He put on his coat and scarf and sombrely told them he would be back later.

Sam lay there, cold and stiff, on a narrow stainless-steel table in the mortuary. 'Yes, that's Sam Taggart,' Paul said, nodding in confirmation to the police officer who stood beside the nurse in charge. He stood for a short while, staring at Sam's face, half expecting him to wake up at any second; it was all so surreal. This intelligent, charismatic man, who Paul liked and respected, was gone forever. The nurse gently explained the fatal injuries were most likely internal; other than the large gash on Sam's forehead, he looked like he was sleeping peacefully.

'Even in death he is still very present,' Paul whispered.

The nurse lightly placed her hand on his arm. 'Yes, it's hard to get your head around when someone is taken so suddenly. Do you want a few moments on your own? We can wait outside.'

'No, I'm okay, thanks. I've to go now and let my colleague know. She and Sam were very close. She's in the antenatal unit… I need to tell her.'

Paul took one last look at Sam as he and the nurse walked out to the corridor. He made his way to the main wing of the hospital and took the lift up to ward five.

64

When Carol picked up the phone and heard Katie's cries on the other end, her first thought was that she'd lost the baby.

'Oh, Katie, love, I'm so sorry. Is Matt with you? I can be there in 15 minutes.'

'It's not the baby, Carol,' Katie said, still sobbing and gasping for breath. 'It's Sam.'

'Sam? What the fuck has he done now? I swear to Christ, Katie, I'm seriously gonna kill him if he even tries to mess with your head.'

'No… oh my God, Carol, Paul from work has just been here… Sam is dead. He was killed in a car crash last night… it's my fault, Carol… it's all my fault.'

Carol couldn't take it in. She wanted to tell Katie to slow down, go back to the start. Repeat what she'd just said. And what did she mean by *it's all my fault?*

'I'm coming over,' she told her friend. 'Be there as quick as I can.'

Katie lay trembling on the bed. She kept replaying Paul's puzzled words in her head: *I wonder why Sam was on this side of town? He only ever stays around the hotel.*

She couldn't banish the image she had in her mind of Sam's body lying on a cold slab in the morgue, not too far from where she lay. She thought of Jill and the heartbreak she'd have to face with the loss of her husband. She thought about how stupid and selfish she'd been in getting involved with Sam in the first place. And she thought about their baby. Sam had asked her for the truth… and now he would never know.

The door opened and Carol stepped inside. She walked towards the bed, leaned over and pulled Katie closely to her.

'I can't believe it, Carol,' she sobbed. 'He was here…'

'*Here?* In this room?' Carol asked, confused.

'Yeah,' Katie answered, her voice trembling. 'I opened my eyes and he was just standing there. He starting asking about the baby… if it was his.'

'I thought he didn't know about the pregnancy,' Carol said.

'Someone at the office must've told him. Oh, I was so horrible to him, Carol! I said the baby wasn't his and told him to get out… he asked me for the truth - *begged* me - but I just ignored him… and now he's dead.' She covered her face with her hands and let out a series of heaving sobs.

'Katie, this is awful, but it's not your fault,' Carol said. 'Come on, now.'

Katie shook her head. 'If he hadn't come over here to see me, he'd still be alive. If I'd been nicer to him…'

'You didn't ask him here, Katie, and there's no way you could have told him the truth. Please try and settle yourself - all this stress isn't good for you or the baby.'

'Maybe I'm going to lose the baby; maybe God is going to punish me for being such a horrible person… maybe I deserve it.'

Carol was disturbed by what she was hearing. 'No. Stop. I'm not listening to this talk. God knows, it was a terrible accident, but you need to stay strong and put this nonsense about blame out of your head.'

They were interrupted by a knock on the door; it was Mr Lewis, the consultant. Katie could go home today, he told her.

'The procedure went well but you need to give time for the cervical stitches to heal properly,' he said. 'I suggest another two weeks at home before going back to work.'

He said his goodbyes and left the room.

Carol, relieved the visit from the consultant had stayed Katie's hysteria, went into practical mode.

'Right, first things first,' she said. 'Phone Matt and tell him you're getting out and that I'm bringing you home. You're obviously going to have to tell him about Sam's accident, but you need to keep it together, Katie: you're shocked at the death of your boss - Matt will expect that - but for God's sake don't give yourself away. C'mon, get dressed.'

Katie quietly got off the bed as Carol started to empty her bedside locker.

'Carol,' she said in a faint voice, 'don't be cracking up with me, but...'

Carol looked up from packing Katie's overnight bag. 'What?'

'I can't leave without saying a proper goodbye...'

Carol, understanding implicitly, simply nodded.

'Do you think they'll let us in to see him?' Katie said, anxiously picking at her nail polish.

'Only one way to find out,' Carol replied. She finished packing Katie's bag, then the two friends made their way to the mortuary.

When they got there, Carol told the receptionist they were colleagues of Sam Taggart's (she made sure to mention the name of the bank) and that they were hoping to pay their respects before his body was taken back to England.

The receptionist smiled sympathetically (Carol was very credible) and called a nurse to come and take them to see Sam. After walking them into the room and over to the steel table where Sam lay, she told them she would wait outside and give them a few minutes alone.

Katie, who had kept her eyes lowered, finally forced herself to look at Sam. Her legs nearly buckled from the shock and Carol had to steady her.

'Oh my God, Carol,' she said. 'Aw, Jesus, look at him.'

She leaned over and touched Sam's cold face and traced her finger across his pale, grey lips.

'Why does his skin look like wax? You would hardly know him.' Her voice was heavy with sadness.

'He always talked about opening his own bank. It's not fair; he had his whole life ahead of him,' she began weeping.

'We had so many good times together,' she went on, the tears flowing freely now. 'And I did love him… in my own way.'

Carol reached out and gently took Katie's hand in hers.

'I know you did, hon. You just hold on to all those lovely memories.'

She let Katie take one last look at Sam, then led her away in silence.

65

It had been two months since Sam's death. Winter had slowly made way for spring, and the air had that unmistakeable feel of the new season being ushered in, with all its customary optimism and brightness.

But, for Jill, there was only darkness and despair. From the moment the female PC had come on the phone and told her that her husband was dead, time had stood still.

She'd taken extended leave from work and spent her mornings in bed and her afternoons on the couch. Her mother, Lily, had become so worried about her that she'd insisted she move in with her for a while; Jill, too numb to care, had passively agreed. That had been a month ago, but, if anything, Jill had become even more withdrawn.

Lily had suggested walks, yoga classes, evenings at the cinema - anything to get her out of the house - but, each time, her daughter had silently shaken her head and turned back to the television screen. Lily was sick with worry. The other evening, when yet another of her suggestions had been rebuffed, she'd looked over at her daughter lying on the couch in shapeless jogging bottoms, her hair lank and unwashed, and something in her snapped.

'For goodness' sake, Jill,' she'd said sharply. 'It's been two months and the only time you've gone outside is to go to the columbarium to visit Sam's urn ... oh, darling, this isn't healthy.'

'I know how long it's been, Mum,' Jill had spat back at her. 'I know how many hours it's been...how many days it's been, how many weeks...' she put her head in her hands and started sobbing.

'Of course you do, darling,' Lily had said, walking over to the couch and sitting down beside her. 'But Sam would not want you like this. He would want you to be strong. Please, Jill.'

But Jill had said nothing; she just lay there, not a word leaving her lips as Lily tenderly, and helplessly, stroked her blonde, greasy hair.

Lily realised she needed to take matters into her own hands. Yesterday, while Jill lay in bed, she'd gone into town and stopped by the Mac makeup counter at Harvey Nicholls and had a conversation with Jenna, Jill's friend from work. She'd only met her once before - at Sam's funeral - but knew they were close.

This morning, she was ready to execute the plan she'd worked out with Jenna. 'Darling?' she called up to Jill's bedroom from the hallway. 'I'm popping out to my yoga class, then I'm meeting Liz for a coffee.

'By the way, I'm expecting an Amazon parcel... could you sign for it if he calls when I'm out?'

With that, Lily swept out the front door, saying a silent prayer that her plan would work.

An hour later, Jill heard a knock. *That must be the Amazon delivery*, she thought. In her current depressed state, the thought of even a brief interaction such as this was daunting, but she knew her mother would be annoyed if she didn't take it in, so she threw on a hoodie over her pyjamas and went down to open the door.

To her surprise (and dismay), it wasn't the Amazon guy: it was her friend Jenna standing there, a lopsided smile on her face and a large bouquet of flowers in her hand.

'It's so good to see you', Jenna said, tentatively stepping forward and embracing Jill with her spare arm.

'I know you need your space... I just... I've been thinking

about you.' She handed her the flowers.

Jenna's act of kindness completely dismantled Jill's defences; instead of shooing her away, she accepted the flowers and asked her inside for a coffee.

Jenna sat at the kitchen table as Jill made the coffee, filling the initial silence with small talk about work. As she chatted away amiably, Jill suddenly stopped what she was doing and placed her two hands on the counter and lowered her head. Her shoulders started to heave and then, as if as dam had burst its banks, she started crying uncontrollably.

Jenna pushed back her chair, rushed to her friend's side and pulled her to her, holding her shaking body and offering soothing words as Jill released two months of pent-up grief, sadness and loneliness.

Over the course of the next few weeks, Jill had slowly started to engage with the real world again. She'd been out for walks and coffees with Jenna and had gone with her to Zumba classes; Jenna had even convinced her that she was ready to go back to work.

But there was something Jill needed to do first. As she sat in the dining room finishing off the delicious Sunday roast her mother had prepared, she knew it was now or never.

'Mum, I've decided to go to Ireland,' she announced, pushing a stem of broccoli around her plate.

'What on earth for?' Lily said, an incredulous look on her face.

'I need to see where Sam died... need to talk to his colleagues and get a proper sense of what happened.'

'Did you not speak to that nice man from Derry at the funeral?'

'I did, yeah, but my head was all over the place and I wasn't taking anything in. I need answers, Mum. Like, who was last to talk to him? Why was he on the other side of town at 5.30 in the evening when he should have been in the office, or even in the hotel?'

'I really don't think it's necessary for you to go all the way over there,' Lily said, trying to sound patient. 'Surely a phone call to the police would clear things up? Darling, you've been doing so well these last few weeks... don't you think it would be better for you if you try and move on?'

'Mum, I *will* move on,' Jill said firmly, 'but I can't do that until I get proper answers about Sam's death.'

She got up from the table, lifted her empty dinner plate and walked to the kitchen. 'I've made up my mind: I'm going to Derry... and you can't stop me.'

Lily sighed; her daughter was every bit as strong-minded as her, so there was no point in arguing.

Later that evening, Jill booked return flights from London to Belfast.

66

Katie was sitting behind the desk in Paul's office; she was holding the fort while her boss was out for a lunch meeting with the new regional manager. Sam's replacement, Mark Sweeney, had arrived at the branch about half an hour ago and, from the minute he'd swaggered into the main office, she knew instinctively he was everything Sam wasn't. He was small and stocky and his short, neat brown hair was slicked back with hair gel. He kept his hands in his trouser pockets as he walked across the floor, his tone unmistakeably smarmy as he said, 'morning, ladies,' on his way to Paul's office.

When Paul had called Katie in to be introduced to him, Mark had immediately stared at her swollen belly and said, 'Oh, by the looks of things we'll be replacing you very soon, too.'

Placing a protective arm around her six-month-old bump, Katie had replied, in a tone dripping with sarcasm, 'I'm pregnant, Mark; not sick. And I'm going nowhere.'

Sensing the tension, Paul had quickly offered to take Mark out for a bite to eat. He would likely have words for Katie when he got back about the tone she'd taken with Mark, but she didn't care; the guy was a complete asshole.

She turned her attention back to the paperwork Paul had asked her to look over, glad to have something to take her mind off the uncomfortable exchange with Mark - as well as the inevitable thoughts of Sam his arrival had provoked. Just as she was lifting her pen to make a note of something, she heard Ruth talking to someone in the main office.

'Mrs Taggart; hello. I'm so sorry for your loss...'

Katie sat bolt upright in her chair. It was Jill.

'Thank you,' she heard her say to Ruth. 'I'm hoping to see Paul, if that's OK. We spoke at the funeral, but...' her voice trailed off.

'Paul has just popped out, Mrs Taggart, but maybe Katie can help you,' Ruth said, walking Jill towards the inner office.

Katie angled her body in front of the computer screen as the two women walked in.

'Katie, Mrs Taggart was hoping to see Paul...'

'Thanks Ruth,' said Katie, nodding at her colleague to leave them to it. 'Hello, Jill. Please, take a seat.'

Katie could hear the tremor in her voice as Jill sat down in front of her, but she had no choice but to brazen it out.

'How are you? We were all devastated to hear about Sam.'

Jill sighed and placed her fingertips to both temples and rubbed hard.

'I have so many questions,' she said quietly, staring at the ground. 'He died alone, in another country, found by total strangers.' She stopped momentarily and then looked up at Katie.

'They said he wasn't paying attention to the road... but he was always such a cautious driver.'

Her eyes were now two sad pools of water with fine lines and dark circles visible underneath. Katie looked at her, feeling a mixture of pity, empathy and guilt.

'Why was he on that side of town?' Jill continued. 'Who was last to see him? Last to speak to him?'

She stopped and stared across at Katie, as if she might have the answers.

And Katie *did* have the answers... but the cost of revealing them to her would be too high. Still, the sight of this poor woman, sitting there tormented with grief, was difficult to watch; especially when she knew exactly what Jill was going through. Before she knew what she was doing, Katie was up off her seat and making her way over to the other side of the table to comfort her.

As Katie emerged from behind the desk, Jill's eyes went immediately to her bump; her mouth fell open. She lifted her head to look directly at Katie, her eyes filled with shock. *And realisation?* Katie thought, panicking. She could see the cogs turning in Jill's brain and had to act fast.

'My husband and I have been trying for 20 years for another baby,' she blurted out as she patted her tummy. 'We're so excited.'

'Right… co-congratulations,' Jill stuttered the words as tears ran down her face.

Katie sat down beside her and put her hands on top of Jill's and rubbed them lightly. Jill allowed her hands to stay there for a few seconds, then abruptly pulled them away. Then she brought them to her face and lowered her head, her shoulders shuddering as she rocked from side to side.

Katie helplessly watched the enormity of Jill's loss, unable to share her own grief for the very same man. Both women sat in silence, each caught up in her own memories of a man who was a husband to one and a lover to the other.

After a minute or two, Jill slowly straightened herself up and dried her wet eyes with the back of her hand.

'Can you take me to the spot where Sam died?' she said, looking pleadingly at Katie.

'Yes, I can take you, Jill.' It was the last thing Katie wanted to do, but she felt she had no choice. She didn't want her speaking to Paul again in case their conversation led to even more questions. She was fairly sure no-one had guessed that Sam had been visiting her the evening he died - and she wanted to keep it that way.

Katie excused herself for a loo break before they set off.

Grateful to find the staff toilets empty, she entered the first cubicle, closed the door and sat on the edge of the seat, forcing herself to take deep breaths to calm herself.

'Please, Sam,' she said under her breath while looking up at the ceiling. 'If you're up there... help me through this.'

Jill had come to Derry to find out about Sam's death, but what if she had also come to fish about her and him? Katie thought back to that evening in November when Jill found the earring in Sam's hotel bedroom. They'd thought they'd got away with it, but maybe Jill had closed her eyes to the truth because she didn't want to lose him. And... her face just then when she'd seen Katie was pregnant. If she put two and two together she could blow Katie's entire world to pieces.

She ran cold water on her wrists as her mind worked overtime. *If I add a month on to my due date, that would mean I didn't get pregnant until December - long after Sam had been in Derry.* She grabbed a paper towel and dabbed her wrists, then hurried back to the office. She needed to do what she had to do, then get Jill back on that plane as soon as possible.

A few minutes later, the two women were in Katie's car. Jill stole a quick glance at Katie's bump while they were fastening their seatbelts, then they drove off in silence towards the scene of Sam's accident. After a few minutes, Jill spoke.

'I'm sorry; I was so upset earlier that I didn't even ask you: when is your baby due?'

Katie was ready for this. 'September, all being well.' She smiled weakly, glad to have been prepared... but she wasn't prepared for Jill's next question.

'Did you sleep with my husband?'

Katie could feel Jill's eyes boring a hole into the side of her face. She had just turned onto the Craigavon Bridge, so she had no choice but to keep driving. She stared at the road ahead; shock and anger racing through her.

'Have you lost your mind?' she said, her voice raised and her tone sharp. *Attack is the best form of defence,* she thought.

But Jill was having none of it.

'Oh, please; don't insult me,' she spat back. 'At least have the decency to tell me the truth; the two of you were having an affair… you planned the whole cruise so you could see each other every day.'

'Sam was a colleague; nothing more!' Katie fired back. 'Who do you think you are, coming over here and making ridiculous accusations? I'm pregnant, in case you've forgotten. I don't need this shit.'

Jill released a mirthless, bitter laugh and said, 'Oh, don't you worry, I haven't forgotten you're pregnant. Actually, about that…'

She paused for a few seconds, and then, with a voice as cold as ice, asked the question that had entered her head the second Katie had stood up in front of her in the office.

'Are you having Sam's baby?'

Jill's words hung ominously in the air as Katie tried to stifle her panic and work out her next move. She was coming to the end of the bridge; she needed to get Jill out of her car. Turning left, she indicated and pulled into the car park by the railway station. She switched off the ignition and turned to face Jill.

'Why didn't you talk to me about this in the office?' she said, her tone bullish. 'You tricked your way into my car so you could interrogate me.'

'Oh, I'm so sorry I took you out of your comfort zone,' Jill hissed sarcastically.

'The only thing I have to say to you,' Katie said, her voice rising, 'is get the fuck out of my car. There's a taxi rank over there; you can make your own way back to the hotel.'

But Jill refused to budge. 'You didn't answer my question. Is that Sam's baby?' she snarled, pointing at Katie's belly.

'Absolutely not! Now... get out!' Katie screamed.

The car fell silent. Katie looked across at Jill, waiting for her to move, but she just sat there staring blankly ahead. As Katie looked at her, guilt rose within her. It was *her* fault she wasn't strong enough to resist Sam; *her* fault she was stupid enough to get pregnant; *her* fault Sam was upset and distracted on the evening of his fatal car crash. And, ultimately, it was her fault Jill had been left a heartbroken widow.

In that moment, Katie knew she had to make a choice: she could give this woman the truth she deserved or she could protect her marriage and unborn child. Much as she hated herself for it, she knew there was only ever going to be one answer. It was something she'd have to live with for the rest of her life, but she could never tell Jill the truth. She would always suspect - that was for sure; but, without proof, suspicion was all she would ever have.

'Listen to me, Jill,' Katie said, her voice softer now. 'You're grieving and I'm pregnant; the emotions and hormones in this car could lift the roof off.'

She took a deep breath before continuing. 'We need to stop this. I will take you to where Sam died, but then you need to go back home, Jill. Go and live your life... and let me live mine.'

Jill nodded silently and they drove the few short miles to the scene of Sam's accident.

Once there, Katie fought back her own tears while Jill sobbed openly and asked more questions.

'How was Sam that day in the office? Did he seem in bad form?'

'I didn't see him in the office,' Katie replied. 'I was off that day.' *At least that much is true,* she thought.

'He always kept within the speed limit, but they said he was speeding... careless, even. Why?'

'I just wish I had answers,' Katie lied. 'I know all this is awful for you, Jill, but I hope this visit brings you some kind of comfort... and closure.'

The two women returned to the car and drove back over to the Cityside. As Katie dropped Jill off at her hotel and they said a terse goodbye, she said a silent prayer she would never hear from her again.

Jill lay in bed that night in the City Hotel, her mind working overtime. *Closure*. Katie's choice of word had been deliberate; she was telling Jill to draw a line under everything and move on.

She thought about the last time she'd been in this hotel. Sam had been lying beside her then, but when he'd reached out to touch her, she'd rejected him. The pain of that memory brought tears to her eyes and she thought, for the umpteenth time since he'd died, what she wouldn't give to feel his arms around her once more.

Katie was the reason she'd ignored Sam that night. She had reluctantly accepted his story that Katie was a work colleague and had only been in his hotel room to drop off paperwork, but, deep down, she knew he was lying. She'd forced herself to believe him because she loved him and didn't want to lose him, but it was always there; gnawing away at her.

That bloody woman, she thought angrily. She'd sensed something about her the minute she'd seen Sam chatting cosily with her on the cruise ship. Then there was all the nonsense in the hotel and Sam holding up that damn earring. But the clincher was today: Katie's bump and how jumpy she'd been acting - even before Jill had asked her outright about her relationship with Sam.

Oh, it's no wonder you want me to get closure, Jill thought. *But this is not over yet... not by a long shot.*

67

In Glasgow, Gerry's house was filling up with family and friends who'd come to pay their respects. After six months in the nursing home, Josie had finally succumbed to her dementia; weakened by a bad infection that her body just didn't have the strength to fight, she'd drifted into unconsciousness and died peacefully in the home, her two sons at her side.

Gerry and his brother Stuart now sat in the living room of the family home; their mother laid out in the coffin before them. She looked so peaceful; all the strain of the last couple years wiped from her face. When their father had passed away, Josie had been insistent he wouldn't be left resting in a 'cold and impersonal funeral home'. She had waked her husband from the family home; it was only right they do the same for her.

Connor was making himself useful by lifting used cups and saucers and taking them out to the kitchen to be washed, occasionally stealing a glance at Gerry to see how his friend was holding up.

Connor knew Gerry was devastated by his mother's death, but he and Stuart were obviously close and they had each other to lean on. Gerry had also been seeing Amy's flatmate, Hannah, these last few months; she was a regular visitor to the house these days and Connor could see they were really into one another. He smiled to himself, thinking how nice it was that love had come into Gerry's life not long after his own had been blessed with the arrival of Chris.

He was brought out of his reverie by the sound of his name being called and turned round to see who it was; it was Amy. It was the first time in eight months they'd been under the same roof.

'Amy,' he said, slightly taken aback. He knew she and Gerry were friendly (even more so, probably, because of his relationship with Hannah) but she hadn't been to the house since Connor had returned from New York in January. It was to be expected that she'd come here for Josie's wake but it was still a jolt to see her after all this time.

'Hello,' she said shyly, placing her hand lightly on the arm of the man standing next to her. 'Connor, this is Greg.'

'Nice to meet you at last, Connor,' Greg said, smiling and stretching his hand out.

'Aye, nice to meet you too, Greg,' Connor said, shaking his hand firmly.

They chatted for a few minutes, mainly about Josie and what a great woman she was, then Amy and Greg excused themselves and joined Gerry and Hannah.

An hour or so later, Connor noticed Amy walking Greg to the front door. They shared a few words, then a little peck on the lips and a tight hug. *They look nice together,* Connor thought. He was glad to see Amy looking happy... *really* happy.

It was midnight on the second night of Josie's wake. The only people still in the house were Gerry and Hannah, Stuart and Jamie, and Connor and Amy. Exhausted by the demands of the two-day open house, they had all sank into soft chairs in the living room while Gerry opened a nice bottle of Macallan 18-year-old Scotch and began pouring everyone a glass.

'Just make mine a very small one,' Amy said. 'I'm driving, but

I'll raise a wee glass to Josie before I go.'

Once everyone had been handed a drink, they all stood up and gathered around the coffin.

'Here's to the best mum ever,' Gerry said, raising his glass. 'Your wee body couldn't take any more and we're glad you're at rest, but Jesus... we are going to miss you.'

'To Josie,' the rest said in unison as they raised their glasses.

'Well, that's me,' Amy said, draining her glass and giving Gerry a hug. 'I'll see you all in the morning.'

Connor followed her out of the living room. 'Wait, I'll walk you to your car,' he offered. She let him take the lead. When they reached the car, Amy was about to say goodnight when Connor cleared his throat.

'Can we talk?'

Amy looked at him hesitantly. She knew they'd had to have this conversation eventually; she just wasn't sure she wanted it to be tonight.

But Connor *needed* to have it. 'Amy, I know circumstances rather than choice have thrown us together over the past few days, but… well... it wasn't that bad, was it?'

He searched her face for some kind of agreement, but she lowered her eyes and fumbled through her handbag for her car keys. He knew she was buying time.

He tried again. 'Greg seems a really nice guy. Hannah and Gerry speak very highly of him.'

She retrieved her car keys and looked up at him.

'Yes,' she said solemnly, 'he *is* really nice… and I know where I stand with him.'

He winced at the last bit, but forced himself to keep going. 'Amy, you *have* to know how sorry I am for hurting you. I think you know we never would have worked, but I really want you to be happy.'

Then, looking at her with a directness that surprised her, he said, 'Are you?'

Amy took her time before giving him an answer. She'd been going out with Greg for six months and she liked him - a lot. More than that: she was falling in love with him. Greg was six years older and some of his maturity had rubbed off on her; she found herself less quick-tempered and less controlling than she'd been when she was with Connor.

She had changed, these last six months, and she realised now, looking across at Connor, that he had changed, too. He had a determined and confident air about him that was so different from the nervous, constantly apologetic young man she'd been in a relationship with. She thought back to the letter he'd written to her: *we can't complete each other*, it had said.

She finally broke her silence. 'Connor, I was hurt. I was completely wrecked by it, if you want to know the truth. I had all these people telling me, "He's gay, he could never make you happy", and that was true... but it didn't change the fact that I loved you.'

He began to respond, but she gently placed her hand on his shoulder; a wordless signal that she had more to say.

'And it's just... you know... you lose who you were... lose all confidence... lose all trust. But I slowly got stronger, Connor; day by day. You were right when you said we couldn't complete each other... maybe we have each found the person who can.'

'Would you look at you, getting all philosophical,' he said, deliberately adopting a teasing tone so as not to betray the emotion that was welling up inside him.

'Yeah, well,' she said, throwing him a lopsided smile, 'I keep *The Power of Now* on my bedside table; I've even learned to take a pause every now and then.'

'I think I just witnessed that,' he said, smiling softly at her. *I like this new Amy*, he thought.

'Maybe this is what the universe wanted for us,' she went

on. 'Because we broke up, you made good friends in John and Andrew... I met Gerry and Josie because you were living with them... Gerry met Hannah because she was living with me... and now we have Stuart and Jamie thrown in for good measure.'

'Not to mention Greg,' Connor added.

'Absolutely. Greg is good for me... and Chris is obviously good for you.'

In saying Chris' name, Amy was finally giving Connor the one thing he wanted most: forgiveness. Unable to hold his emotions back any longer, he let the tears flow.

'So... friends again?' he asked her, his cheeks wet.

Amy nodded and smiled back at him; he took her into his arms and hugged her tight.

'Thank you,' he whispered.

She heard him, and understood.

68

Katie had wanted to travel to Scotland to attend Gerry's mum's funeral but her consultant had advised against it. She'd been diagnosed with gestational hypertension - not uncommon in the latter stages of the third trimester - but they didn't want to take any chances, he'd said.

Although she'd been religiously taking her medication and watching what she ate, her blood pressure continued to rise; that meant a greater risk of complications during labour. Matt was going out of his mind with worry and was constantly fussing over her, making sure she was getting plenty of rest and angling one cushion behind her back and another under her feet every time she lay down on the couch.

They were driving home from the latest appointment at the hospital, where Mr Lewis had told Katie a Caesarean section would be the safest option. They arranged for her to come in the following Monday - one week earlier than her due date.

Katie phoned Carol from the car to give her the latest update and her friend said she'd call in to see her on her lunch break. As Katie was hanging up, her phone pinged with a Facebook friend request… it was from Jill.

She felt like throwing up. *What the actual fuck?* she thought, panic gripping her. But she couldn't give herself away in front of Matt. She hastily put her phone in her handbag as Matt gently patted her knee and said, 'I'll leave you off home, love, but then I need to go back to the office.'

'Aye, that's grand; Carol is calling over,' she said, squeezing his hand in return.

Less than an hour later, Katie answered the door to Carol,

who strode straight into the living room and sat down in the armchair without even removing her coat.

'So,' she said, 'did Matt catch on when Mr Lewis started discussing dates? Is he not questioning the fact you're having the baby so early?'

'No, thank God,' Katie replied, gently rubbing her bump. 'Matt always sits in the waiting room and I've never encouraged him to come in. So, no: he is definitely not questioning anything.

'That's a relief,' said Carol. 'The last thing you need is for him to put two and two together.'

'I don't think he will, Carol. He doesn't pay too much attention to 'women's stuff', as he calls it, and it wouldn't cross his mind to sit down and calculate that, going by when we had sex, I should be due later on in August and not at the start. To be honest, Carol, his only focus is on getting me and the baby through this pregnancy. Each time I take these Braxton Hicks he swears I'm going into labour and all but grabs his car keys and fires me into the car. If it's not that, he's fussing about my blood pressure. I know he means well, but, God love him, he isn't worth tuppence!'

The two women started laughing. 'Sure, you know what men are like with stuff like this,' said Carol. 'Have you told Connor about the Caesarean? Chris is due in Scotland this weekend, isn't he?'

'Aye, Chris is leaving the ship in Rome on Saturday and flying to Glasgow. They're supposed to be coming here on Monday but they might not bother now that I'm going into the hospital early. I'll call Connor later.'

Katie yawned, and Carol noticed how tired and drawn she looked. But there was something else there, too: fear.

'What is it, Katie?' she asked, her voice full of concern. 'Has something happened?'

'I'm hoping it's nothing,' she replied, 'but after I spoke to you earlier, my phone bleeped with a Facebook friend request notification.'

'From who?' Carol stared at her.

'Jill,' said Katie, staring back at her. 'She's going to wreck everything, Carol... isn't she?' Her face was sheet white.

'What the fuck?' Carol exclaimed. 'What is she playing at? I hoped you'd seen the last of her when she was over here in April, shouting the odds!'

'I know, I don't even know how she found my profile,' Katie said. 'I have very few friends on Facebook; I hardly even use it, for God's sake.'

'Right,' Carol said firmly. 'First of all: don't accept her request. Secondly: let her be as suspicious as she likes; she doesn't have proof of anything.'

Then, in a softer tone, she added: 'But don't be sharing any baby pictures on your social media when the time comes, Katie. Just to be on the safe side.'

Katie nodded weakly, but her insides were churning.

She's coming for me.

69

On Monday, July 29th, Katie gave birth to a beautiful baby girl. Matt held her hand nervously throughout the C-section, and both of them broke down when they heard the first healthy cries of their newborn child; they embraced each other tightly and tearfully, overwhelmed with happiness and relief.

When Mr Lewis placed her baby in her arms, all the difficulties and stresses Katie had experienced along the way disappeared in an instant. In that magical moment, there was only love and adoration for this tiny new life nestling against her.

Within an hour, Katie and the baby were cleaned up and taken to their private room. A very excited Matt paced up and down the corridor and rang Carol; she'd opted to work from home that day so she would be available to take the call.

'They're both doing great, Carol, thank God,' Matt said breathlessly. 'Katie was just amazing and the baby is so gorgeous.'

'Oh, Matt,' said Carol, overcome with emotion. 'Thank God is right... and a wee baby girl... congratulations. Oh, I'm so excited for you both. When can I come over and see them?'

'I'd say after lunchtime would be OK. Katie is in great form - though she'll be sore when the anaesthetic wears off.'

'Of course, but they'll manage that with pain relief,' she answered reassuringly.

Later that afternoon, Katie was sitting up in her hospital bed, the baby in her arms and Carol and Matt sat at either side.

All three looked up when they heard a light knock at the door; a massive bunch of flowers pushed through, followed by the excited faces of Connor and Chris.

'Oh my God!' Katie screamed in surprise. They had agreed Connor would wait and come over in a week or so when she'd had the section and was home and settled with the baby.

As he rushed over to her, she threw her free arm around him while Matt, realising this was the first time they'd actually met, got up to shake Chris' hand. Between hugs, and handshakes, and the baby being passed to her big brother, there was a joyful commotion in the room. Katie just sat there, unable to keep the smile off her face as Connor nervously rocked the baby in his arms and Chris leaned in and stroked her little face.

'She's so tiny, I'm afraid I'll drop her,' Connor said, completely awestruck. He looked up at Katie. 'Aw, Mum, she's so perfect.'

Two days later, Katie was discharged from hospital - just in time to say her goodbyes to Connor and Chris before they left for Glasgow. Carol had arrived at the house earlier and prepared a delicious lunch of prawn salad with beef tomato and mozzarella.

'So, Mum,' Connor called through to Katie as he and Chris followed Matt into the kitchen while she organised herself to feed the baby in the living room, 'you thought of a name yet?'

'How about Samantha?' Matt shouted from the kitchen.

'What the fuh...' Katie mouthed to Carol as they looked at one another in shock. If the baby hadn't been latched onto Katie's breast she might actually have dropped her.

'After my granny,' Matt explained. 'Isn't that name 'in' at the minute? We could call her Sam, or Sammi, for short.'

'*Sam?*' Carol whispered to Katie. 'Oh, Jesus, you couldn't make this up.'

'I thought your granny's name was Martha?' Katie called back to Matt, who was now making his way back into the living room.

'Aye,' said Matt, 'but she only got that name because her wee sister couldn't pronounce 'Samantha' when she was learning to talk, so it went from 'Mantha' to 'Martha' and, somehow, it stuck.'

Katie and Carol sat there, not knowing what to say. Katie looked down at the baby contentedly sucking her nipple as Matt approached them. He stopped and lightly touched the baby's soft head.

'Samantha' he said. 'I like it. I think it suits her!' Then, noticing Katie's lukewarm expression, he said, 'No?'

Before she had a chance to answer, Carol intervened.

'What about Maisie?' she blurted out, not really sure where the name came from.

Katie looked up at Carol, a smile playing on her face.

'Yeah,' she said. 'I like Maisie… she kinda looks like a Maisie.'

'Then Maisie it is,' Matt agreed. 'Sure, any name would suit this wee angel.'

Katie stole a brief glance at Carol. 'Thank you', she mouthed silently.

'Right,' said Matt. 'I'm starving. Will we go and eat?'

'You go ahead and lay the plates, love,' Katie said. 'I'll just finish feeding this wee doll and we'll be out in a few minutes.'

When Matt had left the room, Katie looked over at her friend. 'My nerves are shot, Carol,' she said. 'I can't stop thinking about that bloody friend request Jill sent me last week. She didn't believe a word I told her when she came over here in April… what if she hears I've had the baby? She's no dozer; she'll know there's a good chance Sam is the father.'

'That's a lot of "what ifs", Katie,' Carol replied. 'I know it may be easier said than done, but you have to try and put Jill out of your mind.'

Katie looked at her sceptically, but Carol pushed ahead.

'Katie, even if she hears about the baby, what does she *really* know? Maisie could have been born super premature, for all she knows. And even if she thinks you were lying about your due date, so what? It doesn't prove a thing.'

'I know, I know,' Katie said, buttoning her blouse and lifting Maisie into her cot, 'but this wee one is my whole world, Carol, and the thought that Jill could lob a hand grenade into my life at any minute… it terrifies me.'

'I understand, Katie, I really do,' Carol said sympathetically. 'But you can't spend your life stressing about when, or if, the axe is going to fall. I honestly don't think you'll hear from her again, but if you do, sure won't you be able to explain it all away?'

'Maybe,' Katie conceded. 'But she will definitely get Matt's attention. He lets stuff go over his head a lot of the time, but if a woman lands at our door and tells him she thinks her late husband - *my* former boss - is the baby's father, there's going to be trouble. Matt's not stupid: he knows we only had sex that one time, and that we hadn't been able to conceive for the last ten years or more… something like this could be the end of us.'

'Would it, though?' Carol asked. 'Matt is mad in love with you - and with that wee one there. If you had to admit you'd had an affair, could he not find a way to forgive you and move past it?'

'Carol,' Katie sighed, 'I've gone over that scenario a million times in my head. But the thing is, Matt's father walked out on him and his mother when he was still quite young - got himself another woman - and Matt's mother was devastated. He's always said to me he never forgave his father for betraying them… I just know he wouldn't be able to forgive me for this.'

'And it's not just that,' she went on, nodding at little Maisie. 'He absolutely dotes on her. I don't care that he's not her biological father; he's going to be the best daddy she could wish for and I don't want that to be jeopardised. Oh, Carol!' Katie let out a sob.

'It's OK, hon,' Carol said soothingly. 'I know you're driving yourself crazy over this but I think you're worrying about something that is never going to happen. Jill has done the whole angry and grief-stricken widow thing; I really do believe she will move on from this and you can both get on with your lives.'

'I hope so, Carol,' Katie said, not believing her own words for a single second.

70

It was a wet Saturday evening in early November. Jill and Jenna had just finished their shift at Harvey Nics and had run across the road to the local pub opposite, where they often went for a relaxing glass of wine after a busy day on the makeup counter.

After they'd ordered their drinks and sat down at a cosy table in the corner, Jenna eyed Jill with curiosity, one eyebrow raised.

'What's going on with you?' she said. 'Unusual for you to leave the floor during a shift to take a phone call… you were away ages… are you seeing someone?'

Jill's face grew serious and she started to chew the inside of her cheek. 'Something's going on… but it's not what you think,' she said cryptically.

She cleared her throat and started telling Jenna, for the first time, the whole saga about Sam: her suspicions about him and the woman who'd been on the same cruise as them; how he'd never let on he knew her; then the time she'd surprised Sam in Ireland and saw the woman leaving the hotel, and he had to admit she was a work colleague - Katie, her name was; the earring that had been left in Sam's room… how he gave her some bullshit excuse and she'd accepted it; then going over to Derry after he'd died and discovering this woman was pregnant, and how cagey she'd been when Jill had confronted her and asked her outright if the baby was Sam's.

She paused to take a sip of wine.

'Pregnant?' Jenna exclaimed. 'Oh my God… what did she say?'

'She denied it, of course,' Jill replied. 'Told me the baby

wasn't due 'til September, which would have ruled Sam out as he was last in Derry in the early part of November. I didn't believe her, but what could I do? I had no proof. I've tried to put the whole sorry business out of my mind this last six months, but it's just been eating away at me, Jenna.'

Jill looked at her friend with trepidation before continuing. 'So, I contacted a private investigator a few weeks ago - he's based in Belfast. I gave him as much information as I could - Katie's full name, where she works, the dates I think she and Sam were together - and he said he would check out a few things and get back to me. That was him calling me this afternoon.'

'And what did he find out?' Jenna asked.

'He told me Katie had a little girl, born on July 29th,' Jill said. 'He looked it up in the Births, Deaths and Marriages office at the local town hall in Derry.'

'He also rang the bank pretending to be a client of Katie's; asking when she was due back from maternity and how she was getting on with the baby. The woman he spoke to was very helpful; said Katie would be back in the new year and that mother and baby were doing great - no mention of any problems with the birth.'

A solitary tear trickled down Jill's face. 'So, you see, Jenna, that proves it… it must be Sam's baby.'

'You can't jump to conclusions, Jill,' Jenna said gently. 'Who's to say the baby wasn't premature? Didn't you say this woman was in her forties? There tends to be issues at that age. And even if it's true she and Sam were sleeping together, that doesn't mean she wasn't sleeping with her husband at the same time… you just don't know.'

'I know it in my heart,' Jill said with absolute conviction.

All sorts of nightmare scenarios flashed through Jenna's mind. She was very fond of Jill but she knew how highly-strung she was… even more so since Sam had died. She had been demented with grief; truth be told.

Was she going to blow up this woman's marriage by telling her husband the baby wasn't his? Or, worse still, might she somehow try and take the baby from her mother? She felt like grabbing her by the shoulders and shaking some sense into her; tell her she needed to stop all this nonsense.

'Jill,' she said in an even tone, 'I think you should take a step back … this all sounds a bit crazy. I know you have to channel your grief somewhere, but just think of the pain you could cause to someone else… you could destroy an entire family and what good is it going to do you? It won't bring Sam back. And remember: it was *him* who cheated on you.'

Jill flinched at this last comment but said nothing.

Jenna studied her friend's inscrutable face. 'What are you thinking, Jill? What are you going to do with all this?'

'I don't know yet,' Jill said. 'Part of me wants to destroy that woman's life the way she destroyed mine, but the other part of me… well, it's like you said, Jenna: it was *Sam* who cheated on me, and it's Sam I'm most angry with.'

Jenna placed her hand on Jill's, glad her friend might finally be starting to think more rationally. 'I'm just not sure getting revenge would make you feel any better in the long run, Jill.'

'Perhaps', Jill said, taking the last gulp of wine from her glass. 'For *now*, I'm not going to do anything…'

71

When Connor arrived at JFK, Chris was waiting for him. They'd been officially together for almost a year now, but every time he saw him, Connor experienced the same thrill he'd felt the very first time he'd set eyes on Chris on the cruise ship. He was, he realised, deeply in love.

They chatted non-stop on the drive to Chris' parents' home in Long Island, where light dustings of December snow had fallen on the suburban streets and lawns. Beth dished out bowls of home-made spaghetti Bolognese with garlic bread and they all sat casually with their bowls on their laps in front of the blazing fire in the hearth.

Little Carrie was buzzing around the place, thrilled to have her daddy home again and showing off to Connor as she sang and did the actions to the nursery rhyme, 'I'm a Little Teapot'. They all clapped when she finished and she clapped her little hands together with a big smile, delighted to be the centre of attention.

The following afternoon, Chris, Connor and Carrie drove into Manhattan; Chris had promised his daughter a visit with Santa and she had been hyper with anticipation all that morning. An ice-cold wind stung their faces as they walked up 34th Street but Carrie could not have been happier, holding each of their hands as she walked between them and asked for 'another swing, Daddy' at regular intervals.

When they reached Macy's, there was a winter wonderland full of sparkle and colour displayed across the store's front windows. Carrie's little face lit up as she watched the oversized polar bears and penguins singing and dancing and reindeers pulling the beautifully-decorated sleigh.

When they finally got to the end of the very long line to see Santa, Carrie happily sat on his knee, clutching her new toy and beaming for the photographer, who took a lovely picture of her and Santa with Chris and Connor on either side.

It feels like a family photo, Connor thought proudly.

The next day, Chris and Connor said their goodbyes to Carrie and the rest of the family and headed off to the city to spend a few days together; Chris had booked the same AirBnb apartment they'd stayed in last time.

They checked into the apartment at 4pm, leaving just enough time to drop their bags off and get a quick freshen-up before leaving for a meal at Tao. Connor had loved everything about the restaurant when they were there last time and was looking forward to going back.

When they arrived, it was exactly as Connor had remembered: the staff were so warm and friendly and the food was amazing. When they'd finished off their main courses, Connor reached over and took Chris' hand, realising, as he did so, that he felt no fear or apprehension: he had finally accepted who he was.

Chris smiled back at him, and then, clearing his throat, said: 'I've been putting a lot of things through my head, lately, and… I'm thinking of a career change.'

'Go on,' said Connor, surprised and intrigued at the same time.

'Well, I had everything mapped out: study at home, live at sea for three or four months at a time, then back home again, and eventually achieve my rank as captain.'

Chris stopped to take a sip of wine as Connor wondered where all this was leading.

'But then you came along,' he said, gripping Connor's hand tightly. 'I don't want to have to keep sailing away from you.'

Connor's mouth fell open and he stared at Chris in disbelief.

'Yo-you can't give up all this for me,' Connor stammered. 'I don't want to take you away from your dream.'

'You're not,' Chris replied firmly. 'You're broadening my horizons. I've researched maritime colleges in Ireland and Scotland and there are loads of opportunities: I can lecture and complete my studies at the same time. We can have our own careers and see each other every day.'

'What about Carrie?' Connor asked. 'How would she fit into this new life of ours?'

'Well... perfectly, actually. I've spoken to my family: Carrie would continue living with Grace and Ted. Realistically, I'll see her as often as I do now, between me going to New York on vacations and them coming to wherever we end up.'

Connor's heart was racing. He had not expected this turn of events, but now that this scenario was being presented to him, he realised nothing would make him happier.

'Well?' said Chris. 'What do you think?'

'I think,' Connor said, smiling, 'I'm totally on board with it.'

A broad smile spread across Chris' face, then he leaned in to give Connor a tender, lingering kiss.

'I'm so happy to hear you say that, Connor. I love you, man.'

'I love you, too,' Connor replied, barely able to get the words out, he was so choked up with emotion.

Just then, a young waitress arrived at their table and placed a large fortune cookie on a plate in the middle of the table.

'Thought we were supposed to get one each,' Connor said jokingly, bemused by the sly smile Chris had shared with the waitress before she walked away.

'I don't need one,' Chris said, pushing the plate towards Connor. 'I know where my fortune lies... and with *who*.'

Intrigued, Connor cracked open the cookie and pulled out the slip of paper. As he slowly unfolded it, he could barely believe the words he was reading: *Will You Marry Me?*

He looked across the table at Chris, who was staring at him with nervous excitement. 'Well?' he said.

'Absolutely... yes... YES!' Connor replied emphatically.

As they walked back to the apartment that night, a heavy snow shower began to fall and an icy wind swirled around them. The two lovers huddled closer together against the biting cold, but, deep inside, Connor had never felt so warm.

72

(12 months later)

At 1pm on December 10th, two white four-seater carriages, each pulled by a pair of majestic white horses, pulled up at the Tavern on the Green, the infamous bar restaurant nestled deep within New York's Central Park. In the lead carriage were the grooms, Connor and Chris, accompanied by their matron of honour Grace and best man, Gerry.

The second carriage held Katie and Matt and Beth and Joe; Maisie sat on her daddy's knee while Carrie sat between her grandma and grandpa. The little girls looked adorable in their matching white satin dresses and fur gilets. Carrie was excited at being her daddy's little flower girl and was happily playing the big sister role to Maisie, ensuring that the wee one's pretty pearl and rosebud hairband stayed in place.

As the carriages came into view, the guests who had been waiting for them made their way to the entrance and stood along both sides of the red carpet that led into the foyer. A loud cheer rang out as Connor and Chris, smartly dressed in tailored silver-grey Italian wool suits with slate grey waistcoats, crisp white shirts and red open bow ties, stepped out of their carriage. The boys waited on the others to dismount; then, placing the cute little flower girls between them and each taking a small hand in theirs, they led the procession into the magical, historic venue.

A roaring fire welcomed them as they entered the hallway; two huge Christmas trees with coloured baubles and fairy lights standing at either side of the door leading into the wooden-panelled bar. Flute glasses arranged in champagne towers were placed around an ornate oval table and a string quartet played as the guests mingled and enjoyed the beautiful surroundings.

An hour later, everyone moved to the smaller room off the bar, where the registrar, a bubbly gentleman with a great sense of humour, conducted the marriage ceremony.

The service was lively and enjoyable - though a few tears were shed by the two mums, naturally, when the vows were exchanged. Loud shouts and clapping reverberated around the room when the two boys shared their first kiss as husband and husband, then the guests were herded out to the dining room as Connor and Chris stayed behind to do all the necessary form-signing.

After a few minutes, the *maître d'* silenced everyone with a tinkle of a silver spoon on an empty glass and announced the arrival of the two grooms. The room exploded again as Connor and Chris walked in, hand in hand, looking so handsome and bubbling with happiness.

The food was delicious, the staff so attentive, funny speeches were recited, glasses were raised and a five-piece band started up; it was everything they had all hoped for and more.

Katie could not have been a prouder or happier mother of the groom. She sat back in her chair, feeling utter contentment, and watched the happy scenes on the packed dance floor. Amy was looking radiant, snuggling close to Greg as they enjoyed their slow dance, while Hannah was chatting up into Gerry's open face as he smiled lovingly back at her.

Matt held Maisie high in his arms and slowly waltzed her around the floor; she was his pride and joy. Katie had long ago made peace with herself about not telling Matt the truth; watching him out there with his little girl, she believed it had been the right decision.

She had also made her peace with Sam and said a silent prayer to him in gratitude for the beautiful life they had created: *Our baby is so beautiful… I hope you can see her, Sam - she has your chin dimple - and, oh, how she is loved and cherished by everyone!*

And, finally, she had made her peace with Jill. For a year after Maisie was born, she was constantly looking over her shoulder and tensing up every time her phone rang, convinced the axe had to fall; that Jill would expose her lie to the world. But then she woke up one day and realised the constant knot in her stomach had disappeared.

There was still an underlying fear there and Katie knew it would never go away, but she had learned to live with it; just as she had learned to live with the mistakes she'd made and the hurt she'd caused.

'Mum, mum, come over...' Connor broke into her reverie. 'Chris is going up for a song,' he was laughing in disbelief.

Up on the stage, Chris nodded confidently to the lead guitarist, who started up the intro to 'The Voyage' by Christy Moore, then Chris took his cue:

'I am a Sailor, you're my first mate,
We signed on together, coupled our fate…'

A hushed silence descended on the room as Chris' eloquent voice sang out so clearly and lovingly. After the opening few lines, he took the microphone off its stand and walked - still singing - down on to the dance floor, never once taking his eyes off Connor. On reaching him, he took his hand just as he was about to launch into the chorus:

'Life is an ocean and love is a boat
In troubled waters it keeps us afloat
When we started the voyage, there was just me and you

Now gathered round us, we have our own crew…'

The energy in the room was electric as everyone joined in with the chorus and formed a circle around the newlywed. Tears of pride and happiness overwhelmed everyone and there was barely a dry eye in the room.

At eight o'clock that evening, Grace came to find Chris and Connor, who were among the younger crowd at the bar knocking back a few shots.

'I'm ready to leave any time now, Chris,' she said. 'The girls are getting tired. Now might be a good time to tell them?' she said, taking two small boxes out of her handbag and handing one to her brother and the other to Connor.

The three of them walked over to where their parents were sitting, then Connor scanned the dance floor looking for Carol. Sure enough, she was out there with Amy and Hannah, giving her all to 'Dancing Queen'.

'Can I borrow her for a few minutes, ladies?' Connor smiled as he whisked Carol away.

'What's up, Con?' she asked.

'You'll see…' he answered, giving her a playful peck on the cheek.

When they reached the booth, Maisie was sleeping on Matt's knee while Carrie was sleepily watching *Frozen* on Grace's iPhone. Katie pushed them tighter together and motioned for Carol and Grace to sit down.

'Hold on, Mum,' said Connor, producing the box from his jacket pocket while Chris did the same with his. 'We've something for you and Beth.'

They each handed a box to their respective mums as Grace stood quietly beside them.

'We want you to open them at the same time,' Connor insisted, winking at Carol.

The excitement mounted as Katie and Beth ripped off the gold wrapping on their boxes and each of them took out a small photo. Katie was the first to catch on; jumping up from her chair, she clutched the baby scan photo to her chest and gave a small shriek of joy. She looked at Connor, then Chris and finally Beth, who had also worked out what it was.

'Yes, Mum,' Connor confirmed, 'we're having a baby!'

A hundred questions bubbled up in Katie's mouth as she stared at the photo and then at Connor and Matt. Carol was rendered speechless. It was Beth who was first to speak.

'So, you have a surrogate? But… is she genuinely up for this?' On the one hand she was overjoyed, but on the other, she knew surrogacy didn't come without risk.

Then Grace spoke. 'Yes, the surrogate is genuine… you're looking at her,' she said, placing her hand on the barely perceptible bump on her tummy.

'I'm carrying Connor's daughter and Chris' niece, and when she is born, I'm giving her to her parents… these two beautiful young men here.'

Katie and Beth rushed to Grace and threw their arms around her.

'I'm so proud of you, Gracie,' Beth said, planting kisses all over her face. 'What an amazing thing to do for your brother.'

Carol grabbed Connor and Chris and danced them round on the spot, shouting, 'I can't believe it!'

Matt and Joe just sat there smiling, taking in the scene in front of them.

'Well,' Joe said to Matt, 'I'll be damned! Congratulations, Grandpa.'

'Right back at you,' Matt said, laughing, as both men shook hands warmly.

Matt's smile got even wider as he looked across at Katie, then down at Maisie sleeping soundly on his lap. He leaned over and kissed the top of her head. 'You're going to be an auntie,' he whispered.

When Katie reached Connor, she held his two hands in hers and stopped to look up at him, not quite knowing how to express the love and happiness that filled her heart.

'Oh my God, Connor,' she said. 'You're going to be a daddy… this is simply the best day of my life.' Then she turned back to look at the people gathered around the table: her extended family… her future.

And, in the middle of them all, was Carol, who was walking towards her now with her arms outstretched. Her rock. Her confidante. Her best friend.

'We're going to be a granny, Katie,' she said, her voice filled with awe as they hugged each other tightly.

No more words were needed.

Acknowledgements

Over many years of stopping and starting when I was writing this book, I often doubted I'd actually get to type the words 'the end'. Now that I have, I'm already missing my fictional characters!

I will be forever grateful to, and thankful for, those people who had faith in me from the very beginning.

First and foremost, I wish to express my deepest gratitude to my immediate family, my extended family and my friends, who all read my drafts with interest and showed me encouragement throughout.

Special thanks to my long time friend, Eamonn Lynch, a talented writer who gave me the confidence to finish what I started.

A huge thank-you to my editor, Mary-Anne McNulty, for her expertise and guidance in helping me refine my work into its best form.

To Martina Doherty, for her beautiful, skilled work on the front and back covers, and to Paddy Leonard, who laid the pages of my manuscript out so meticulously.

And finally, to whoever is holding my book in their hands right now, a very big thank you; I hope you enjoyed reading it as much as I enjoyed writing it.

Best wishes,
Cassie x

Printed in Great Britain
by Amazon